As the River Runs

Stephen Scourfield, author, travel editor, writer and photographer, has travelled extensively throughout the world. His journeys in Australia, including more than a million kilometres on roads and tracks around Western Australia, have given him a deep understanding of the continent's human and geographic landscape. The relationship of humans to landscape has become a central theme of his writing.

His first novel, *Other Country*, was the fiction winner in the WA Premier's Book Award 2007, shortlisted for the Commonwealth Writers' Prize and longlisted for the 2009 International IMPAC Dublin Literary Award. Stephen Scourfield is a recipient of a United Nations Media Award and has twice been named Australia's Best Travel Writer, in 2011 and 2009.

# As the River Runs

# Stephen
# Scourfield

UWA PUBLISHING

First published in 2013 by
UWA Publishing
Crawley, Western Australia 6009
www.uwap.uwa.edu.au

UWAP is an imprint of UWA Publishing
a division of The University of Western Australia

THE UNIVERSITY OF
WESTERN AUSTRALIA
*Achieve International Excellence*

National Library of Australia
Cataloguing-in-Publication data:

9781742584904 (pbk.)


Scourfield, Stephen.
As the river runs / Stephen Scourfield.
A823.4


Typeset by J & M Typesetting
Printed by Griffin Press

This project has been assisted by the Australian Government through the
Australian Council, its arts funding and advisory body.

*In time and with water,*
*everything changes.*

– Leonardo da Vinci

# One

The snake moves like mercury poured on the ferociously red gravel. It grips the back of the lizard's neck and syringes venom in calculated overdoses. Scuffed arcs either side show where the blue-tongue has put up its fight, but now it and the two-metre king brown are absorbed only by death. The lizard froths at the mouth, cells saturated by poison, but obstinate survival instincts force its tough little body and crazed mind to resist. Every now and then its tail arcs, signalling both insolence and complete hopelessness.

'She can take some poison. I'd'a been well dead by now,' breathes Vincent Yimi, hanging back, mesmerised by the spectacle. The sun is silver on its ringlet body.

'Reckon,' replies Dylan Ward.

'Don't you get too close,' says Vincent, watching uncomfortably as the young bloke crams in so that he can see the diamond in the snake's eyes.

'She's too busy to worry about me.'

Dylan had been watching, almost motionless, for minutes when Vincent noticed him and wandered up.

'I don't like them snakes. Should leave 'em well alone,' he murmurs, scuffing the red Australian dirt with his boots, adjusting the silver Elvis sunglasses he found on a street years ago and that are now his trademark. They cover yellowed eyes crusted with glaucoma. His black skin, so deep and dark that it sucks in the sunlight and leaves his face almost featureless, is glistening with an oily, nervous sweat. Uncle Vincent Yimi. 'You don't want snakes of no sorts around you.'

The lizard's stumpy legs suddenly run in the air, and the king brown's head picks up the rhythm and squirts in more lethal sap. *Pseudechis Australia* doing its thing. *Tiliqua multifasciata* – the central blue-tongued skink – finally getting the message.

'You know about us Aborigines' Dreamtime snakes?' The rainbow serpent that made the universe, and another one that made the rivers, pools and springs. Vincent changing the subject. 'Dreamtime snake is like our mother, the earth. The story of this place.'

'I could sit here all afternoon. Watch it ingest.' Dylan is still fascinated by the moment, anticipating the snake dislocating its jaw, contracting its body in waves, sucking in the corpse to fizz and dissolve inside it.

'It's givin' me the creeps.' Vincent, chilled by the macabre theatre.

'Blackfellas and snakes.'

'Bloody right,' says Vincent. 'Haven't got through 40,000 years in the bush by mucking round with them things. Anyways, better get back inside. They can't settle this without us.'

Dylan and Vincent file back into the mining company's boardroom, where their eyes had picked one another across the negotiating table.

'So we're all agreed in principle on expansion, royalty payments, local labour and conservation,' says chairman Eric Garson eventually. 'We might leave these two to work on the fine detail,' nodding towards them. The locals are a tricky bunch, Garson thinks, but Ward'll fix it up.

'Thank you, gentlemen.' They all troop out, dismissed.

Vincent and Dylan blink back out under the cerulean sky. Vincent shakes his head as he scans the mine's conveyors and passing vehicles, then he turns to Dylan. 'Got any plans?'

'Make sure everyone wins.'

'Nah,' says Vincent. 'I meant, got any plans *now*?'

'Nope.'

'Then how about a lemon squash down the pub?'

'The pub? In Carter's Ford?'

'Yeah. Bit of a drive, but I'll bring you back after.'

'Sounds like a plan to me,' says Dylan. The outback town is more than two hours' drive, off the high plateau and down into the Duncan River valley, and it's a chance to see the landscape alongside the elder. And Dylan knows that's what Vincent is really suggesting.

'Good-o.'

Vincent shambles over to an old four-wheel drive dual cab and humps his bulk in. He scoops rubbish off the passenger floor and seat and throws it back over the headrest.

They go through the security checks, then break free of orange overalls, hardhats with nicknames in black marker, beeping, backing vehicles and the neurotic smell of money.

Vincent glances back towards the mine's dropping boom gate and shakes his head again. 'As long as they're happy in there.'

The ute lumpily builds to ninety kilometres an hour, where the engine rattles settle down. Vincent hums a hybrid mix of tribal chant and country music. 'Funny in there,' he finally says. 'All so damned worried about making squillions. Silly bastards.' There's only a short silence before he corrects himself. 'But ours not to judge...'

'That's right,' says Dylan. 'Some of them are just doing the right thing by their families. Buying their homes, looking after their kids, paying the bills. I know some of them feel they're contributing to the greater good. Providing raw materials for the things we all want. Iron ore for our vehicles. Gas for our energy. Commercial diamonds for lots of things. And some of these guys really do just love mining. I guess there are many ways to be a servant of the landscape.'

Half an hour later, a young bloke with his back to them is playing with a dog by the roadside. Vincent stamps on the brakes, the left disc gripping harder than the right, skewing the Toyota off the edge of the bitumen and onto the dirt. Four hundred and twenty-five thousand square kilometres of the Kimberley, three times the size of England, and only about 35,000 people in the whole joint, and here, on a deserted road in the middle of nowhere, they might just hit one of them.

'Whoa there, girl,' sings Uncle Vincent, manhandling the vehicle to a slithering halt, just in time. The young bloke shambles up to Dylan's wound-down window and sticks his smiling face in. He has long, tightly curled hair with bronze tips, and a headband of bean beads strung on wool.

'Hiya Uncle. Howzit?' He wipes his right hand on his left shoulder then sticks it in through the window towards Dylan. 'Henny. Henny Breeze. G'day.' He wears a green and purple striped shirt and a muggy cloud of body odour.

Dylan takes it and shakes. 'Dylan Ward.'

Henny scoops up the puppy and goes to jump in the back.

'He...' Vincent's snarl sounds forced... 'goes in the tray.'

'But he's only a little tacker. He can sit on my lap.'

'*The tray...*'

'But Uncle, he might fall out. You know how many dogs die every year like that? Well, I can tell you it's a damned lot...' Henny likes to talk.

'Alright. Alright,' says Uncle Vincent. 'But, on yer lap.'

Henny coos to the pup as they pull back onto the bitumen.

Vincent looks straight ahead but talks low to Dylan. 'He likes to come out for the ride, but the mine gives him the shivers. Reminds him of jail, he reckons. So I leave him in the bush a cupla hours.'


Carter's Ford sits in a valley of wispy grassland so wide that the edges show the curve of the earth. Most of the year it's gaspingly dry. Even the most timid, try-your-luck willy-willy wind can whip the red dirt upwards in a spiralling plume.

The valley is dotted with boab trees that have white tucker in olive-green nuts the size of mangoes, fizzy like sherbet. There are bloodwoods with thick, hard branches kinked right to make killer boomerangs. Their oozing ruby sap antiseptic for wounds. Red bloodwood tree boiled to use for colds and flu; bark of emu bush for sores; snake vine for headaches; a paperbark tree, cadjubut, for cooking and carrying, and white eucalypt leaves to flavour fish and meat.

Bush oranges have fruit the size of tennis balls, packed with vitamin C.

Over to the side is the wide, slivering cut of the Duncan River itself. The water from 95,000 square kilometres drains into it and wriggles five hundred kays to the coast. Despite the aquifer beneath, in the Dry season there are just a few tell-tale greening pools left in the riverbed, way below the road bridges; but every Wet season, the northern monsoon's thundering rain combines with gravity to create an awesome force. Early every year, the Duncan River briefly carries more water than India's Ganges.

Uncle Vincent stirs the gearstick and crunches down though the notches long before they pass the town's entry sign. WELCOME TO CARTER'S FORD. The engine settles to a fifty-kay whine and Vincent hooks an arm over the window sill, Henny doing the same in the back. A gaggle of youngsters waves and shouts and Henny jabbers loudly back, circling his hand like royalty. He rocks with laughter.

'Uncle, Uncle. Let me out,' he squeals, and the dual cab's almost padless brakes grind it to a slow halt on wonky discs. Henny slews his cap round backwards, drops one flip-flop and shuffles a foot in.

'Did you lose a thong?' asks Dylan.

'Nah, I found one,' grins Henny. He yells 'see-ya' to Dylan and Vincent, and greets his mates with slappy handshakes. They lurch off down the road together, arms hung around each other's shoulders, the puppy following. 'Cop-ya-later,' chirps Henny, not looking back.

Dylan feels the paradoxical comforts and nervy excitement of extended family and mobs of mates.

'I dunno,' says Vincent. 'That boy's cup is always half full. The other day him and his mate had one thong each. Henny hadn't got any, so Cyrus shared his.'

And then, in a confiding tone, 'Young fellas. You gotta worry about them.'

'I do,' says Dylan. He knows this is a hard place for young blokes to live and an easy place for them to die.

Vincent studies him and nods once.

Now that he's back over the border, in his own country, Vincent Yimi relaxes his grip on the wheel. Carter's Ford: love it or hate it. A few thousand people in the wide grid of streets alongside the river, galvanised to the place by histories. The natural crossing was just outside town and blackfellas used it, following songlines. Then whitefellas came for pasture and gold. But when the river was up they all just had to wait, put in their place by nature; something Aborigines already knew and Europeans still had to learn.

They built the road bridge and trucks followed. Beasts and crushed boulders going out; Fanta and fridges coming in.

Truck airbrakes suck outside as they stand in the tarted-up hotel, Uncle Vincent holding out a twenty-dollar note, waiting to be served, others in and out before him.

'What's yours?' says Vincent. ''Fraid we don't have them fancy city boutique beers. Kangaroo'd eat the hops.' His own joke.

'Want to talk about the mine?' asks Dylan.

'Nah,' says Vincent, moving his elbow back from the damp bar towel. 'No need. We'll get something out of this. You'll help those blokes get to the right thing.'

Dylan looks quizzical. 'You know that?'

'We know you.'

'You do?'

'We know all about you,' says Vincent mischievously. 'They hire you but they don't buy you. Us mobs talk a lot. Just not everyone can hear.'

# Two

The tropical north-west feels as different as its story demands. Eighteen hundred million years ago, it drifted in and welded itself onto the ancient landmass of Gondwana. Later, much of it was covered by a warm, shallow sea. A fringing coral reef hundreds of kilometres long now stands as sharp hills. Then there was ice several kilometres thick. As it thawed, it cut the Duncan River valley and gorges through the limestone ranges.

And, deep down, the geology of the place had been creating other treasures.

The land around the mine has long been crisscrossed by surveyors' lines – the welts of fiscal initiation. Geologists' plastic sample bags accrued in forgotten heaps, hardened and cracked in the sun. They left coloured plastic shards and spilt their contents back to the earth. They had an inkling that this was the top of a lava tube, spewing up diamonds from twenty kays down. Core samples on trolleys were wheeled into the

Scimitar Project's city boardroom to impress prospective investors; as wide as a thigh and their surfaces pocked with diamonds, uncut and rough like sugar cubes. Presentations and gourmet finger food, hard sell and handshakes. Eric Garson's final trick was to mix one of the uncuts into the silk bag of handmade chocolates that he sent home for wives. A seductive rough diamond.

Then the whole resources sector started to boom. Marginal projects got the green light. Iron ore was shipped to China as fast as the country could be loaded into bulk ships; liquefied natural gas went out in deals worth billions; mineral sands were scraped off the land. Uranium and diamonds became hot runners on the stock exchange and the Scimitar Project's share price rocketed.

Soon white demountable buildings stood in rows. Amber lights flashed on vehicles. Blasting crews blew the guts out of the joint. Power shovels loaded forty-five tonnes a time into haulpak trucks that carried enough rock to fill a house. It was crushed, ground and sifted, and out of it all came tiny nuggets held between tweezers under a magnifying glass.

The initial local negotiations had been tricky and Eric Garson wasn't planning on doing that again. He needed someone the traditional owners would go along with. So he'd put out the word and come up with Dylan Ward.

Most mine site offices have bare walls with holes punched by fists, or girlie and fast-car posters, or the kids' drawings, but Dylan's feels like a gallery. On a shelf in one corner there's a handmade wandoo mandolin and two finely carved boab nuts. A painting by Mabel Scarletfinch hangs on one wall; the creator spirit's big face has two dark eyes and no mouth and its round head seems to throw out light. Near it, there are two old hats with holed crowns and gnawed edges, spattered with diesel or blood. One was Mabel's, and the other was worn to death by Jimmy Skinner, who had dreams and painted them, and who taught Mabel to work in ochres, when she asked to learn. Everything in the room has meaning.

Dylan is at a silver laptop, attaching his final report and emailing it to the chairman.

Garson is impressed. Ward seems to have put together the basis of a watertight royalty agreement. He reckons the local labour clause is a load of baloney, but it's no skin off his nose. When it falls in a heap, he'll just bring in more hard-arsed Maoris. Ward has outlined a separate traineeship plan to be developed with the local community – cooked up with Yimi, no doubt. Classrooms, lecturers, broadband. Garson types hard with two fingers, 'Thanks for the email. A mutually beneficial option.'

But don't hold your breath, he thinks.

Dylan has just received Garson's reply when the phone rings.

'Vincent Yimi here.'

'Good to hear you. What's up?'

'We're going up-river,' says Uncle Vincent, straight to the point. 'You can come if you want to.'

'I'd like to. Thanks.' Knows not to over-enthuse.

'Henny'll come along. Keeps him out of strife. Airplane too.'

Dylan's confused. 'By aircraft?'

There's no change in Vincent's voice. 'No,' he says. 'You go up the river in a boat. Nelson's got one. But we'll take my uncle, Airplane Cuttover. He wants to see them gorges again, and we need him with us. He's from Minjubal people.'

'Coupla days,' continues Vincent. 'Bring a swag, that's all. We'll have all the tucker an' that.'

Dylan rings and books a room at the hotel in Carter's Ford – it's only a couple of hours' drive, but he reckons he'll spend an extra night there when they come off the river.

And then he dials another number. The phone is quickly answered. 'Erindale Station. Amy speaking.'

'Hi Amy, how are you? It's Dylan Ward.'

'Dylan – how lovely to hear you.' And Amy Parkes means it. 'How have you been?'

They talk for a few minutes, ranging easily round subjects. More than the commonplace. 'Were you after Billy? He's out in the shed. I can put you through to him out there now – he's wired it all up.'

'Thanks Amy. It's been lovely catching up.'

'For me too. Any chance of you coming by this way soon?'

'I'll try.'

'Well, whenever it is, we'll be pleased to see you. Bye then.'

He waits for Billy to come to the phone, and conjures up an image of the work shed it's hanging in. Dylan remembers the story of how station boys Billy and his big brother Ace had fled a rotten father when they were young. How they'd set out to break the pattern of the men in that family, but how Ace had been dragged back into it. How he'd bitten on the barrel of a gun and pulled the trigger in a shed probably just like the one Billy is in now. Of Billy's agony at the loss.

'G'day Dylan. How's it hangin'?'

And they chat easily, too. News and views. Life and limb. Billy tells him how things are on Erindale Station, his million-acre spread that's run smart and diversified away from just cattle, then ranges out into other issues down the east end of the Kimberley. Dylan fills in bits on the west of it. Tells him he's just off up the Duncan River with Vincent Yimi, Henny Breeze and Airplane Cuttover.

'That'll be interesting. An invitation like that's not to be sneezed at. They're the men.'

It's a hullabaloo. Nelson Milson has tied his yellow polyethylene boat to the riverbank and is stalking around it in bare feet and bright blue overalls, sleeves rolled high up his thin biceps. Wisps of hair spiral off his mottled white head. He's exasperated. He coils pieces of rope which are too short for any real purpose, shifts the red fuel tank a smidge one way, then back to the original spot, stows the boat hook — made from an old broom-handle with a bend of wire taped to it — then gets it out again. He shouts orders at Henny, who is lugging gear. Uncle Vincent tells Henny to carry the swags down the steep bank, then Nelson orders him to take them back up. 'Heavy stuff first,' he barks, turning back to his tidying. Henny lugs down the big coolbox, but then Vincent tells him to stop fussing with that and get the water jerries in pronto.

By the time Dylan arrives, it is at fever pitch.

'Sorry I'm late. Flat tyre,' he explains. The mine vehicle's right rear gave out halfway into town and he eventually found the jack jammed under the back seat.

'No worries,' says Vincent. 'We're still getting organised.'

'Come back tomorrow,' chimes Henny cheerily, 'and you won't have missed much...'

'Less of the cheek, you,' shouts Uncle Vincent, feigning annoyance. 'You lot just stop ginning around and get that esky into the boat.'

'Let me give you a hand,' says Dylan, darting forward to grab one handle of the big plastic coolbox.

'Cheers,' says Henny. 'Nice to have someone who's not giving orders. Got enough of them.'

'Cheeky young bugger,' chips Uncle Vincent.

'Lost control of that boy,' says Nelson, bending to shift the fuel tank back to position B.

'Never had it,' says Henny. Water off a duck's back.

'You could use a little respect, my lad,' says Nelson.

'I could use a drink,' says Henny. 'And a pretty girlfriend along, instead of you old fellas.' He swallows down great gobs of air as he laughs. *Old fellas.* 'And you blokes could do with pretty girlfriends along too, I reckon.'

'When you get to my age,' says Uncle Vincent, 'you're happier with half an ounce of tobacco. Anyway, what could be more perfect?'

'If the river was made out of nice, cold beer,' says Henny.

'Nah – that'd be no good.'

'Why's that?'

'You'd have to piss in the boat.'


'Dylan Ward.' Dylan introduces himself to Nelson as he slithers down alongside the gunwale. 'I'd shake, but...' He hangs on to the esky.

'Better off doing a deal of work with a hand than poncing around,' says Nelson, now with too much of a head of steam for niceties.

'You'll come to love him.' Henny stage whispers to Dylan. 'He's really as sweet as pie.'

'Don't push your luck, you...' says Nelson furiously, clenching his right hand into a fist and wheeling it back over his left shoulder, ready to strike, pointing a thin, bony elbow threateningly at Henny. 'Or you'll get what-for.'

Dylan expects another smart-arse answer from Henny, but that's where it stops. 'Yes sir,' he says, signalling to Dylan with raised eyebrows.

'C'mon you blokes. Stop arsing about,' says Uncle Vincent, 'or it'll be dark before we get away.'

They one-two-three lift the esky over the side of the boat and, oddly, within minutes everything is loaded and they are all but ready to go. Dylan clips his car keys onto the karabiner inside his daypack as he heads back down to the boat, carrying a small black case with him.

'You gonna bury the cat down there?' asks Henny.

'Mandolin,' says Dylan.

'Yay,' sings Henny.

'Better get Uncle. Bring him down,' says Vincent to Henny. 'An' we'll be off.'

Airplane Cuttover sits in the passenger seat of Vincent's four-wheel drive, calmly staring ahead. Unbearded but unevenly shaved, his dark chin is spiked with stray whiskers. Black hair flour-dusted with grey starts from high up on his forehead and cascades backwards and well below his shoulders. Surf-style sunglasses with shiny maroon frames are pushed up on his head, held by the neoprene band that is tight around the back. His loose white T-shirt, with THE BIG KAHUNA written across in yellow spangles, has been worn to a soft thinness. He could be an old forty-eight or a young eighty-four.

Henny talks gently to the elder, telling him they are ready, and the old man snaps out of his trance. He swings his left leg out of the door; a thin calf and bony ankle jutting from his baggy pants. When Airplane stands, Dylan senses a tribal body under the western clothes, not only in the shape, but in the stance – the slightly bowed legs, pelvis tilted forward, elbows hooked out but arms held long.

Henny walks a little behind Airplane as he heads towards them with high and slightly unsure steps.

Vincent introduces Dylan and the old man nods without looking at the newcomer. Then Henny takes Airplane by one arm and gently helps him into the boat. 'There, Uncle,' he says, leading him to the pile of swags. 'You sit there, comfortable-like.'

Henny jumps back out of the boat, shapes the thumb and third finger of his right hand like a crescent moon and sticks them between his teeth. He whistles a long, shrill note. 'Ready to cast off, Admiral Nelson,' he says in best Pommy.

Nelson Milson splutters, 'Just let go that line.'

'Aye, aye, Cap'n Blackbeard, ye old pirate,' drawls Henny. And then he adds, 'Hey Cap'n – you know how to make a pirate irate?'

Nelson gives him a withering look.

'Take the pee out of him,' continues Henny, unabashed.

'Get it? The 'P'? Pirate? Irate? Learnt that one in spelling class.'

'All the money the taxpayers spent on yer education, and that's it?' growls Nelson.

'Yep,' grins Henny proudly. 'I guess it is.'

'Whatta circus,' mutters Vincent.

Airplane sits silently in the bow and looks ahead.

Some parts of the river are edged by tall melaleucas, the paper-like bark hanging off like sheets of sunburnt skin. Wild pear, corkwood and coolamon – *Gyrocarpus,* which kids throw high in handfuls, to watch them propeller against the blazing sky. Black flying foxes hang by the hundred in the eucalypts, one or two letting go, circling on membranous wings and reattaching further along. Three Johnson crocodiles sun themselves on rocks, like plastic toys, their cold-blooded lives revolving around temperature as they have done for 150 million years. Using the high sun now, the shade later, and the cooler water.

The river flows serpentine through lower country and then into gorges, where red rock walls rise either side until the boat is dwarfed. Two short-eared rock wallabies scamper ledge to ledge for cover.

Nelson, sitting at the stern, twists off the throttle grip and the Yamaha outboard idles. The monumental walls are fractured, a few big fig trees rooted in the smallest crevices. The eternal optimism of *Ficus.*

There are four distinct colours: rock already reddening with the falling sun, the lush green edging, the dark blue of the water, and the white wake streaming out in smooth arcs behind the boat.

'Good country,' Dylan shouts to Vincent, over engine noise.

Vincent nods without taking his gaze off the river ahead. The place holds hearts and beliefs.

In a big Wet season, the Duncan River's catchment might get 1600 millimetres of rain, and more than a million litres of water a second come down the river, but now it is calm and the late sun paints it an oily gold.

'This is it,' Uncle Vincent shouts to Nelson over the Yamaha outboard. 'We'll camp here.' He points to his right, on the outside of a bend, where the vegetation gives way to a sandy beach. Two hundred metres back, through *Pandanus* and *Livistona* palms, the sandstone rises in a sheer face with a deep vertical crack. In there, the vegetation looks even lusher.

'Tie us off,' Nelson shouts to Henny as they bump the bank, and Henny leaps into ankle-deep, gravelly sand.

Airplane Cuttover bends for a smooth, washed-up stick, clacks it on a flat rock to test its stoutness, and sets off cautiously towards the rock face behind.

Henny and Dylan are lifting gear out of the boat, while Nelson is stringing out ropes to trees and burying the anchor in the sand. 'Henny,' Uncle Vincent calls. 'You can leave that. Go with him now.'

'Yes, Uncle,' he says, compliant, and jogs up the sand to follow just behind the old man.

'I'll give you a hand.' Vincent nods to Dylan. 'They got business up there.'

'You got a woman?' Vincent is pottering at the river's edge.

'Not at the moment,' Dylan answers, caught off-guard by the blunt question.

'I thought there was something wrong. Good-looking young bloke like you should have a woman.'

'What do you mean "something wrong"?'

'Something not settled in here,' the older man bangs a fist on his own heart. 'Ever been someone special?'

'There was once, but it didn't work out. Perhaps it wasn't the right time.'

'Well, even a broken clock has the right time twice a day,' says Vincent.

'Maybe it wasn't that it was the wrong time, then, or even the wrong thing,' Dylan says. He pauses. 'I just *did* the wrong thing.'

'We can all let ourselves down sometimes.'

'Yeah, well I really did. Let myself down – more, importantly, I let her, Jules, down. We were young and really caught up in environmental stuff. I met her through the forest protests down south...'

'Old-growth stuff. I heard about that,' says Vincent.

'It got nasty – the police and government departments in there burning our camps, protesters living on platforms up trees, chaining ourselves in the way of bulldozers. And then there were the dragons.'

The last word is almost drowned by river-sound.

'Dragons?'

'Car bodies. We got car bodies and cut a hole in the bottom just big enough to put a hand through. Then dug a pit underneath and concreted in a cylinder as long as your arm. Fixed a dog collar in the bottom so that you could clip it round your wrist. Then we concreted the cylinder – and the whole car – in the ground. You laid in the car, pushed your arm through and "locked on". It was all made so you couldn't get your arm out.'

'Scary.'

'Yeah, it was scary alright, but we were so caught up in the thing. We believed we were doing it for future generations; that we could change the world. We just wanted the place protected – turned into a national park. Lots of us wanted to do a dragon.'

'You did it?'

'Yes, I did.'

'They got you out, though. I can see that.'

'Yeah, they got me out. The others ran off and it took the police and emergency guys nearly a day to cut and dig me out. Compressors running big angle grinders and jackhammers to break up the concrete. And I got frightened.'

'I'd-a been bloody frightened, too.'

'Not really scared of being hurt or anything. I just got terrified of the repercussions. The guys were talking to me about it. I panicked about getting a criminal record – it suddenly became real. Not a game. A lot of the protesters had records. They were put on a good behaviour bond first time, then sent to jail the second time. I was studying, had a future. I worried about what it would do to mum and dad.'

'So?'

'So I did a deal.'

'I see.'

'I got off. The others didn't. Jules got the worst of it. She was already on a bond and ended up in a women's prison for six months.'

They sit in silence.

'I kidded myself it was the right thing because I'd be of more use if I didn't have a police record. But that wasn't the truth of it. I just bailed on her.'

Vincent turns quietly to him. 'Well, you wouldn't have been doing this negotiation for the mine if you'd been in that sort of trouble. You've helped us mob and others before us.'

Dylan doesn't answer.

Henny stumbles back into camp with an armful of firewood and Dylan moves to help him unload.

Then Henny holds out his fingers and Dylan sees a stodge of green ants. 'Here, try these. Old Uncle just showed me.' He looks thrilled. 'They taste like honey. Learnin' cultural stuff here.'

'Never had them before?'

'Must be kiddin'. More of a burger man, me.'

'How's this?' Nelson appears from behind rocks, holding up a barramundi almost the length of his arm.

'Good going,' Vincent says.

'Too easy,' Nelson replies. He cleans the fish downstream, watched by a white-breasted sea eagle which eventually swoops in to hook up the guts as they float away. Nelson lays the silver fish out on the sand near the fire, goes to the boat and sprays his finger with water-dispersant oil. Dylan's look questions it.

'Catfish barb,' says Nelson. 'Caught one before this and he got me. Best thing for it, CRC.

'Anyway,' he says. 'Someone better cook this lot up. I could eat the crutch out of a low-flying duck.'

The fish has been grilled over coals and they have eaten the two hard, slightly black-crusted homemade loaves from a cardboard box. The billy can has been boiled twice and the meal washed down with strong black tea.

In mellow mood, they lie back on their swags as the rising moon picks out the bends of the river in silver. The water has a constant song.

'When the earth was just born, the great Dreamtime snake came here,' Airplane says suddenly in a strong voice. He looks from Henny to Dylan and back again. 'He moved through this country, making this river. That's the story here. This snake, he's the big creator. Big boss spirits helped him bring laws and kinship.' Then the old uncle seems to vanish again back into the dark.

There is silence for a long time, then Henny murmurs a country song and Dylan starts to strum a soft accompaniment on his mandolin. Henny smiles appreciatively and sings a little louder. When the remembered words have petered out, he hums a bit, then lies back and listens to the mandolin's sweet chords and the sound of the contented elder breathing heavily as he drifts into sleep.

'The old man's comfortable in this place,' Vincent tells Dylan under his breath. 'No-one above him here – only the spirits themselves. He's an important man in this country, and the place knows him. Feels at ease too.' His eyes are amber in the firelight, and he fixes them on Dylan. 'And he likes you.'

'He does?'

'Oh yes, he likes you.'

'How would you know if he didn't?'

'He wouldn't be like this.'

Under the great sweep of stars set in velvet, Dylan dreams he is meandering. He can't separate his mind and body. There is just this more abstract sense of him – the concept of his whole self – being gently sucked along an arcing path by a silvery gravity. He is not scared and not resistant. Just enticed by the feeling of being guided. He glides through his colubrine unconsciousness.

Dylan wakes in the dark with the feeling still in his head.

'Been dreamin'?' Vincent is almost invisible in the night, sitting near coals that are now only the faintest red.

'Yes,' says Dylan.

'Good dream?'

'I think so. I don't often dream – or, at least, I don't remember my dreams – but when I do, they're usually bad.'

'About the girl?'

'I suppose so. Guilt.'

'Every right-thinking man has it, I reckon. I read stuff from the suicide psychologists saying guilt's a useless emotion, but I don't reckon so. I reckon you get guilt from conscience, and if you haven't got one of *them* you're not the full ticket.' Vincent pokes the red cinder bed. 'Mind you, you'd probably sleep better without one, and be less likely to hang up your boots and take an early shower. The bead grows brighter. 'What now for you?'

'Home for a bit,' replies Dylan. 'Time with mum and dad. Give them a hand around the place. See what happens. Look out for another contract.'

'The city? Good luck,' grins Vincent. 'That place is no good for anyone. There's too much trouble down there.'

'You think so?'

'Yeah. It's just gravity, I reckon. The sludge gathers at the bottom.'

'The city?'

'Yeah,' Vincent says, meeting Dylan with a steady gaze. 'Too much bad stuff. Too many people burgling, stealing to swap for drugs, running in mobs, stealing cars, hurting folk. You know it, I know it.' Then he smiles, like sun breaking through dark cloud. 'Besides, there's a lot of this country in you now. You'll miss this place more-n-more.'

'You can take the boy from the country but you can't take the country from the boy?'

'Something like that.'

Something more than that. Country. A word. A place. But the Kimberley has become more than either of these things to Dylan. It is a learnt place for him, but has such substance that it has become a complete entity. This country permeates, percolates, diffuses through him. He has absorbed it and they have become fused. It subsumes him.

This country is not just a place. Not just geography or geology, but an amalgamation of landscape and sentiment. He is steeped in the country. It is that simple; that complex.

When Dylan walks into the hotel's reception, there's a folded sheet of paper waiting for him. The receptionist slides it over and he opens it. 'I'm in town. If you have time, give me a call. Maybe we can catch up. If not, no hassles – maybe next time you're here or I'm there.' There's a mobile phone number, and Billy Parkes's name across the bottom.

Dylan immediately presses in the number and Billy answers.

'What are you doing here?'

'After we talked the other day, I thought I'd come down, just on the off-chance. In case you had a bit of time on your hands. Used it as an excuse to pick up some gear in Kununda, too.' In fact, Billy has driven seven hours down a corrugated dirt road awash with gravel to the town of Kununda, fuelled up, and then another six hundred kilometres on the bitumen. Billy knows how to value friendship, and the importance of connection.

'Well, I really appreciate it,' says Dylan. Not shy to fix him eye to eye. 'I really like our friendship.'

Billy and Dylan look a little alike. Though Billy is a few years older, in his mid-thirties, he's on the same wavelength, and for Dylan he's been a personal conduit into the northern landscape.

'I love the place and I might know a bit about it, but I'm not really from here. I've never lived here,' Dylan had once told him. 'I'm not local. I've never really lived here for a long period.'

'I don't see how any of that matters,' said Billy. 'You get the place.'

'Yes, but you know it in a different way. An everyday way. And you've seen the use of the landscape change — you've been part of it, instrumental in it.'

There's a trigger in the sentence that fires off memories for Billy. When he and his brother Ace were boys, many of the stations were overgrazed dustbowls, but Billy could see the possibilities of diversity. And here it is — more careful grazing, tourism, conservation. 'You know, when I was a kid, you could drive from one side of the Kimberley to the other and only see three or four vehicles on the way. People would stop in the middle of the road to chat.

'Now you'd get mown over. There are hundreds. Thousands. It's a huge shift.'

It was a shift that Ace couldn't make, that tore them apart, and which led to Ace's violent end. A wound that Billy still carries, but which friends like Dylan help to heal.

# Three

The bottleneck tidal estuary of the Duncan River is inundated by eleven-metre tides as the moon pushes water into its gawping mouth, then drags it out again, leaving crabs and mud skippers to clean up what's left on the grey sludge. Mangroves discard garlands of salty leaves.

And three hard days' drive away, the city has its own tidal ebb and flow. In the early morning, a workaday flood of urban humans washes in, between concrete canyons. At night, office towers are solid blocks of light; the cleaners are busy at work. Fluids are pressure-hosed off bus stands, rubbish inhaled by drive-around vacuums. Security cars do laps but the kids hanging around the railway station have mostly disappeared. The 24-hour burger diners are oases.

A pre-dawn lull is broken by the squeal of bus brakes as the incoming tide of white- and blue-collar workers starts again.

Kate Kennedy waits for the pedestrian lights to blink green and propel her across with their tick-tick-tick-tick. A sideways glance at a tinted office window shows her white shirt, straight black skirt, pale skin and dark hair pinned back. Elegantly tall, classy posture, killer calves.

Michael Mooney likes an early morning meeting with her, if he hasn't got another appointment. The Minister wants his takeaway coffee from the same place – double-shot long black, piping hot – and expects Kate to pick it up. Ronaldo shrugs as he adds it to the tab.

She swings in and then out of the Parliament House lift, pushes backwards through the office door, drops her bag on her desk, taps on the door to Mooney's office and hands him his coffee. 'Ah. My little heart-starter.' He draws on flirtatious memories.

'Good morning, Minister,' Kate replies, sometimes cool and formal, occasionally with warmth that's a souvenir; playing it a little.

Michael Mooney's two portfolios – Planning and Infrastructure, and the new Water Resources – put her right in the fray, and she likes that. She could have ended up Chief of Staff in Housing or Veterans Affairs or something. And Mooney's sharp. He'll end up State Premier, or go federal, with her taken along for the ride. And she knows how much he'd like to do that again, remembering her one-off indiscretion as an intern at her first conference, with a then frontbencher clearly going places.

The Minister's responsibilities combine in the story splashed across the front page before him – WATER CRISIS DEEPENS – but first he reads the second lead, FIRST BLOOD ON ELECTION TRAIL. It's a flop of a report about a 'leaked' opposition election promise and he knows the paper's only run it to get the ball rolling. His coffee and the news are equally stimulating. The spotlight makes him feel frisky.

'Any word from Jack Cole?' he asks.

The name catches Kate by surprise, but she's careful not to show it. The Premier only recently lifted his ban on having any contact with Cole. Officially pronounced persona non grata for members of parliament by the previous incumbent, Cole has wheedled his way back into the circles of power through persistency, bullying and blatantly calling in favours. Part lobbyist, part consultant, part adviser, part dealmaker. The new young Premier, Simon Whittaker, arrived like a breath of fresh air – open-minded, egalitarian – and let him back in. A show of confidence. But Cole knows that idealists get only a short honeymoon in government. The voters like the dream, but when the wheels fall off, the party factions'll turn to the old guard, with Mooney certain to take over, and him sitting pretty.

Cole is powerful, manipulative and he's trouble, Kate thinks. 'We haven't heard anything. Would you like me to get hold of him?'

'It's OK,' Mooney says. 'I'll do it.' The mobile phone when she's gone, he thinks. That's better.


'Jack Cole.' The voice is abrupt and there's car noise in the background.

'It's Michael Mooney. Can you talk?'

'I was going to ring you. Did Peter van Hoot contact you about the rail link contract?'

'Yes. I'm seeing him next week. But there's something else. I want to meet.'

'Sure…but just on van Hoot…it's important to get this thing ironed out. You'll like him. He can get it done. You can lose the other tenders somewhere, can't you? There must be enough piles of paper to tuck them under.'

'It doesn't work like that…'

'Sure, I know,' oozes the perfidious Cole. 'I'm just trying to help everyone out.'

Mooney knows about Cole's fat retainer from van Hoot. 'As I said, I'm seeing him.'

'Good man. And what can I do for you now?' Cole is adept at keeping the ledger going.

'It's sensitive,' says Mooney. 'I'd rather not talk on the phone. Dinner at the Aegean?'

'Sure. I can clear this evening if it's urgent.' The Minister's cautiousness is exciting.

'Eight, then. Franco's tizzed up the wine list. It's on me.'

On the taxpayer, thinks Cole, and who better? 'Eight it is.'

Mooney leaves the government car parked behind Parliament House and takes a taxi to the restaurant. He gets the cabbie to drop him off in an adjacent street, and uses the back door.

'I see what you mean about the wine list,' says Cole, already ensconced in a curtained booth, not rising as they shake hands. 'I took the liberty…' He raises the glass of red. 'Bloody good one.'

The Aegean is full. In the middle, there are be-seen-at round tables with white cloths and noisy groups leftover from sales lunches. Women flashy as whitebait accept Krug sent with messages.

But the real point of the Aegean is the booths. It looks like a quaint, old-fashioned idea, but in a boom-and-bust economy, privacy is imperative. Cockerel today, feather duster tomorrow. Franco, the Aegean's owner, knows the value of seclusion. He leans into the booth, offers a thin handshake and welcomes the Minister. 'And what do we think we might eat tonight?'

Cole has already dissected the menu, but Mooney says: 'I'll leave it to you, Franco.'

'Certainly. Tonight we have very good specials.' He pauses effectually, closing one hand over the other. 'A little gnocchi to start with. I have a new man from Italy and very good at this.' He smiles too sweetly. 'Then a coral trout.' He pouts like a fish. 'You leave to me.'

'Lamb rack,' snaps Cole. The little man annoys him. 'Oysters to start. A dozen.'

'But of course, signor. Naturel?'

Cole glances at him witheringly.

'Certainly. *Gracie.*' Franco shows his palms and tilts his head, in blessing.

'*Prego.*' Mooney doesn't mind playing games.


It's eight o'clock when Kate finally flicks on her apartment's lights, careful not to drop the aluminium takeaway container. The place looks desolate and the lasagne's grease is staining the edges of its cardboard lid orange. She leaves it on the counter, drops her bag on the chair in the bedroom, kicks off her shoes and starts to peel off clothes that smell of offices and politics. Quickly naked, she walks on the balls of her feet into the bathroom, unnecessarily locks the door, and cranks the shower on full.

'God,' she murmurs, to no-one but herself, gripping either side of the hand basin while the shower water warms in a cascade behind her. What a day. She lifts her head and is shocked by her own exhaustion. In the fogging mirror, she looks done in. She drops her head again, and watches the curve of her breasts from this unusual angle. Well, at least *they* look pretty good. Then she stands straight, takes one step back and confronts her midriff, which in her critical eyes is starting to lose the tautness of a more athletic youth. She looks softer. There's nothing like the naked truth, she thinks, and this is it: You're in a rat race, it's wearing you out, and at the end of the day, you won't get any prizes. She's starting to wonder what it's all about. And she's trying to ignore the stir of a clock ticking somewhere, unexpected and unwanted.

Half an hour; that's a decent shower.

'*You wouldn't think there was a water shortage,*' her father used to call through the bathroom door when she did this. What drove John Kennedy insane was not the waste of water, but having his daughter behind the locked door. He'd storm into the kitchen. 'It's not normal. That long in the bathroom.'

'Use the other one,' said her mother, Alison, swinging a business jacket on and eating toast at the same time.

'It's not that.'

Kate revelled in privacy behind the locked door – these moments when no-one had control over her.

Michael Mooney takes an hour to outline the proposal to Jack Cole. 'Water is the pressing issue and the voters are looking for a vision.' It already sounds rehearsed. 'They don't want to take shorter showers, they don't want their lawns to die and they don't want to pay more for it. There's a backlash on desalination – it looks short-term and it's expensive. There is the power use, the greenhouse gases and the super-saline outflow. The voters think it will affect their fishing and crabbing in the Sound.'

Cole knows not to stop a pollie in full flight. He pours another generous glass of red and tops up Mooney's.

'After two terms, we've established our credentials with the handling of the economy and, as I say, it is time for some visionary government.' It's already a sound-bite.

Mooney draws breath dramatically and sips from his glass.

'And that's where the northern water pipeline project comes in.'

Cole can barely believe what he's hearing. 'Piping water from the north? You know how many people have fallen foul of that old idea?' It comes out more blunt than he planned, but political careers have drowned before in a hysterical response to the idea.

'Times have changed,' says Mooney. 'Technology has changed. The city's water situation is critical. Our understanding of the effects of climate change means it's not acceptable to the electorate to keep putting in more desalination units. That no longer looks like a long-term strategy. But this is.'

'It's a gamble, but I see where you're going.'

'Be clear...' Mooney drops into the voice he uses for clinchers. 'Piping water two and a half thousand kilometres is a long-term, visionary solution. There's more water in the north than you can imagine and only thirty thousand people. When the Duncan River is flowing, more than seven gigalitres of water – enough to fill a football stadium to the top of its goalposts seven times over – would flow over the top of a dam every day.' Cole knows he is listening to a media statement being rehearsed. 'I've had the figures done – it's highly confidential, of course.'

Mooney sips and continues. 'For the two million people in the metropolitan area, it's a big answer to a big problem. And that is not only good, strong government, but, if we sell it right, it'll certainly guarantee us the election at the end of the year.'

Mooney breaks into a smile. He hasn't tried this pitch on anyone before – but speaking it aloud fills him with confidence.

Cole latches on to just one word. 'A dam? They're political dynamite.'

'The water source has to be sustainable throughout the year,' says Mooney, still practicing. 'That was the flaw with previous proposals – they didn't grasp the nettle. You need to draw all year round from a reservoir in the Duncan River valley to make it viable.'

The voting numbers are good, thinks Jack. Two million 'for', probably only five thousand in the Duncan River catchment 'against'. But it's still politically risky. Greenies, Indigenous groups, graziers – they can all be noisy. 'What do you want me to do?'

'We need to do our groundwork. I don't just want to know who would be affected – I need to know who they are, what connections they have and what sort of noise they could make. Station owners, Indigenous communities, conservation groups, tourism. I need you to gauge the worst-case political fallout from them. The miners might end up being the trickiest lobby – but all the diamond stuff and big operators are way outside this area – only a few independent miners would be affected. But you know as well as I do what sort of lobby they can raise, so we'll leave them out of this little exercise. Handle them separately later.'

'I can't see the locals being keen to share heart and soul with me,' says Cole. 'Asking questions around the place will stir up trouble.'

'There is another *device* to deal with that,' says Mooney. 'Carter's Ford and just about all the communities in the valley still use diesel generators. Some are getting on – none of it is very efficient. So far as people up there are concerned, you'll be looking at the viability of replacing diesel with sustainable power. A pilot project. If there's any doubt about the success of hinging the campaign on the water pipeline, we can always drop solar in as part of the platform. It's not strong enough to hang things on, but it's good enough for a media release.' He adds, 'It's another reason for not calling on the miners – the story wouldn't wash with them.'

Michael Mooney has surprised Cole with a sharp scheme. 'Who knows the detail of the water project?'

'Planning and Infrastructure had the preliminary scientific and engineering work done years ago – a feasibility study of the technical side of building the pipeline and putting in the pumping stations. Never made public. Forgotten on a shelf somewhere. I've had someone update and add to it and it's strong enough to hang the announcements off. There's an obvious dam site – it was identified when they were trying to get cotton grown there, years back. You might remember the fuss about that.' Cole does indeed, and understands Mooney's caution now.

'I've got someone coming up with a costing for the whole

thing,' continues Mooney. 'Someone I trust.'

'And the Premier and other Ministers?'

'Not yet,' says Mooney.

'Whose seat it is? Will McCaffrey? What about him? After all, he's a country member.'

'Yes, I remember. That's why he won't get to hear about this. This is my little project.'

Cole bristles with excitement. Mooney clearly has his sights on Simon Whittaker.

Yes, thinks Cole. I'll hitch my wagon. 'What about logistics?' he asks.

'My Chief of Staff, Kate Kennedy, will set it up personally. You know her. She'll come along and make it all work.' Behind every political leader, a chief of staff lives in the shadows. Unrelenting hours, enormous pressure, alert to the ever-present threat of political disaster, but with a guaranteed seat in the inner sanctum. Their pay-off's in power. Kate is the intermediary between Mooney, his ministries, the backbench, the bureaucracy and the party. She makes the call on day-to-day decisions, and is there as a final rubber-stamp for Mooney's conclusions. 'What do you think, Kate?' How often had she heard that, knowing Mooney just needed a final, but probably superfluous, ratification?

'Kate Kennedy?' Cole thinks she's a lightweight.

'She's been with me a long time,' says Mooney, but Cole involuntarily raises an eyebrow. 'I trust her,' Mooney says decisively and a little too loud. 'She's smart and she's ambitious.' Knowing the lengths she once went to. 'She knows the lie of the land.'

'Decorative, too,' smiles Cole, backing off and changing the tone.

Michael Mooney realises he's pitched an unexpected attraction. 'She'll find someone who knows these people and can get you into places, but only you and Kate will be aware of the real nature of this little excursion.'

Mooney musters chill to his voice. 'This mustn't backfire, Cole. In the election run-in, that'd be a disaster.' Cole nods slowly, weighing up the real value of what Mooney is saying.

'Cost for the trip isn't a problem,' says Mooney. 'We don't need to tender on this. You can invoice me and I'll see to it. And I'd consider it a favour.'

A favour. Better than cash, thinks Cole. That's really something to bank. Get this mob re-elected for a third term, then help ease Mooney into the Premier's seat.

With Cole on board, Michael Mooney has slept well, and by the time his heart-starter arrives, he's keen to place the next piece of the jigsaw.

'Good morning, Minister.' Kate has knocked, and swings in through the door with his black coffee.

'Ah, Kate.' He tries to make it sound warm and confidential, but ends up sounding almost surprised to see her. 'There's something I want to run through with you. Close the door would you.'

He talks through the sustainable power plan, gauging her receptiveness.

'It's a good project,' she says. 'Clean energy, relatively inexpensive.' Then she pauses. Her radar is working. 'But it's not big enough to hang an election campaign on.'

'You're quite right.' Mooney acknowledges her shrewdness with a nod. 'But it's a good back-up.'

'Back-up?' She thought so.

'It's something we can use if we need to.'

Mooney starts with the city's demand for water, talks up the pipeline and ends with the dam. The spiel unfurls even smoother this time.

It's visionary, all-or–nothing politics and she's on the inside, where she wants to be.

'You need to find someone to put it together on the ground,' Mooney is saying. 'Someone to give you an "in". And Jack Cole is coming along.'

Kate winces. She'd assumed it was all hers. Cole is a cocktail of ego, confidence and power – not without its attractions, but he makes her edgy. There's a jumble of emotions, but mostly Kate's just plain fed up. She knows Cole will take over and assume she's just there to run around after him.

But she tells herself she's still in there, and being on the inside of this, she'll be there all the way. She tells herself to swallow her pride and get a win out of it.

Kate learnt how to succeed in a man's world by watching her mother. Alison's life had been in two parts, the first smothered by John's self-opinion, uncompromising business drive and the sexual indiscretions that he barely tried to hide. And then came the second part of her life. *No more* she said to herself, and then to her husband.

'What exactly do you have in mind?'

'Change,' she said, and he shuddered, knowing the alternative would bankrupt him.

'It will ruin everything.'

You already have, she thought. 'I am going back to my career. I will look after Andrew and Kate. You can pay the bills and come and go as you please. But we will live separately, in every sense.'

'Is that it?'

'That's it.'

And it was. John Kennedy became absent from the family and Alison eased back into a city accountancy firm through old contacts. Nothing was said, but the teenagers saw it all clearly. Kate's brother Andrew got his law degree with honours and a good offer from a firm in Scotland, and Kate learned to not equate men with morality. Later she began to think that they were like parking spots with the best ones taken and the rest handicapped.

Kate concentrates on the map spread across her desk. She hasn't even heard of half the places. 'Always get a plan,' Alison had taught her. Mt Goode, Daydawn, Barker River, Warramorra. The most important thing is to find someone who knows them. She writes 'Department of Industry and Resources'. Even though Mooney doesn't want to include them, miners are the best bet when it comes to this sort of stuff.

'Kevin. It's Kate Kennedy.' She smiles to make herself sound more amiable. 'I'm good, thanks. How about you? Good. Have you got time to meet? I need to pick your brains. Lunch – on me.' Carmichael suggests the next day at the glassy sushi restaurant, where they're sure to be seen. No-one turns down a lunch date with Kate Kennedy. They all reckon she's one to watch.

'Dylan Ward's the man to show you round up there,' says Carmichael, lifting raw tuna and touching it on wasabi.

'Dylan Ward, by a country mile.' He eases one knee forward to brush hers under the table. She pulls her leg away.

'Who's he?'

'He was out at Solder Range mine site doing their environmental and Aboriginal stuff. He did some work in Laverley. A bit hippy, but he does a good job. But his last contract was at the Scimitar Project – near where you're talking about. He got between Eric Garson and the local community and pulled it off. They like him. There's no-one to touch him as the go-between in that region now. You'll need Ward if you've got that prick Cole along.' Kevin Carmichael looks sceptical. 'Even if it's a good-news sustainability thing.'

'Do you know how to contact this Dylan Ward?'

'Yeah, I've kept track of him. He's the sort you want to keep tabs on. I heard he wasn't up to much at the moment, so he'll probably be keen enough. I'll send an email with the contact details.'

Kevin Carmichael decides to try his luck. 'I like the dress, by the way. You're looking great.'

Kate walks back into her office slightly lighter than she left. Carmichael's a drip, but any interest's a compliment, she supposes. And at least he's given her Ward.

When Cole calls to tee up a briefing meeting, she's frosty. He suggests the Aegean, on him, but she says there are 'maps and things' and they'd be better off in a parliamentary meeting room.

'Tomorrow at ten then,' he says over the black Range Rover's hands-free phone, making his voice softer. 'I look forward to it. Put the kettle on.'

Jack Cole strides towards his reflection in the parliamentary admin building's glass doors. His barrel chest inflating a well-cut Italian suit. He equates size with power. He's had colour put through his hair so that it's close to aubergine. He looks really quite magnificent, he thinks, as the doors open automatically.

She doesn't offer coffee; just gets down to business. 'I haven't approached Dylan Ward yet,' Kate is saying. 'I thought we should meet first.'

'Quite right,' replies Cole, lost in the slightest suggestion of cleavage. 'You're across the whole...brief?' Even though Mooney's told him she's on board, he likes to size things up for himself.

'Yes,' she says. 'The whole brief. I've got some technical info and costings on photovoltaic cells, inverters and installation coming. All the solar stuff. I like the scheme.'

He nods and smiles a little approval.

'...on the water issue,' she continues, more quietly, 'as I understand it, it's just about getting a measure of the locals...'

'And doing that quietly,' he adds.

'Obviously.'

'So what do you suggest now?'

'I'll contact Dylan Ward and get him on board.'

'I can leave all that to you?' Cole at his most charming.

'Sure. It's what I'm here for.'

'Far more than that,' Cole replies, with a well-measured smile.

'Thank you.' She tilts her head flirtatiously.

# Four

Back from the bush, Dylan moves into his old bedroom. It is unchanged since his childhood, but everything surrounding the house is different. The rural rim of the city is getting chopped up; people have sold out, blocks subdivided. Developers have pushed, appealed, paid lobbyists to lean on the right people and got their way. Dylan's parents, Mitchell and Elaine Ward, never knew that was the way the world worked, and it has come as a shock to them.

They are surrounded, but trapped by good history and a dream remembered. A stomach ulcer feasts on the acidity in Mitchell's innards.

Dylan lies on his bed, running his eye along the CDs of his teens – singer-songwriters faded back to country pubs and RSL halls – and spines of cherished books. As his father made a special shelf for them, he had marvelled at the rhythm of the hand plane and the thinness of the curly shavings.

He thinks back to the gift of a gentle childhood and doesn't know how to ease his parents' distress.

'We're not selling,' says Elaine, when he tackles her quietly. 'We're not leaving our home. Wherever we went, it would be the same. It's just about the number of people here now.'

He holds her hands over the kitchen table, rubbing in the emu balm he's bought for her arthritic joints. She already has hard gobstopper knuckles.

'I worry for you both,' he says. 'The stress is no good for you.'

But when Dylan tries for the same, quiet discussion with his father, he sees the terrible rage and resentment within him. Fists clench. Mitchell Ward's breathlessness comes from the grip on his heart. 'Developers,' he says. 'They'll be the death of us all.'

Dylan responds straight away to Kate's email, cautious but eager. 'Power supply is a vital issue for the Duncan River valley. Some places truck in 200,000 litres of diesel a year. Madness. So a project that secures reliable and sustainable power is interesting. I'd be happy to meet as soon as possible, wherever suits.'

But it's still government, he thinks, and who can trust that?

Enthusiastic is good, she thinks, but the earnestness sounds a bit pathetic.

From her high office window in Parliament House, Kate looks out across the road to eucalypts in the big park opposite. Their leaves flicker, one side dark green, the other almost silver. Light jumps off the river in diamond shards as it twists away from the city's lung.

The river. Turning into a salty bleed from denuded agricultural lands. Super-fertilised by the suburbs. Slicked up by oily water from boat bilges. A real estate value-adder: 'river glimpses'.

In tribal minds, the Dreamtime snake wriggled through here, making the waterway. And a more powerful rainbow serpent had created that snake to shape the river, springs, billabongs and all the animals that lived off them. Then it went grinding inland, leaving gullies and round, sumpy lakes. Its body scoured the course for more rivers and its rubbed-off scales became the forests. Its droppings became the rocks scattered over the hills. And the scarp itself, they say, is its body. Where it came to rest.

The sting has already gone out of the afternoon's heat when Dylan chooses a green apple with a scab, leaving the perfect ones for others, and picks the label off. He adds it to the flower on the kitchen wall, which blooms from the first petal of avocado stickers placed by his mother, like the insides of a kaleidoscope. Elaine is resting on her bed and he calls up that he's off for a walk. Outside, he fills a water bottle from the rainwater tank and drops it in his daypack. He pulls on his elastic-sided boots and follows a childhood track once full of cubbies built from sticks and ferns, leaning up against granite outcrops. The smell of garlicky undergrowth, eucalypts and good earth triggers cellular memories.

Five years of drought have taken their toll on the country. The jarrah forest looks stressed and brittle, the under-scrub thinned out. Needley sheoaks, grey and haggard, have dropped their bundles, scared witless. There are holes in the birdsong.

To the west, down on the plain, trees in parks are dying from drought. Showcasey rows of eucalypts are left with gaps. Out east, farmers on their dustbowl wheat and sheep stations have started shooting starving stock. Ragged corpses pile up. Many of the grain growers haven't even seeded as it's not worth gambling the two hundred grand.

Dylan crunches through the scarp's dry forest country, his mind roaming. Receding polar ice, summer floods in England, Pacific atolls drowning, South American villages starved as high glaciers melt.

Usually the granite outcrops would have moist mosses, but they are dried to a curly crust, like those of the famous gardens of Kyoto. Dylan shrugs off the pack and drops flat on his chest, like the child he once was, toes dug in, chin on the grainy rock, face so close to this other-world that it takes on the foresty dimensions of the planet around him. In its desiccation, he sees a post-apocalyptic nightmare.

In one long push-up, his body is horizontal off the ground, fingers straight and white, boots scuffing. Then he sets off fast, consciously pulling on the optimism that lives in him.

The country falls away and Dylan follows it, enjoying the encouragement of gravity. Grooves cut by the sluice of hard rain are long filled with baked leaves and honky nuts.

He skis the ball-bearing gravel down the final bank into a dry creek bed and finally bursts out of the crackling forest.

Here, as a boy, he had made rafts from fallen branches, bound them with string and pushed them out onto the small reservoir. He ran in and out of the water so much that it made a wet slipway. Eventually it was so soft and slippery that he could slide the gel of it into the water. His mother and father sat with the picnic, in the shade, watching their only child turn terracotta.

Now, down in the sump of the reservoir, twenty metres below him, there is just enough pollen-dusted water for birds to peck. Goannas and geckos, skinks and snakes sip at it. It looks like a banked raceway, sides crazed – the wall of death from the greatest show on earth. At the far end, the dam wall towers above this empty crucible.

The dugite is coiled clockwise like a black spring, eyes wide, a vertical slash through the lens. Its body is dry and shingled amid the sheoak needles and its jaw is slightly open. Its tongue darts out to taste an oasis almost gone. A raptor circles above.

Dylan hunkers down for a closer look. He recognises its demeanour; it is warm but will not strike. They both look across the dried reservoir. So, it has come to this.

There was barely a pathway through the hills that Dylan didn't know as a child. In winter, he built dams in the streams. In summer he put up cubbies in shady spots. He and his friends were bushrangers, red Indians, Olympic equestrians on imaginary horses. On long summer holiday days they made up plays and then performed them for their parents in the relative cool of late afternoon. Ushered into a natural granite amphitheatre near their homes, the families spread blankets and were served homemade lemonade and over-baked star biscuits made by the kids. And with the final bows, the parents clapped and clapped and clapped.

In the same spot now, for six days a week, there are beeping earthmovers relentlessly clearing the bush. Their engines hawk up black diesel smoke as they strain against trees.

He breaks through a final stand of jarrah trees and sees the scalp of the land before him. The forest has been scraped to one side.

A single tuart tree has been left sentinel as a showpiece, but around it, Tuart Crest has been razed, timber pushed to the bottom of the slope. The forest fringes it in straight lines, trunks exposed. Unbelievable, he thinks. Bitumen roadways curve in cul de sacs, curbs squeezed out like toothpaste. Rows of 'Lot for Sale' signs indicate the narrowness of the blocks. Dylan tries to imagine family homes with kids and dogs. It's obscene, he thinks. They can't all be house blocks.

He heads down the slope and onto the end of one of the bitumen roads, reading the Action Real Estate lot number signs. A lot of people. It'll be a lot of people. Human population, the core of environmental issues.

And they'll be on Mitchell and Elaine's back doorstep. Developers, he thinks. The Lord save us from property developers.

'Everywhere will be the same,' says Mitchell Ward when Dylan describes most of the scene. 'We're better off staying here. "Fire fighting." I'll build a decent fence along the end of the block. We built this place with our own hands. This is where we belong. We're not shifting.'

'But the stress and the hassle, Dad. It'll be too hard. It'll affect your health.'

Elaine lifts the floral teapot, looks for signals and pours more English Breakfast into the cups. It seems to Dylan that tea binds his family together. When he was old enough, his father taught him to make steaming mugs of it, which he did as a treat for his parents. *Two cups of Crocodile Tea, and make it snappy...*one of Mitchell Ward's old jokes. *Two cups of Kangaroo Tea and hop to it...two cups of Snake Tea and get a wriggle on...*

Afternoon tea on the back verandah with the good China, a plate of biscuits and small blocks of light fruitcake. Elaine has a need for elegance.

'If you can be where you belong, you are lucky,' she says simply and carefully.

Dylan sees the reassurance in her eyes, but his father's rage is only just being overpowered by rationality. 'The developers have called it Tuart Crest, but I hear they've got rid of them all.'

All but one, thinks Dylan. And he hopes his father never sees it stranded there.

Kate decides to meet Dylan halfway. She thinks neutral ground's better than bringing him in to the CBD. She's done her research and doesn't want him spooked by the idea of being sucked into the government machine. Anyway, it will be good to take a government car and get out of the office. There's a nice little lunch place on the river, half an hour out of town towards the scarp.

———

Dylan's dark green Subaru Forester is a familiar sight round the back roads of the hills. It stops occasionally, its occupant getting out to chip-dried red sap from a gum tree, watch the morning sun turn granite into a silver sheet or scrutinise a fox carcass on the side of the road. But today it just passes through the undulating forest, and soon seems to tip over the edge of the scarp and start weaving down the zigzag road to the flatlands below.

She guesses it is Dylan Ward. He is tall and his black linen pants are pulled tight by a belt that shows a slim waist. There's a tight grey T-shirt with a V-neck under his denim jacket. It is only when he turns away to speak to the waitress that she sees a kangaroo embroidery on the back, the animal at full stretch.

After they greet, he takes the jacket off and slips it over the back of the chair, and she can see it has been sown on by hand – the delicate look of handwork.

'It's an unusual jacket.'

'A friend of mine in a community out near Laverley did the embroidery as a gift. I stitched it on.'

He's a bit painful. Not what she's used to. A bit too enthusiastic and a bit too *interested* in everything. Dylan wants to know all the ins and outs of the solar power project, but she sees 'done deal' written all over him. She catches herself thinking that perhaps it's not that he's pathetic, just that he's not cynical. Imagine that.

'Going up there is just about getting to key stakeholders,' she says. 'The government is serious about its policy of community consultation. We want to get everything right.'

Kate rolls out the cover story and never bats an eyelid. She adds, 'To be honest, I've never been that far from the city.' (Elaine has always warned her son about people who begin sentences with 'to be honest'. ('They are obviously capable of being dishonest.')

'Not that far out of the city?'

'Well, not out of the northern suburbs, really.' She finds herself embarrassed, and finds that strange.

'Really?'

'I've been busy.' The words sound thin.

'Well, the north is fantastic. I'll be surprised if you don't fall in love.'

Mooney is pleased. Kate's done well finding this Ward character. He likes the fact that Ward has told her straight that he doesn't want to be seen up there as representing government, just facilitating. He wants to stay on the outside, and that means he'll just do the thing and clear out. No residual. Cole has done some extra homework, too, and, though Ward's been in some trouble in the past, he reckons handling him'll be a pushover.

From what he's dredged up, Cole reckons if anything does hit the fan, Ward's likely to duck for cover.

'Get a letter to him, Kate. Cost whatever you think's right for him. But you don't have to put it through the full system. It can come out of the discretionary budget. Just send him the letter then pass the invoice to me and I'll sort it out.' He smiles reassuringly. 'No need to make it complicated.'

She ignores the alarm bells.

Michael Mooney's name pops up in the screen of Cole's mobile phone and he lets it ring five times, catching it just before it goes to his message bank.

'Cole.'

'Mooney.'

Cole likes to inflect a tone of surprise even for his known callers. 'Michael. I was going to call you today.'

Mooney ignores the niceties. 'I need to catch up again, over the next couple of days. There's something I want to run through. Not on the phone, though.'

'Sure. Let me just check my diary.' Cole covers the mouthpiece and waits, staring into space. 'When did you have in mind?'

'This evening. Won't take long. Perhaps just in the side bar at the golf club. Sixish.'

They are all instructions. 'Sixish?' Cole muses. 'Let me see, Michael.' He pauses, but not as long. 'Yes,' he says, 'I've got something I can shift. It should be OK. Six at the club.'

'Half an hour,' says Mooney. 'Just shift that appointment half an hour.'

Cole feels like his bluff has been called.


Jack Cole knows the rewards of memory and preparation. He presents himself as casual and naturally knowledgeable, but behind it are hours of homework. He's put in time on sustainable power – finding even himself surprised by the advancements, advantages and cost-effectiveness. Break-even over a shorter period than he had expected. He is interested in the front edge of the wave of technology and the number of places that have adopted it, from large-scale solar farms in Denmark to solar wells in Africa. It'd clearly be good for the Duncan River valley – and it doesn't hurt to have a win in the bag already.

Then there's the bigger goal – the water. He's put in even more time on Michael Mooney's plan, and has turned his research assistant, Jill, onto it.

The Duncan River rises in the Drassic Range and heads five hundred kilometres west to the Indian Ocean. It slices thought the Prince Oswald Range and Gecko Gorge, then twists through jagged country, straight across plains and on to Admiralty Sound, where tides are pushed by a moon so big it has veins. Its valley is so wide that it takes half an hour to drive across on the highway, which is up on levy banks. It is running; the old tribals call it jila, living water. In the Wet season, this land goes under – inundated by the sprawling, brown river. This is warramba, torrent water. Flat out in flood, the Duncan River could fill Sydney Harbour in twenty-one hours. In the Dry, it trickles through, then stops completely, leaving deep, gravelly sand and rocks under crackling sheets of dry algae. Over a year, the Duncan River spews five billion cubic metres of water into the Indian Ocean. To plenty of people, that's just a damned waste.

Even back in the 1950s, the government looked at damming the Duncan River, with Emerald Gorge as the site. But the election came and went, and costs suddenly looked astronomical, and it rained on the city.

But now climate change forecasters say that in the same time the city's rainfall decreases by sixty per cent, the Kimberley's will rise by thirty-five per cent.

Times have changed. Around the world, wars are being fought for water. And no wonder – scientists reckon that if the planet's water was a litre, only half a teaspoon could be drunk by humans.

It's all too obvious to Cole.

A dam at Emerald Gorge, a bit of country flooded out, hook up a 3,700 kilometre covered canal or a pipeline and you've got 200 gigalitres of fresh water a year delivered to the city. Two per cent of the river's annual flow, but forty per cent of the southern population's long-term needs. Just a couple of billion dollars or so. It's a no-brainer.

Golf is a sideline at the Royal Riverview club. Prospective members are filtered for connections and the buy-in is dear. Old money gives a musty smell, new-rich entrepreneurs cook up cartels over beef Wellington and pinot and sycophants hang off merchant bankers. Retired CEOs who have done their six-year dash, hiking up share prices to walk away with millions and Mercs, plan cruises together. Politicians are necessary connections with use-by dates.

The interior is timber and tartan.

'The usual, Sir?' A double Chivas with ice. Riverview is one of few places where a barman remembers an infrequent drinker's choice.

'Evening, Ron.' Michael Mooney ponders a life of subserviency.

Cole sticks up fingers. 'Good timing. Make that two.' He straightens his suit jacket, perches on a stool, shakes Mooney's hand and cracks his knuckles. 'Place is empty.'

'Yes.'

'Sounded urgent.'

'Just wanted to clear a few things up.'

'Fire away.'

No pretences.

Michael Mooney pauses as the barman returns and puts down a second mat and two heavy cut-crystal glasses. He proffers a leather folder, which Cole is quick to take and sign to his tab.

'Thanks,' says Michael Mooney.

'No problem.'

Michael Mooney launches into it. 'I want to make my thinking on this little assignment up north very clear. It must be handled with great care.'

Cole sees Michael Mooney has had second thoughts – he's jittery. Cole sees his vulnerability and likes it.

'I'll be blunt...' Mooney pulls in closer and fixes Cole with a stare so icy, he's taken aback by the threat in it. 'If the ice on the water idea looks too thin, I'll just go with the sustainability announcement. The water pipeline is visionary but, well, open to backlash. We have the numbers, obviously – a big population in the city that could be facing a complete water ban next summer. They won't even be allowed to water their lawns. You know what it will mean, politically, when they can't even take a decent shower. And we'll have industry down our throats when it comes under the pump.'

Cole would like to point out the pun, but knows better. He draws his mouth into a crescent moon frown. 'There are only a few hundred people in Duncan River valley area who would be directly affected. But there's an element of exposure in covering off the bases that's beginning to bother me. The worst thing we could do is give the game away.'

Mooney has done more than he planned; he has shown his fear.

Kate has emailed Dylan to say that the budget's not an issue – the main thing is to get up there quickly and be comprehensive. She presumes they'll fly north and jump in a hired vehicle, but adds, 'I'll leave all that up to you.'

'I appreciate your confidence,' he types back. 'I suggest you and Mr Cole fly to Shoal Bay, but I'll prepare a vehicle here and drive up to meet you. It's better than trying to hire one and flying all the gear up.'

His Inbox immediately bings. 'That's fine. Seems a long way on your own.'

Dylan thinks it's a treat.

He clicks Contacts and starts an email to Vincent Yimi, but thinks better of it and picks up the phone. It rings until he thinks it will ring out. Then it's answered and there's a rustling sound and distant voices. The phone is being held in mid-air while another conversation is shouted to conclusion. Then the voice is loud in his ear. A woman barks, 'Who there?'

'Dylan Ward. Is Vincent Yimi there, please?'

'Who?'

'Vincent Yimi. Uncle Vincent.'

She rasps something Dylan can't make out, then the phone clicks off.

He dials again and this time the receiver is picked up straight away.

'Carter's Ford Community Centre.' The man's voice is calm, but there's still commotion beyond it.

'Vincent?'

'Ya.'

'Dylan Ward.'

'Hold on,' says Uncle Vincent, unable to hear clearly. He places his hand over the mouthpiece, but Dylan still hears him yell, 'Shut-up-you-mob-I-can't-hear-this-bloke-speak. Out, the lot of yer. Go on. Outside.' *Blessed Mary*, Vincent breathes to himself.

'Now,' he says down the receiver. 'Who're you, again?'

'Dylan Ward.'

'Hey, mate. Good ta hear you. Things haven't changed here.'

Dylan tells Vincent all he knows.

'Be good to get rid of those old gennies,' agrees Vincent. 'Lot of people been struggling with the power. And the cost of diesel. But half a million bucks for solar is a helluva lot to find, even with the grant.'

'From what I gather, they're talking outright replacement,' says Dylan. 'No cost to the user. A pilot project. Investment in the regions and carbon credits.'

'So they'll want their bit of publicity out of it,' says Vincent, snorting hot air.

'Sure, there's all that,' agrees Dylan. 'But that's just a flash in the pan, and everyone will be left with long-term benefits.'

'Yeah. I get it. Election coming up...'

The men wait for the words to settle. 'Well,' says Vincent eventually. 'You'd better bring these city types up and let us have a look at 'em.'

Dylan says he'll email a suggested itinerary later and Vincent says, when he gets it, he'll do a ring-around and clear the way. 'You know how it is when "govie" people turn up...'

Ngalgardi Aboriginal community, Mt Goode Station, Daydawn Biosphere Reserve, Barker River Station, Warramorra Peninsula and Mt Jane Station on the way through. A couple of days around Carter's Ford, five hundred kays inland.

Dylan sends the list and Vincent, hooked up to a satellite and typing two-fingered, flicks one back. 'I'll talk to 'em.'

And then another email bings into the Inbox. 'When you setting off? I got Henny a lift down to an Indigenous youth leadership do at Drifter's Bay Retreat. He could use a ride back to Shoal Bay.'

Dylan can picture the messy back room at the community centre. Mismatched chairs, piles of boxes full of legal contracts and potato crisps, with its relentless ping-pong and pool-ball clatter. And Vincent, elbows out, prodding out words on the keyboard, bottom lip locked over the top one, Elvis glasses pushed up on top of his head. Finishing up and cursing the old printer next to him – out of ink, low on paper, Device Manager blipping errors on his screen. Maybe one day his prints would come.

Two worlds. North and south, there and here. They seem like the equal parts of Dylan and he likes the duality.

Dylan rings around car hire companies, getting quotes for a diesel LandCruiser with two spare tyres and a cargo barrier.

He plans to sort out his own camping, mechanical and emergency gear, hire anything he needs for the other two, and set out four or five days before he has to meet them, driving the 2,500-odd kilometres up the inland route. He's warned Kate that it might take a couple of weeks to get around the places they need to visit. When she tells Cole, he says he can't afford that sort of time and she might have to finish off on her own. He might come back early. But not to tell the Minister – 'he needn't be bothered with that'.

When Dylan picks up the LandCruiser it has only one

spare tyre.

'You'll have to pick one up from our servicers,' says the bloke who hands him the keys.

'I asked for it to be in the vehicle.'

'They're just round the corner.'

Whatever happened to good old-fashioned service? He wonders and realises he is beginning to sound like his mother.

Dwayne is more used to dealing with the drop-off drivers from mining companies. Dylan is not their usual type.

'Where are you off to?'

'Far north. Duncan River. Carter's Ford,' says Dylan.

'I worked up at Carter's for a year or so,' says Dwayne. 'Fixing tyres, mostly.' The revenge of the Kimberley's gravel roads. 'Tyres kept the whole business going. That and selling chips and Coke to the local kids.' He pauses. 'I like the place.'

'Me too,' says Dylan. 'I'm not so keen on hired vehicles though.'

'I know what you mean. Tell you what, spin it into the workshop and I'll give it a once-over.' He moves a battered HJ75 personnel carrier out of his bay, guides Dylan in, pops the bonnet.

'All good,' he says eventually, rubbing his hands on a rag. 'But the jack handle was missing, so I've put another in. People nick 'em. I'll bill the hire company for it.'

'Thanks,' says Dylan, reaching for his own wallet. 'What do I owe you?'

'Nah, that's fine,' says Dwayne. 'Just say hello to Carter's Ford for me. It gets into you.'

'I know the feeling.'

'Cut me open and I'll swear red dirt'd pour out.'

Dylan grooms and refines the pile of gear as it grows, but won't start the pack until he has everything finalised and in one place. Then he'll put it in, together and in the right spot.

'Got everything you need?' Mitchell is comfortable in the sheds and garages and likes the growing bulk of equipment.

'Getting there. I'm probably over-thinking it.'

'Anything I can help with?'

'Nah.' But Dylan sees his father's disappointment. 'Actually, I could use a hand here. The fridge's canvas cover's split. I was just going to try to fix it.'

'Got just the thing,' says his father, happily fossicking in a drawer. 'Here. Best tool for it.' He unscrews the knurled chuck of his canvas stitching awl and threads whipping twine through it and up the grooved needle, making sure there isn't too much tension on it. Over the years, Dylan has often held fabric taut as his father mended school bags and the family tents.

'Just a tick,' says his father. 'I'll get my specs.'

Under the sharp light of a work lamp, Mitchell pushes the needle through layers of heavy canvas, threads the twine, withdraws it, and sews in a neat, even line. Each stitch is pulled to a consistently firm tension, but not so tight it will pucker. Dylan appreciates the gentle control his father has over his own strength. He feels comforted by the experience in him.

'Always neat and always firm,' says Dylan.

'If a job's worth doing...'

A comfortable ease as the stitches march on.

'You'll be happy to be up north again.'

'Yep, I will.'

'You don't seem completely relaxed about it all, though.'

'It's an important thing.'

'The government types might be difficult people to do it with?'

'It's sort-of that,' admits Dylan. 'I feel a bit jittery about them. Kate seems alright, but I haven't met this Jack Cole fella.'

'We've all read about him in the paper, though.'

'We have that.'

'Bother you?'

'I'm not sure.'

'Sounds like a prize arsehole.'

Dylan laughs. Trust his dad to put it succinctly.

'I'd be worried too.'

'Not worried, so much, just wary. Cautious.'

'Good thing, I reckon.'

'Not too cynical?'

'Sensible. Watch him.'

Mitchell Ward pulls the last stitch tight, ties it off twice and snips the twine.

'Thanks for the advice. And fixing the cover.'

'You're welcome. On both counts.' Mitchell and Dylan both lean forward, and throw arms around one another.

Dylan sits outside his parents' house in the dark, cleaning Mitchell's boots, then his own.

'Another Sunday,' says Elaine, closing the door quietly behind her and easing down on the stump beside him.

'I love them,' says Dylan.

'I know.' She draws arcs on the mossy bricks with her toe. 'Did you see Jules in the paper?'

'Jules?'

'She's heading up some conservation group. She seems to be in charge of it. She must have managed to put prison behind her. I thought you should know.' His mother pauses. 'I thought I should tell you.'

'Thanks. Yes,' he says, looking for words. 'I'm pleased for her.'

'While we're talking like this…about Tuart Crest…it's just best for us to accept it. It will be best for your father, in the long run. It's going to be worse if we move. The whole place is changing. You can't beat money. We can't win.'

Dylan is stunned. 'How can you say that?'

'I must have told you the golden rule: the people with the gold make the rules.'

# Five

Kate sleeps until 10am, luxuriates briefly in white cotton sheets that she insists are pure Egyptian sateen with a 1,400 thread count, then gets up, makes a cup of tea and takes it back to bed with the Sunday paper and her laptop. She dozes under the white doona while the tea goes cold, and only wakes again when the sun swings in through the window. She grimaces at the tepid tea, then gets up to make a fresh cup.

The apartment is silent except for the muffled rumblings of other lives. A radio through the wall, someone talking too loud on a phone on a balcony, a drill in plaster as a picture is hung, the crescendos of Christian TV, raised voices and a slammed door.

Her flat suddenly seems very white and too empty, and the day seems to stretch out pointlessly before her. The one day of the week she doesn't go into the office has started to feel pointless. There just seems to be too much of the day before her.

She wishes briefly that Tom was still there. In moments like this, there's a craving just to have someone beside you. To feel contact. To feel related. To have another connection to the world; through another person.

But these moments are few. Her working life bulldozes through her relationships, leaving a trail of stood-up dinners, cancelled weekends away and the sort of exhaustion that repels physical approach. The sort of distraction that leads to other temptations for a partner being ignored. It's happened four times – at first leaving the relationship flat, then burying it altogether – and even when she's seen the bulldozer coming, complete with flashing lights, she hasn't been prepared to fend it off. But she's learnt her lesson from it. She can't have it all.

Most of the time, it's fine being alone again, being single. The low-hassle of it. No-one to appease, no-one to call when you're going to be late, and no-one else's interests to endure – God, those tedious days at the V8 car races, and then the noise of MotoGP bikes screaming round and round on the lounge room screen.

But she knows that if she looked deep enough inside, even past that nasty biological clock that she can mostly force herself to ignore, she'd see that she isn't looking for fear she might just find the right one.

Sundays were never a family affair for the Kennedys. Kate's father might have been out early in his lycra cycling gear, then come home to shower and change for golf, or meet someone useful for lunch. Later, he'd spread his risk-assessment reports across the table and work until it was time for dinner and a bottle of red. Or else he might say he was going to the office, but no-one would dare ring him there.

Her mother spent Sundays in arcs, skirting her husband. When he was out, she was in the kitchen, when he came back, she seemed to glide around the periphery of the garden. When he settled into the dining area, she took ages showering upstairs and then popped over the road to June's, which took an hour or more. After serving dinner, she would phone someone and talk for a long time, sitting either on the back patio or upstairs on her side of the king size bed. The room was still maintained, visually, as one shared.

She controlled her emotions and read magazines into the night.

———

Jack Cole sits at the table, knees spread wide, white towelling robe gaping, letting the fresh air in. These are the few hours of the week when his shape is not sharpened by Brioni suits, or he hasn't ratcheted in chinos and covered the growing bulge with a loose polo shirt. He studies financial papers, business magazines, investment sections, gossip pages and appointments columns, highlighting in green, underlining in red, and writing instructions on stick-on yellow notes. He tears out whole articles with a quick, whipping action using a ruler clamped down tight. He might study a picture from a football club sponsorship event in a social page and notice that while most are there out of sufferance, one chief executive is wearing the club badge on his lapel. Partners at events, comments on mergers, the phrasing of forecasts to investors. Each detail will be keyed into the database and cross-referenced by his research assistant. Dossiers on everyone and everything.

His assistants invariably falter under the workload and his bombastic style and that's part of his plan. They are all gone before they know too much. So he pays over the odds, always gets applicants, then just burns them off.

People are too simple, he thinks.

As much as Cole stores information about others, he hides it about himself. He hires a different accountant for each part of his business, and contractually obligates them not to have contact with one another. Only Cole knows all of Cole's business and he knows that if ever it hits the fan, no-one but himself would be able to unscramble things. He keeps track of everything in his head. He sees it all as one shape.

On this Sunday, Cole highlights a picture of John Kennedy, snapped at a charity auction for a newspaper's social page, a girl much younger by his side. He studies the body language, puts a yellow sticker on it and instructs for it to go into the Kennedy database. Another family dissolving.

It prompts him to read again the email from his researcher that has 'Dylan Ward' in the Subject line. Cole wasn't surprised when she finally dug up the fact that Ward had once dobbed himself out of a good deal of trouble. Everyone has a flaw somewhere.

By noon, Cole has drained three mugs of excruciatingly black coffee and exhausted the papers. He lays light pants, Italian moccasins and an orange Ralph Lauren shirt on the unmade bed, drops the robe and stands looking in the mirror for a while. He likes the big, furred form of himself, black hair flying off his shoulders.

With his sculpting brush in his right hand, and the left one smoothing, he draws his dyed hair, front to back, into an immaculate, set helmet. It's as thick and stiff as strained wire. He scrutinises the growth starting up again between his eyebrows and makes a mental note to book a waxing.

And then he stands back and smiles at himself.

Cole is glad to be living alone in the apartment for the moment. Women have come and gone. And he reckons they're all basically – well, they're just made to look different so you know which one's yours. Come November, he'll look for someone for the busy function season. His financial generosity and the scent of power will draw them in.

He pulls back one of the heavy slide doors, and leans on the high verandah's stainless steel rail, looking out over the river. The water seems stainless and steely too, with yacht sails strewn like petals. Around the sandy foreshore, families picnic among the peppermint trees and children run in and out of the water, or float in tethered inflatable boats. Dogs sit by empty ice cream containers holding water. A windsurfer's sail flops from side to side as dad gives it a go, his stringy teenage sons geeing him up and then exploding with laughter as he's dunked. Grandparents sit in plastic chairs in the shade, enjoying the tableau of their families.

But Cole is engaged only by the sight of a vacant block around the bay that he hasn't noticed before. He will need to find out what its zoning is.

The day has stretched out around Kate. She's phoned a couple of girlfriends, but they are tied up with their boyfriends.

She has done a couple of loads of washing, a stack of ironing in front of the TV, drunk a river of tea and watched a movie that she didn't really care about. She convinces herself that she deserves an early night.

# Six

By the time Dylan leaves his parents and the city, it has all felt like a bigger goodbye than it should be. He grinds up through the gears at traffic lights and mumbles through school zones full of fancy four-wheel drives dropping off kids. Mum's taxis. Cost a mint going to the shops. There are lines of trucks in the left lanes, souped-up Subarus behind him, builders in V8 dual cabs sipping drive-by coffee and talking on mobile phones. Cashed-up bogans.

It's only when Dylan bursts out of the sprawling suburbs that he seems to reinhabit every corner of himself, and another four hours north-east, when he's broken free of the cleared land, that he starts to feel freed. He calls it 'crossing the line'.

There are two ways to the far north, but he's always liked going up the inside and coming back down the coast. He cuts straight inland and plunges into open savannah plains, the low trees of the deserts and super-heated red rock. He likes seeing signs that say 'next fuel 300km'. Or more. And he likes having nearly 2500 kays in front of him, his swag on the rack, and tyre pliers and so many spare tubes and patches that he could go on forever, however many punctures the Dunlop Road Grippers get. His mandolin's in the back, there's a box of talking book CDs, a bag of snow-peas beside him and a carton of chilled coffee-flavoured milk stuffed familiarly between his thighs. A stack of seriously-blue long-sleeved shirts are stowed in the rodeo bag he bought up in Kununda.

He likes it all, he thinks to himself. And then Dylan corrects himself. He absolutely loves it. All of it.

He loves bursting over the eucalypt-mulga line that Mt Ferris station straddles, where the southern trees give way to the hard, gnarled mulga of the desert country. The natural salt lakes, white cockatoos hanging and squawking in the trees, crazy as froth in the wind, and the road leading in a straight line to a non-negotiable spot on the horizon. He loves the outback roadhouses with their bad food – pies like floor tiles, Chiko rolls full of runny grease, poor hygiene, bad attitude, suspect Aboriginal art, polyester sarongs, stubby holders with sexist slogans, guarana shots for truckies and dusty country music CDs. He loves ridiculous fuel prices that make city whingers seem obscene, massive distances, the contortions of roadkill, and road trains with a sleeper box and three trailers, 'My Dream' painted across the bonnet complete with scrolls.

He loves sleep pushing his eyelids down, and not trying to shake it off, and stopping because he has to.

He loves seeing old folks dragging caravans over the Tropic of Capricorn, young foreigners in rented campervans with graffiti or maps of Australia on the side. He loves seeing local traffic; a lopsided four-wheel drive ute with no rego plates and two dogs running from side to side in the tray, brand new Toyotas with mine-site lights on top, Aboriginal families crammed into dinged Mitsubishis. This is where the old Magnas go to die.

And he loves it all because he knows it all, and it makes him feel that he inhabits the whole, remarkable million square miles of Western Australia. So big that, if it were Europe, the city he was leaving would be in Spain, and the Kimberley'd be in Norway. HA! Imagine it. His backyard.

Dylan loves the momentum of travelling. At first he's thinking too fast, the vehicle's too slow; the trip seems to drag or race past. His biological tick, the speed of the vehicle, the engine noise and the journey's pace don't match. And then, after he begins to let stuff go, it all starts to mesh; it gels into a pace of being, where his thoughts and appreciations, reactions and forecasts match the roll of the country past the windows and the metrical cadence of the engine.

It all makes Dylan feel wealthy in a way few get to appreciate.


'Where're you off to, mate?' The old bloke is eyeing the new LandCruiser as Dylan fills it with diesel at the fast-flow truck bowser.

'North-west,' says Dylan. 'Kimberley.'

'Shoal Bay?' he asks.

'First-off.'

'Always wanted to go to Shoal Bay. Never got there.'

'It's pretty nice.'

'Pretty nice here, too.' The old bloke looks around him,

and shifts so his weight slews from one leg to another. He stands lopsided on a spine contorted by physical work and hard knocks. 'A man's lucky to find somewhere to end up.'

The service station's forecourt is a desert of concrete the size of a footy oval that spills out from the solid rectangle of shade cast by the canopy over bowsers. It has diesel puddles, seismic cracks and drifts of chip packets.

There are big gas canisters by the main road, trucks ticking over while their drivers buy burgers, and two rows of dark-green dongas. Each of the converted sea containers' little rooms has a window, single wire-mesh bed and lino-covered floor space the same size, and a white plastic chair.

And beyond that is the patchy grass, uncertain shade and power stands of the caravan park. There, dry-cleaned overnighters with superannuation-funded rigs (*Footloose, Just Roamin', Spending the Inheritance*) rub shoulders in the ablution block with long-stayers who unhitched once and then couldn't think of anywhere else to go to, or just plain ran out of steam. With the first piece of corrugated tin put up for shade, or the first geranium planted in a border soon edged by stones and watered with the cold dregs of the teapot, they became permanent. A pedestal fan outside, a collection of odd chairs and a gleaned card table. Shadecloth hanging down from the new roofing. Before you knew it, a cobbled-up shed and long-in-the-tooth outdoor freezer.

These are lives of long silences and curled-up paperbacks from the exchange rack. There's odd-job work cleaning the dunnies, unloading stuff for the servo's shop or cooking hot chips. Four-o'clock beers with one of the neighbours. A bit of fuzzy ABC radio; high-pitched Aussie Rules commentaries, but bugger the news.

'Yep, lucky to find anywhere as good as this,' says the old bloke. The sense of belonging, the scent of some sort of family. Home. Dylan sees it in him, but can't help hoping for more luck for himself.

The bowser's handpiece clicks off as the second tank gurgles down a last mouthful and then belches fullness. Dylan goes inside to pay, leaving the man looking at the vehicle, which gleams too-white against this oil- and time-stained patch of humanity.

*On the road again…*Dylan doesn't know the words to the whole song, but chorus lines tend to leak out of him on highways heading north. Already he has lapsed into the rhythm of travel. Being on the road. The romance of it has got him. Travelling makes him want to cry for joy as he begins to feel whole again.

At his next roadhouse stop, from behind the square mesh of its cage, a sulphur-crested cockatoo screeches *'ello'* and abseils down the side on a beak as strong as wire-cutters.

'Hello,' Dylan half-mimics.

'*Gis a beer,*' the bird gags.

'Bit early,' says Dylan.

'*Case-a VB, not a case-a VD,*' the cocky chirps.

'It's just his set piece,' says a bulbous bloke in a grubby apron, pushing backwards through the kitchen doors, a tray in his hands. 'It's not as if he's smart or anything.'

'*Ello, gis a beer,*' the bird screeches in a fury.

'Fucker needs a plucker.'

'*Case-a VB, not a case-a VD,*' challenges the bird, menacingly.

Dylan pays for the fuel, exchanges drought chat, then makes himself a takeaway mug of tea at the truckies' table. The back wall is plastered with mega-rigs pulled from magazines. In one picture, a girl in pink hotpants and a cowboy hat strains up to clean a windscreen. Another, with a low-cut top, leans forward and fondles wheelnuts.

'Cute, eh? Wouldn't-ya go it?' coughs the bloke, seeing Dylan's glance.

Dylan clamps his stainless steel mug between his legs and takes off in second gear while he's still hooking the middle finger under the seatbelt's chest strap and pulling it down to the buckle. Clicking it with his thumb. He gets a bit of speed up before checking the road, steering onto the bitumen, snicking the gearbox from third to fourth and letting the torque work.

*On the road again...*

The country changes in the slow increments of long-distance travel on straight roads that vanish into shimmer. With shifts in soil type or drainage, flora quickly runs out of range and is replaced by something related but not quite the same. Constant subtle shifts. The appearance of the landscape evolves with latitude and the patterns of climate. It is smooth and seamless but Dylan sees the changes as clearly defined chapters. He senses the bigger shift coming as he closes in on the heart of the Pilbara.

It is late morning and Dylan, hazy in the head, stops in a layby for a breather and to hear the sounds that go with the view. A break from engine-hum.

The couple who have put out their folding table and chairs next to their caravan in the rest bay are enjoying tea and biscuits.

'Journey going well?' Dylan asks, smiling.

'Very good,' says the woman, who has soft grey hair and wears a floral frock.

'The fuel's pricey, though,' chips in her husband, good-naturedly.

'Yes,' says Dylan. 'We should feel guilty about complaining about city prices, when it's so much more out here, and the distances are so much greater.'

The man stands, revealing a neat outfit of shorts pressed with a knife-edge crease and a laundered short-sleeved shirt.

'John Phillips.' He steps forward and holds out a soft hand with a few sunspots.

'Dylan Ward.'

'Phyllis,' says his wife, her head bobbing like a bird's. 'Perhaps you'd join us for a cup of coffee, or tea if you'd prefer. And a biscuit.'

'Phyllis bakes a wonderful biscuit,' praises John. 'Gluten-free. I'm intolerant.'

Dylan feels he has rarely encountered anyone who is obviously less so.


John and Phyllis reverse-mortgaged their house in Port Macquarie, bought the three-year-old four-wheel drive and modest caravan, and set out to see the country. They never really thought of it as running away.

Polite and private, they struggle with the chumminess of caravan parks and avoid dragging their chairs over to the groups that form for five-o'clock drinks. They resist giving away much about themselves and cherish one another's trusted company. Even on hot evenings, they prefer to sweat it out inside. Curtains are drawn by carefully gracious degrees, so that they appear to have been shimmied along their rails for shade, rather than pulled to shut people out.

'Perhaps you would like a particular type of tea?' Phyllis asks Dylan, who has accepted their invitation, instinctively feeling comfortable with their niceties.

'Just normal's fine thanks.' His voice has shifted into a softer timbre and he intonates his words more carefully, reflecting those around him; away from the rasp of the roadhouse.

'We have Earl Grey, Irish Breakfast, Prince of Wales and, rather fittingly, Russian Caravan blend.' Then she halts herself, raising the delicate fingers of her left hand to her lips as if to gently silence herself. 'But don't let me try to persuade you,' she says. 'English Breakfast it is.' Phyllis excuses herself and steps lightly up the caravan's steps to put the kettle back on the gas burner.

John has vacated his chair, and got a spare fold-down stool from inside. He holds out a palm, indicating for Dylan to sit in the most comfortable one. 'It's such an incredible view,' he enthuses in a conspiratorial whisper. 'This country really is amazing.'

'Yes indeed,' says Dylan. 'I've been through here a number of times, but I still find it very exciting.'

'Are you in the resources industry?' asks John.

'I was previously, but not as a miner, as such. I'm more involved in sustainability. Environment and community.'

'How very interesting.'

'And you? May I ask?'

'Retired. But I was in a small insurance office for many years. Well, for my whole career, actually.' He pauses and says more quietly, 'I'm not sure why I'm embarrassed about that.'

'Being in one place for a long time is wonderful, I think,' says Dylan. 'It's funny how we have come to undervalue consistency and commitment. I'm not sure why that happened along the way. Just fashion. Odd, isn't it.'

John Phillips has cheered up instantly. 'Odd indeed. It sounds a bit boring, doing the same thing all those years, I suppose.' Phyllis rejoins them. 'But I had a wonderful wife, a comfortable little home and my health. And I was happy to thoroughly know what I was doing, and to keep doing it. With all that experience, you would have thought I'd have known better…'

John and Phyllis look at one another, shocked to hear their secret so easily stream into the air. It seems to curl before them like smoke.

'Some difficulty?' asks Dylan, sensing not only the wisp but also a moment when he has a role to play.

'Well, yes actually,' confides John, to his wife's surprise. Neither has spoken of this to anyone else. But now, in a roadside rest area, parked on a sunny afternoon, they release it like doves.

'You see, I lost the lot. All the superannuation. I had been working and saving for over forty years, and I moved it into a real estate development company. We lost the lot.'

'It wasn't your fault,' his wife quickly insists. 'It could have happened to anyone.'

'It was my decision, Phyllis,' he corrects gently. 'It is my responsibility. Unfortunately it has also affected you, and I wouldn't have had that for the world.'

'Surely there are protections. Isn't there some hope of recovering some of the funds?' says Dylan.

'We decided that to fight would take years and probably kill us,' says John. 'We are not confrontational people. We decided that we couldn't see the point in lying awake every night, or of talking about nothing else. We decided to live minimally, take money out of our home to buy this...' He looks towards the caravan. 'It has given us what we wanted. We enjoy one another's company and take pleasure in frugality, if you can believe that.'

'I understand that completely,' says Dylan.

'I'm sorry,' says John, sitting himself up a little more upright. 'I'm not sure why we've burdened you with our private business.'

'I feel inspired rather than burdened,' says Dylan. 'Sometimes a passing stranger may be what we need.'

'More tea?' asks Phyllis, as her husband offers a biscuit and a warm wind stirs the air into rising spirals.

Dylan can't get the story out of his head. How to liberate oneself? Not become a casualty? And set against that, the injustice. He knows that, somewhere, the company directors who ripped the guts out of these mum-and-dad investors live the high life and sleep soundly at night.

Dylan can't get the harmony between John and Phyllis out his head and he doesn't want to.

# Seven

On the map in front of him, Michael Mooney's eyes follows the contours of the landscape, skirting ranges and tracing the lengths of valleys. He can almost see the glint of a silver pipeline against rock. Drawn as a red line, it cuts, colubrine, inland through gorge country to Kennedy Gap. Nearly 2,500 kilometres.

He flicks over the page to the next map, and sees the far more serpentine route proposed for the alternative, a covered canal. More sensitive to the rise and fall of rock, dune and plain, it turns that 2,000 kilometres into more than 3,500. Michael Mooney turns back to the executive summary of the plan, and the phrases he has already run his highlighter over...

> *The Duncan River is the preferred source for both pipeline and canal options. While the study acknowledges the government's 'no dams' policy, the water flow is, however, variable and a dam or significant off-stream storage would be required in order to provide a consistent year-round water supply. The dam is the most economic and reliable option...*

*The pressing need was to first establish the technical and economic feasibility of the proposal. This is a precursor to investigating the environmental and social issues...*

*With regard to social issues, a canal would prove a significant permanent barrier to movement of the local population. A pipeline is somewhat less intrusive, but both have a significant visual impact...*

*The fundamental requirement to dam the Duncan River would have a significant impact on the region. While it was not our brief to gauge local reaction, we would anticipate a lack of support from the Kimberley communities...*

Three taps. Liz's distinctive fingertips, then the door opens and she peeps around its edge. 'Professor Pearson is here,' Mooney's personal assistant announces.

'Send him in. Thanks, Liz.'

Mooney rolls the thick report closed, steps around the table and greets Peter Pearson with a neat smile and handshake. Pearson's trousers are too short, displaying beige socks poking from brown shoes that have seen so many kilometres they have split down the sides of the toe joints. They have seen so much polish and hard brushing that they glint. He wears a shirt with short sleeves that are wide and flap around his thin, speckled arms. His hair has thinned to a wispy, grey nest and he has a lopsided goatee. His spectacles are gold-framed, 70s-style aviators, the lenses covered in a thick film.

It all irks Mooney, but he knows Pearson's mind is incisive, and he's organised, methodical and unshakeably trustworthy. Tell Professor Pearson that a study and report is to be kept confidential and not only can this be completely depended upon, but Pearson's single-minded commitment to the objective infects the rest of his team.

'Minister.'

'Thanks for coming in, Peter.'

'My pleasure.' Pearson tilts his head, in the manner of a subject proffering reverence.

'Please, sit.' Mooney indicates one of the seats now opposite him across the table. 'Can I organise something for you? Tea, coffee? Water?'

Professor Pearson laughs nervously, wary of ever venturing towards humour. 'I rather thought I was organising the water for you, Minister.'

'I appreciate the comprehensive nature of the report.' Mooney has rocked back in his chair, hands behind his head, fingers knitted together. 'But I rather wanted to hear it from you personally, too.'

'Very well, Minister.' Again Pearson nods in deference. Mooney might think it a compliment, but Pearson sees only the historical importance of the office of which Mooney is custodian. His nod of respect is to the Westminster system.

'Just your gut feeling. An overview. How you feel it.'

The words jar against the meticulous nature of the Professor's science. A carefully considered and worded document sits between them, and now the Minister's asking for a touchy-feely verbal potboiler. He also senses a slight nervousness in Mooney.

'Well, Minister, as you will read in the report...' Pearson raises his eyebrows and glances down at it, as reprovingly as his reserve will allow, '...the whole issue revolves not around the delivery method, but around supply.'

As I suspected, thinks Mooney. He'll tiptoe round in academic circles. 'In other words...'

'In other words, Minister, there are five options for delivery. There's the land pipeline, which has sovereignty and engineering integrity, but is the most costly option.

'It would also be possible to lay the pipeline offshore around the coast. This negates some of the issues regarding land tenure, but adds greater distance, and ongoing maintenance is a rather different issue.

'The option of building a canal is achievable, but there are engineering issues. For a start, the canal would have to take a rather more tortuous route following the land contours, which would add to the distance. Overall, the water would have to be lifted a total of half a kilometre. Although this could be done in five or six stages, it would require significant power. The canal would have to be lined – double-lined, in fact. In the early stages, it was calculated that, as the water would take ninety days to run the distance, transpiration and leakage could virtually account for all of it...'

'Nothing would come out at the end?'

'Mmm. Precisely,' confirms Pearson. 'In fact, without a cover, it has been calculated that we would lose about six and a half millimetres a day – that's 125 gigalitres a year. So we have done all our calculations based on the fact that the canal would have to be covered with a membrane. There are significant maintenance issues with this...' he pauses, unable to resist, '...which are also detailed and costed in the report before you.'

'Please continue.'

'Fresh water is transported to the Greek islands, for example, by water-bag. These are filled and towed in the ocean behind tugs. The biggest ones currently available hold 25,000 litres, but we propose that we would require half a million litres in each to make it a viable option. Bags of that size would have to be developed and tested. Our coastline and weather patterns are rather different to the areas where these smaller bags are used and, basically, we doubt the suitability.

'The purchase of 500,000-tonne tanker ships to transport the water turned out to be a fairly economical option, but there are concerns regarding consistency of supply, and they need minimum water depths of thirty metres, which can make port entries difficult. But then, at $200 million for a useful life of twenty-five years, as I say, they provide a comparatively economic solution.'

Mooney cuts in, 'But the overall preference is for a pipeline. One on land.'

'It is not the cheapest option, but it is deemed the most secure and long-term.' The Professor stops to gather his thoughts. 'But, as I have said, the report records that the whole issue revolves not around delivery, but supply.'

'Damming the Duncan River.'

'Indeed.' Pearson pauses, then tackles the crux of the issue. 'While the government has had a "no dams" policy for eight years, in a purely technical sense, there is no question in my mind that the combination of a dam, reservoir and pipeline is the full solution. Without a dam, the scheme would require off-stream storage of anything up to, well, almost 400 gigalitres. For that, from recollection, we are talking about moving some twenty million cubic metres in earthworks. We'd need a series of smaller dams for these man-made lakes and the whole thing would cost, conservatively, half a billion dollars. And then, the off-stream storages would still cover more than fifteen square kilometres.

'No,' says Pearson, suddenly very confident, 'damming the Duncan River is a sensible and reasonable proposition. The preferred site for this is Emerald Gorge. In layman's terms, it would take a relatively small dam wall to produce a very big reservoir.'

Mooney winces involuntarily, 'The only real difference being that the reservoir then is along the course of the Duncan River, rather than being precisely where we want it, by putting in off-stream storage.'

'May I speak candidly, Minister?'

'Of course, Professor.'

'I know dams can create political problems. Public emotion becomes involved. But, if the government is looking for a long-term, stable solution to the city's water supply, one really must accept the outcome of the report. The onshore pipeline is by far the superior delivery solution and a dam and reservoir are by far the preferred storage method. If you want the Rolls Royce model, that's it. It doesn't come without some difficulties, but once you have it, you have it for a very long time, and it won't break.'

Pearson draws breath as Mooney places his elbows firmly on the desk, locks his fingers in front of his chin and leans in, taking a finger knuckle between his teeth.

Pearson continues, 'And there is one other thing I might raise, Minister?'

Mooney looks at him over an octave of joints. 'Yes, Peter?'

'As you are aware, the terms of reference for the study were purely technical. Under that mandate, I have assessed and analysed purely practical issues. But at some stage there will need to be a parallel study of social and cultural impacts and a cross-referencing to benefit.'

Mooney raises an eyebrow. 'Meaning?'

'Well, Minister, obviously one will need to weigh the needs of the many against the preferences of the few, if I may be so bold.'

'If we propose to further the scheme, certainly we will have to look at local impacts in the Duncan River region,' Mooney ventures more guardedly.

'And weigh the needs of the many against those of the few,' insists the Professor. 'And it is only a few, as the map showing the projected average waterline of the reservoir makes clear.'

Mooney is careful not to comment. 'Yes, that map,' he says. 'Could you let me have a couple of loose copies of it?'

'I'll get them to you by close of business tomorrow,' says Pearson, pleased by the notion of his own efficiency.

'That'll be fine. Mark the waterline in red, thanks, so there's no confusion. That would be useful.' Something to tuck in that fancy Italian briefcase Cole always carries.

'Certainly, Minister. Certainly.' The Professor senses a plan stirring.


Liz has brought coffee and Mooney unwraps the lunch roll on the tray with it. He pulls the local daily newspaper closer and flicks through the first news pages. Hospital waiting lists growing, perverts in court, footy players in brawls, some new diet fad, the daily cartoon, some columnist burbling on about political factionalism. He gets to the international pages and is drawn by the headline NEW WORLD CRISIS IN WATER.

In 102 countries, there is a risk of violent clashes because of water-related crises and climate change. Two-thirds of the world's population faces conflict over water. The United Nations wants the looming crisis over water shortages to be put at the top of the global agenda and calls for action to prevent violence. 'Too often, where we need water we find guns instead,' says the Secretary-General. 'Population growth will make the problem worse. So will climate change. As the global economy grows, so will its thirst. Many more conflicts lie just over the horizon.'

It validates everything in his plan. Something in the fact that he might just be saving his part of the world appeals to deep Christian roots. Mooney, the only begotten son of severe Roman Catholic parenting.

He doesn't read the story underneath it, reporting that since the building of China's Three Gorges Dam, the water level of the Yangtze River has fallen by up to fourteen metres in some places, affecting shipping, fisheries and water supplies.

# Eight

Two hundred kilometres from Shoal Bay, Dylan finds Henny Breeze living it up at Drifter's Bay Retreat, at the end of the conference. After all the gabbing. Henny's been there for four days, but his big safari tent – *with ensuite* – is as tidy as when he arrived.

'Comfortable?' says Dylan, walking in on Henny sprawled on the bed, looking up at the ceiling.

'Dylan! Mate! I'll say. Never been on my own like this. I was rattling round in here like an egg in an esky the first day, but I reckon I like it now.'

Dylan can imagine the Breeze household in Carter's Ford, full of family; brothers and sisters, and uncles' and aunts' kids who got left there for one reason or another, and then just got mixed into the stew. Rellies staying for weeks, loud conversations, partying, arguments. All the stuff that happens when a big, extended family is crowded in.

'A bit busier at home, then?'

'Say that again.' Henny pauses, levering himself off the bed. 'You heard about overcrowding in Carter's Ford?'

'Sure.' Heard about the twenty people living in one house. 'Heard about it, but I haven't lived it.'

'Well I have and it's shit. It leads to trouble. And my old man can't do nothing about it because there's no work; no real money. Just the pension and welfare. I know people whinge about us, but we can't fix it.' And then Henny smiles broadly. 'But I've been sleepin' like a baby these past few days.'

'And how was the conference?' asks Dylan, helping himself to a rattan chair, expecting one of Henny's cool, smart-arse replies.

But his eyes blink wide. 'Brilliant, man.'

'How so?'

'Dunno, really. Just good stuff.'

'Not just jabba-jabba?'

'Nah,' says Henny. 'Thought it was gonna be. First morning was a bit like that. People going on about "housekeeping". This one sheila could talk the ear off a deaf donkey. Always *breaking* for this and that. But then it got going.'

'Get anything in particular out of it?'

A considered expression settles across Henny's strong features, wide forehead and deep-set eyes. With big thoughts running through his head, his wiry hair shocks upwards as if he's been plugged in. 'Not feeling alone,' he says. 'I met all these other people. Young Aboriginal people doing all sorts of stuff. Marko and me got on. He's in a black patrol in a country town, picking up kids at night before the police do. The police even call them first – get them to go along and sort things out before it turns bad. Other people doing different things. Running groups for kids, doing tourism – guiding and stuff, and telling people the tribal stories they're allowed to. Getting into politics. All sorts of things.

'You know, Dyl, I saw hope. Not like a word on a poster in the Rec Centre. But an actual thing. It made me feel I didn't just come from a bunch of losers.'

The words flow with a force, not the usual staccato jive, learnt from rappers and TV.

'Mate, that's brilliant,' says Dylan.

'Mate, it's a first. Just got to take it home now.' Henny grins.


They set off to drive the straight kilometres up the shoulder of the Long Drift Beach. Henny is staring out of the side window, lost in country.

'This vehicle smells wrong,' he says, out of the blue.

'Wrong?'

'Just wrong.' No whiffs of kangaroo carcass and oil cans, pie wrappers and pindan dust, old sports shoes and basketball vests. 'Just too clean.'

'Sorry about that,' says Dylan.

'It's good, but,' adds Henny, appeasing. 'Got some grunt. Big engine.'

'Four-and-a-half-litre V8. They reckon it's got 200 kilowatts under the bonnet.'

'Better not open it then,' warns Henny. 'You gotta look out for them killer wasps.' Then, jumping straight to the next thought, 'Anyway, what's with these dudes you're picking up in Shoal Bay? Uncle says you're showing them round the power sheds or somethin'.'

'They're doing an assessment. The government's looking at putting in new electricity right through the valley. Solar. As a pilot project. It's good for everyone.'

'So what's the problem?'

Dylan takes his eyes off the bleached road ahead, looks at Henny and raises an eyebrow.

'You're trying to sell it, man.' Henny shrugs, amused by being asked to state the obvious.

Talk about perceptive. 'There's no problem. It's all good.'

'Is it?' Henny has hooked his left foot up into the corner where the dashboard meets the windscreen and Dylan can see its pinker sole. The other long leg is curled under him. His shirt is buffeted by wind and he stares out of the window, eyes fixed somewhere above the horizon. You'd think he was half asleep, miles away, daydreaming, in la-la-land, not thinking about anything at all, and yet Dylan feels the incisive accuracy of the question.

'What are you getting at?'

'Not getting at anything, bro. Just picking up.'

'Picking up on what?'

Henny swings his head towards Dylan and fixes a glance on him, over his sunglasses. He looks like some mad headmaster, talking to the naughtiest boy in the school. 'You, bro. You.'

Amid the noise, the wind, the engine's plaintive whine and the road roar, there's an intimate silence.

'Nothing's wrong. Everything looks good. It's just government, sometimes...'

'...and that'd worry the bejesus out of me, too.'

'Yeah, well that's just being cynical, and there's no evidence for it.'

Henny pulls his mouth into a show of faked agreement and looks out of the window then swings back wildly, subject over, mood changed. 'So, any chance of some decent music in this truck?'

'CDs on the back seat. All country and western and classical, I'm afraid. You choose.'

But soon Henny nods off, lullabied by the vehicle's steady engine anthem, his head lolling. The landscape glides through his dreams. He dozes for only a quarter of an hour, then wakes with a start. 'Pass the Adam's ale. I'm dying over here.'

Dylan hands over a water bottle.

'Ta,' says Henny, popping the top with his teeth and squirting the water in so fast that it spills out of the sides of his mouth, down his neck and gives his T-shirt a wet bib. 'As dry as a dead dingo's donger.' Henny gasps for air. 'Are we there yet?'

Eventually they turn left at the big roadhouse and into Shoal Bay Road – the last twenty-four kilometres – and they sing *We are the champions…we are the champions…of the weeerld.*

Windows down, still chorusing, they cross the mangrove flats and swing a leftie into the town, for the mango and pawpaw smoothie with nutmeg on top that they started talking about an hour ago. 'Jeez, someone hand me a towel. I'm drooling.' Henny grins at homecoming.

Arriving in Shoal Bay is like falling against a palette of oil paint that has just two colours: turquoise and the red of cut muscle. For it is dominated by red earth – a stripe of land as dense in colour as soft tissue – and a line of iridescent turquoise ocean. It looks as if a paintbrush as thick as a wrist has smeared them horizontally, next to one another.

The town itself sits tentatively on the cusp between the two, tin roofs shimmering by the low-lying mangroves and sea that teems like chowder. It is blasted by enough bleachy sunlight to burn retinas.

Past the fast-food joints, fuel stations and car-hire mobs, sarongs hang on nails outside tourist shops, jiggling as the hot air moves. There are T-shirts on racks, eskies in stacks. A travelling feral sets up a plank on two crates, covers it with a piece of cloth and lays out the jewellery she has threaded together sitting on the step of her Kombi, parked up at Red Beach. Glass beads mix with ruby-coloured desert seeds, threaded on wool or leather. In the next street, girls lean into the shop windows, putting out the pearl displays. Backpackers sit on benches, eating bakery-bought breakfasts. Filling up fast, ready for the next leg of wild four-wheel drive singles coach tours: 'A bottle of red, a bottle of white, a different girl every night.'

A small tide of people has eased into the centre of the little town. A blue Mini Moke with a bohemian wannabe parks round the back of his legal practice; a road crew stands around looking at potholes and contemplates heating bitumen; shop doors start to bang open, brass hooks fastening them back in the vain hope of breeze. Mango smoothies, trucked-in salads, cattle station utes being loaded with slabs of beer at the drive-in bottle shop. A mother pulls a little boy along by the hand; all over the world, boys resisting school. Dark groups of Aborigines sit in circles under the boab trees.

It used to be a sleepy little joint; just a park-up for the pearl luggers that latched onto the wooden jetty in the mangroves as the bay drained twenty kilometres over the horizon into the Indian Ocean, leaving a jelly of grey ooze quivering with mud skippers.

Then holiday-makers found it, and oil and gas prices sky-rocketed, and resources projects boomed. It was like someone hit the turbo button.

But there are still the two colours. 'If I could bottle that, I'd make a fortune,' says some bloke from the city, facing the view.

Sometimes the big tides come in so fast over the bay's rippled mud that it sounds like shards of glass pouring down a drainpipe. It pushes back wader birds before it – millions of them, come down the Asian flyway from Siberia, some to poke in their needle-like bills as they goosestep on brittle-looking legs, others to pick over the surface, scavenging the ocean's leftovers. More than 300 species drawn by a natural abundance.

The tides wash over footprints left 120 million years ago by a brachiosaurus grazing when this was soft forest floor. It weighed eighty-five tonnes and was heading north-east. Its footprints – a whole set of them, a steady gait apart – were set in the soft ground and it turned to rock. Just some of 140 fossilised dinosaur footprints, more than anywhere else in the world. The patter of planetary history in the most biodiverse bay in the world.

When the tide goes out, it leaves water between the crests of the undulations, and a rising full moon spills light into them, making a stairway.

The local Aboriginal tribes fed on crabs and seafood, and tiptoed the bay with bendy fish spears. Over generations, they traded shells and discarded those from their meals, forming distinctive domes. Middens.

Then divers came for the pearl shell. Japanese, Chinese, Filipino, Malay, Koepanger, Makassan and Aborigines; willing or not. Desert people rounded up and brought to the bay and a watery world, wondering what the hell had happened to them. Free-diving for *Pinctada maxima* until their ears bled, then sent back down for shell, or a handful of sand to prove they'd hit bottom.

Hard-hat divers went as deep as seventy-three metres, walking the bottom at an angle with a net bag until a migrating whale snagged the air hose out of their helmet and the pressure tried to suck their bodies through the hole, turning them into guacamole in the bowl of it, feet left dangling.

Or they got the bends. Nine hundred Japanese divers in the town cemetery.

It's so damned exciting lobbing into Shoal Bay. Seeing the two colours. All the bougainvillea and fruit and corrugated tin and history and newness. All mixed into one. Gone through the blender and come out with a distinctive flavour.

'I've always been lucky in Shoal Bay,' Dylan tells Henny, as they sit outside the fluoro pink and blue ice-cream parlour with their smoothies. He's seen rock bands at the Phoenix

Hotel, ballet on the beach and heard congregations ringing out anthems, hymns and songs at the little corrugated iron cathedral.

In the Wet, he's seen clouds pumped with electricity and pulsing like cartoon brains, and the blessed, sweet rainfall. Kids splashing in gutters and women running from one shop canopy to another, a newspaper covering their hair. Grass growing five centimetres a day – two inches in the old measure.

He once found a weird split of rock on a beach south of the big port jetty and then, half an hour, two hundred metres and a million rocks away, found the other half. He keeps them on a shelf, now seamlessly one again, and still wonders at the chance of it.

'I've been lucky in Shoal Bay,' he repeats, 'and I think I always will be.'


'They say you make our own luck.' A familiar voice, and Dylan spins on his seat to see the happy grin of Billy Parkes. Dylan jumps up and they both step forward, shake warmly and then each throw a strong left forearm around the other's shoulders – shake'n'embrace in the fashion of comfortable and confident modern men.

'What are you doing here? It never crossed my mind that'd I'd see you.' Dylan's opener.

'I live just down the road, remember.' They both laugh.

In fact, Erindale Station is 300 kilometres up the bitumen and another 500 down a rough-as-guts gravel road.

Dylan introduces one to the other. 'Of course,' says Henny when he hears Billy's name. 'I heard-a-youz. You're a chap they talk about.' A bouquet.

'And you're from the Crossing. The Breezes there?' Billy carefully repays the compliment of recognition.

'Yup. That's us.'

'Well, it's good to finally meet you. Dylan talks about you.' He smiles. 'I just came in for a mango and pawpaw smoothie, but I see you beat me to it. Anyway – what are you two up to, lurking in our ice-cream parlour?'

'Girding our loins. I'll order that drink for you, then tell you about it.' Dylan is quickly inside, through the veil of clattering thick-plastic flyscreen strips and soon back at the table.

'I've just driven up from the city – picked up Henny on the way. I'm showing some government reps around. They are flagging a sustainable power project for the region.'

'Ah – the public meeting coming up in Carter's Ford. I'm hoping to get to that.'

'Yep, that's part of it. We're doing a lap of a few places first.'

Billy has swung a glance at Henny. 'Not me,' the young man says. 'I'm just goin' home. He's on his own with them types.'

'Not coming as far as Erindale?' Billy asks Dylan.

'Unfortunately you're way outside the area they're suggesting – or certainly we would have.'

'No hassles. We're pretty well set up for it anyway.' Putting Dylan at ease. 'I did a lot of research on it, and keep up with it pretty well, so it there's anything I can do to help, just call any time.'

'Thanks, mate. But they'll be doing all the work on it – I'm just getting them around to meet a few people. We're going to Nick Goodson's at Barker River.'

'Oh, good.' Billy is genuinely pleased.

'I thought I'd heard you two were mates.'

'Yeah – Nick's a good lad. Got good ideas. He's the sort of guy who'll have an impact up here. His old man – Peter – is a bit stuck in the old ways, but Nick'll have his say, I'm sure.'

*The old man. Stuck in the old ways.* These are echoes that have shaped Billy's life. When he was just a youngster, he and his older brother Ace just took off from their old man's place near Nine Mile. Set off to make better lives. To break a bad, destructive cycle that generations of men in their family had been stuck in. It was Ace who led; the heroic brother, always feeling he was saving little Billy. But it was Ace who got dragged back into it, even though they had Erindale by then. It was Ace who sank in mud. It was Ace for whom bureaucracy was one of the last straws. When that telco car turned up and the uniforms got out – all over Ace for fixing up a phone line because they hadn't – something in him finally broke. The tide swept over him. It was Ace who knelt with the barrel of a rifle between his teeth. And it was Billy who moved on and found other country within himself. Good country. Found peace, found Amy. Found kindness.

'Anyway, who's the "they" from the government?' Billy asks. 'If you can say, of course…if it's confidential, fair enough…'

'Oh no,' says Dylan. 'There's no secret about it. I've been dealing with a young woman from the Department of Premier – Kate Kennedy. She's good, and she's coming. And a consultant, Jack Cole.'

'Jack Cole?' The chill in Billy's voice speaks volumes. 'Well there's a name to be reckoned with. Interesting track record.'

'You certainly keep up, for someone who lives in Woop Woop,' says Dylan.

'Mate, there's this thing called the internet...'

'I'm sorry — I didn't mean that.'

'I know, I know. Settle. Just ridin' ya. So, Cole's running it.'

'Not really. It's the Minister, Michael Mooney, behind it. It seems to be very much his project. He's the one pushing it along.'

'Even more interesting.'

'Is it?'

'Oh yeah. I hear that Mooney might even have the numbers for a run for Premier.' Graziers' association, farmers' federation, primary producers' cooperative, agricultural advisory committees, exporters' council, sustainability forums, landcare initiatives, rural funding panels. There are plenty of ways for the motivated in the bush to be plugged directly into the power of the city, and Billy is. Intelligent, industrious, energetic, indefatigable, he's not only part of a web of contacts, but central to it. Billy attracts, inspires and influences.

'Really?' Dylan's interested that Billy knows more than him.

'Yes. This solar thing'd be another nice little feather in his cap. A good-news media release always helps.' Billy's drink has been placed on the table, and he sucks the cold, crystalline blend of fruit, ice cream and milk up its straw. 'How are you getting on with Cole?' A pointed question.

'I haven't met him yet. They're flying up and I'm meeting them.' He pauses. 'To be honest, I'm a bit jittery about all those days in the vehicle. Just the interpersonal thing.'

'I know what you mean. That stuff can be a bit awkward. But everyone's got something in common. It'll work out. And you're in the Kimberley – that helps. Always something to talk about here.' Being supportive.

Dylan turns to Henny. 'See – he's just like you. Looking on the bright side. Being positive.' A forced, beatific smile.

'I'm positive, alright,' says Henny. 'I'm positive you're in *trouble*...' Laughs like a kookaburra.

'You'll be alright,' says Billy. 'It's good to work with the system – contribute to it. That's where change really comes from. Change comes from within. Besides folks are generally just folks.'

Billy Parkes. Always looking for the good.

# Nine

Jack Cole is starting to feel niggly about the whole trip. He has to catch tomorrow's early morning flight to Shoal Bay, and knows he'll be up most of the night finishing work. He sips neat scotch and fires out email missives.

'I understand we can't bank on mobile phone reception once we've left Shoal Bay, and there won't be much facility to pick up emails,' Kate had responded precisely to his question. It suddenly seems like a long time to be out of touch. Deals going through, the Hills subdivision at a crucial stage, and his new black four-wheel drive – with all the options – to pick up. Then he remembers Mooney and refocuses.

——

Michael Mooney sits with his forehead on his desk, tablet under his tongue, trying to relax. Damned heart. This is getting more frequent, and each attack feels more severe. Not now, he tells it. Not now. Not when I've got everything going for me.

Breathe slowly. Think of a colour – that's what they say. A nice, cool, icy stripe of turquoise.

As the grip on his chest eases, he sucks in air more easily and he starts to straighten, until his chin is a fist's width off the desk. The map of the Duncan River valley he was looking at before the attack is in his face, as if he has dropped straight into the country. Like a fast-forward zoom. He's submerged in it and, for the first time, sees a dark, shaded area following the course of the Duncan River, outlining the river in flood. Off to the north-west, where the river system enters Admiralty Sound, it comes to a sharpish tail, then heads south-east across the country in two loops, fattening. Just before Carter's Ford, where the floodplain bowls out, it rounds to an oval before finishing with a sharp, tongue-like sliver which passes through the town and then ends in two prongs, up the two creek systems that feed into the main river.

Mooney is transfixed by the grey serpent before him.

———

Cole decides on another scotch and reads again the brief for the proposed solar power project. He gets it off pat.

In fact, Cole still thinks, it's a bloody good plan; pulling out all the old generators and putting in good energy sources. If there were any real votes in it, that'd do. But nothing compares with bringing limitless water to the city. Nothing.

Cole stares into his wardrobe. He'd better finish packing. It is nearly 2am and the world has taken on the beige hue of whisky. His eyes are as pink as a surfer's and his face is puce. Sweat beads on his forehead and he feels gnarly, the alcohol acting like acid. He makes a pistol of the index and middle fingers of his right hand and runs the barrel along the soft sleeves of his suits. They are all navy, black or charcoal. The way they recoil from this lightest brush shows the quality in the fine wool fabrics. Italian labels that make him look taut and taller. A good suit with a white shirt and a confidently striped tie is a weapon in the war for power and money.

Everywhere has a uniform and part of the trick of being accepted is to be in the right gear. He's going to be out of his environment, he knows that, and dressing like a dickhead'd make it more difficult.

There are two more pairs of chinos at the end of the rail and he gets out a pair of old brown leather shoes to go with the moccasins. He wishes he had boots but knows that new ones are laughable. He hauls out half a dozen polo-style shirts, making sure none have stripes. Just flat, muted colours.

Jocks, socks, boxers to sleep in. He puts in a loose singlet and a pair of shorts he used to wear in the gym. A cap which he manages to snip the golf-ball brand badge off with a pair of hair-nose scissors. His cream fedora. Shaving gear, wash bag. He looks along the shelf in the bathroom and selects an aftershave, squirting one irresistible little cloud into the air.

Notebooks, ballpoints, A4 pads, laptop charger and spare battery, hard-drive for backing stuff up. Phone charger. The maps that Mooney sent him.

Cole glances at his watch. It's nearly 3am and he has booked a taxi for 6.30 to take him to the airport. One last scotch and he lies on the bed with the curtains open and watches the vague halo of citylight across the ceiling.

———

Kate's bags are at the front door by late afternoon. She's bought two new pairs of khaki-coloured linen pants, which have loose legs, suede boots and a big cotton hat that she thinks is cute. She's put in two nice, soft old long-sleeved shirts that Tom left and some T-shirts. She's tucked in a couple of bright bandanas for colour. She packs her full bathing suit with the high front, but she takes her favourite underwear – the good stuff she treated herself to.

For evenings and as nighties, she's wound up some of her favourite silk dresses and slips, which she can wear layered, and a cashmere throw in case there's a cool evening.

'Hi Mum. I just thought I'd give you a ring before I go,' says Kate. 'Yes, all packed.' Her mother runs a check. 'Yes. Yes. Yes, I've got insect repellent, too.'

As they talk, she hears the phone beep with another incoming call. 'I'd better go – someone's trying to call. It might be urgent about tomorrow. Love you.'

She puts down the phone and it rings immediately. 'Hello,' she says, not announcing her name, as she does in the office. 'Oh, hello Kevin.'

Kevin Carmichael says he'd made a note in his diary that she was off tomorrow and just thought he'd give her a ring to say he hopes things go well, seeing as he'd helped to put in the groundwork. He must have searched out her mobile number in the emergency contact directory.

'Thanks, Kevin. Everything seems pretty well organised.'

'Should be a good junket,' he says.

'I don't think of it like that.'

'C'mon. It's just a vote thing. They're flying a kite. If they get back in, it'll just be one of those promises they'll never keep.'

'In other words, you think I'm completely wasting my time.' Keeping up the pretence.

'You're getting paid and going to the Kimberley. I wouldn't complain about that too much. Just make sure Cole's kept happy. That's what Mooney wants most.'

Infuriating, she thinks. The drop-kick is infuriating.

She listens to Kevin's cooed suggestion. 'Yes, a catch-up when I get back would be good,' she answers without conviction.

Kate spends the evening pampering herself; it is her way of preparing herself to go into the unknown. She has a long, hot shower, washing and conditioning her hair and then winding it up in a big, soft towel. She puts on a face pack and sits in her white robe on the sofa, spreading another towel on the pouf and propping her feet up so that she can paint her toenails. Soapies parade across the plasma screen, one merging into the next. She treats herself to chocolates and hot milk.

# Ten

Armed with two trolleys, Dylan and Henny hit the supermarket as soon as it opens in the morning.

'I'll give you a hand before I shoot through,' Henny had said. 'Be interesting to see how the other half lives. Champagne and caviar for those govie types, I suppose. They wouldn't eat the same tucker as the rest of us. You might even find a bit of red carpet at the hardware.'

'Cheeky brat.'

But Henny won't leave off. 'And before they come, you'd better brush up on the way you speak.'

'What do you mean?'

'Well,' says Henny, all earnest, 'what's the stuff you're breathing?'

'Air?' says Dylan.

'And the stuff on your head?'

'Hair.'

'And what do foxes hide in?'

'A cave?'

'No, yer dick – a lair.'

'Alright, a lair, then.'

'Good-o,' says Henny. 'Now string 'em all together.'

'Air, hair lair…'

'I say, a jolly good greeting, old boy,' says Henny, as if he's sitting on an icy pole. 'Now, that's how I want you to say oh-he-llo to the nobs.'

'Twit,' says Dylan, bringing his left hand up to clip the back of Henny's mop head.

Dylan's worked out a menu for breakfasts, cold lunches and snacks, and the nights he thinks he'll have to cook dinner for them all. He's factored in plenty of hard fruits and vegetables, which he'll wrap in newspaper and stow in cardboard boxes to keep fresh. He's keeping stuff to be cooled to a minimum as he's only got the small Engel fridge for essentials and to chill beer and white wine down, if they want it.

'No need to shortcut on costs, apparently,' Kate had told him. 'Especially on the wines. The Minister would like Mr Cole to be hosted well, and informs me that he has a somewhat educated palate.'

Henny's on best behaviour in the supermarket, steering the trolley carefully behind Dylan as he chooses items and ticks them off the list, though he's dying to treat it like a grand prix and see what this chromed-up baby'll do across the hard, slick floor and through the chicanes of table cracker displays.

Dylan pays, tucks the receipt in his wallet and they pack everything into boxes from a pile near the door and carry them out to the vehicle. He takes half an hour to wrap and stow everything exactly where he wants it, Henny standing quietly by his side, taking things and passing them back.

'Good job. Thanks Henny,' says Dylan, turning to him. 'Appreciate the help.'

'No probs. Any time.' Then Henny looks up the road. 'Anyway, bro, we'd better go find Uncle Vincent. Me 'n' him gotta get back to the Crossing today.'

'By the way,' Dylan asks Henny as they amble off down the street, 'how's that puppy of yours?'

'Got a name now. Malacite,' Henny jives, grinning forwards. 'And he's riding in the cab, man. Riding in the cab.'

Vincent Yimi is sitting out the front of the ice-cream parlour.

'Hey, Uncle.' Henny waves from way off and the old bloke nods back.

They hook in to easy talk.

'How are things at the Rec Centre?' asks Dylan.

'Pretty busy,' says Vincent. 'And I been on the phone for hours setting this stuff up.'

'Everyone ready for us?'

Yimi grimaces a little. 'Ya know.'

'Yeah, I know. Different calendar up here.'

'Should be OK.'

'No problems?'

He shrugs.

'Government types?'

'Yeah. You know.'

'I know.'

Henny says he's got to get some stuff before they go, and he'll be back soon.

'You put the wind up me,' says Vincent, when they're alone.

'How so?'

'That stuff about the car bodies. What you told me. Every one I've seen since has scared hell out of me.'

'The thought scares the hell out of me too, now,' says Dylan, suddenly transported from blue and red landscape to green.

'I been thinking about all that.'

'Couldn't we just drink our milkshakes…'

'Nah.'

'Please?'

'No – I gotta say something about it. I been thinking about all that – what happened to you…'

'What I did, you mean.'

'Well, I reckon we all got half a dozen big things we're not proud of, if we're lucky. But we need them. They sit in us, staring at us. They might be the parts we don't like, but we got to have them so we know what we don't like in ourselves and we can change it. It's like we need salt.'

'Salt?'

'We can have plenty of sweet things, but there's gotta be salt in our lives. I want you to think about that. Be more comfortable.'

Before starting the vehicle, Dylan dials home on the mobile. A last call before he heads out to the airport.

'Mum. Hi, it's me.'

From the way his mother says she's glad he's called, Dylan knows something's up.

'The hospital was really good and did the tests on dad straight away,' she says. 'I thought it was a full-on heart attack or a stroke or something, but they say it was arrhythmia. Your dad seems fine now, just a bit shaken.' She hears the urgency in her son's reply. 'No, of course you won't come back,' she says. 'There's absolutely no need for that. He'll be fine, but I just looked in on him and he's asleep, so I won't wake him. I'll tell him you called.' Again he says he'll get on the next plane home – everyone will just have to understand. 'No, Dylan. I won't hear of it. It's ridiculous. He'll be looking forward to seeing you when you've done what you have to do there, but there's absolutely no question of you coming home now. Mitchell will be fine. I think he's just got himself too worked up over this subdivision – getting all het up over something he has no control over.'

Mitchell Ward: Believer in Natural Justice. It's a hard lesson, thinks Dylan.

'I'll call as often as I can,' says Dylan. 'Are you OK? Bearing up?'

'Yes, I'm fine, love. You're not to worry. We'll be fine.'

'Love you,' says Dylan. 'And tell dad I love him, too.'

'He knows, but I'll tell him.'


Everything in Dylan screams at him to get on a plane and head south; every thought or word about caring for others, every good intention, every belief in family, every bit of love and gratitude.

Talking is one thing, doing is another. It feels like a betrayal of everything fundamental to him. It rips at him. He thinks of calling her back, but knows he'll get nowhere. Developers, Dylan thinks, hitting the steering wheel with the palms of his hands so it shakes.

# Eleven

Row 1. Kate is sitting in the window seat on the right side of the plane, Cole opting for the aisle so that he doesn't feel pinned in. There's deliberately no-one between them and Cole claims the seat with his fedora. He rips his way through the morning paper, making a big event of each page; snatching the right-handers by the top corner before shaking the paper violently three or four times to snap the creases out of it. After ten, eleven, maybe twelve turns, Kate comes to dread the next. She braces as she senses it coming. A deep groove of concentration cuts a furrow between Cole's eyebrows as he dissects, analyses, categorises and selectively memorises the events of the day before. It is as if he is not reading but searching. He quickly dismisses most, but it is as if some have a tiny, shiny, barbed bream hook in them. Maybe a name, maybe just three or four words strung together in a particular way, maybe something that cross-references to a previous happening, leverage to be had.

He searches the death notices, casts an eye through the prostitution ads, scrutinises the government tenders, takes note of the stuff listed in company auction sell-offs and who's sponsoring the various horseraces of the day. He plunges on through the sport, folds the paper in half and tosses it on the floor.

Then Cole twists the corm of his torso, hooks his right elbow up on the headrest of the empty seat between them, and sets off on his next task: making charming chat.

'So, how long exactly have you been working with Michael?' Jack Cole is careful not to say *for* Michael – he thinks she'll like the compliment.

Inside she groans. It wouldn't be so bad if it was just a creep making small-talk, but Kate has told herself to be wary of Cole at all times. And, having watched him devour the newspaper, she's now more sure than ever that she's right; that he doesn't do anything without some underlying agenda. If he were to find out about, well, certain things, goodness knows how he'd use it.

'I've been with the Department of Premier, one way and another, a couple of years or so. Other departments before that,' she says, trying not to show the bile behind her smile. She could give him one of her favourite lectures, about her working first and foremost for the people of the state, and then for the incumbent government elected by those people, and not specifically for any individual or political party, who are just custodians of an office which has a continuity of its own, but she doesn't bother.

'Not many little missions like this one, though?'

'No, not like this.'

'Well, I think we can pull it off. Our little secret.'

The plane tracks northward up the coast, following the rim of Long Drift Beach, and blond sand gives way to jade mangroves scored with channels of salty bisque. It wheels out to sea and turns into the offshore wind, lining up the Shoal Bay runway. And it is now that Kate sees turquoise ocean against low bluffs of pindan earth, like fresh blood mixed into concrete. A primal statement in landscape.

My God, she thinks, seeing the two incredible colours vibrating against one another. The horizontal weld between earth and water. She has become used to not sharing such moments. She has developed the knack of being tough on herself.

Cole puffs out hard and checks his watch. Now it's happening, he realises he's not at all looking forward to the next couple of weeks. And something in her mannerisms tells him she's going to be a hard nut to crack.

Light and hot air assaults them as the plane door is opened. Passengers duck their heads and blink down the rattly aluminium steps, holding hats, clutching bags, feeling for the hot rail. They swim into the light, misjudge the distance from the bottom step and land with a judder on ancient ground.

The cabin crew thank each passing stranger and point them across the dazzle of tarmac to the terminal. Purple and white bougainvillea, scarlet and white lattice. Cole leads the way with a wide-elbowed walk, chin jutting forward. Kate sees he is making a conscious effort to impose himself, perhaps on her, perhaps on the place, but definitely on Dylan, whom he is about to meet for the first time.

From the terminal, Dylan sees Kate first, though Cole is several paces in front. Out of her hard-cut business wear, she looks delicate under the deluge of sunshine, and has charming, fluid movements. Long-sleeved shirt with the collar hooked up, soft pants, suede boots. Cleverly feminine; not try-hard.

There's the usual hubbub of greetings, introductions and bag-grabbing. Jack Cole gives a firm handshake, but only glancingly meets Dylan's eye. And then they are out in the car park, Dylan dragging stuff over the gravely bitumen to the four-wheel drive. He clicks the doors unlocked and Cole walks to the front and gets in the passenger door.

Kate leans to unlatch the rear doors. 'Let me get that,' Dylan says, reaching forward faster.

'I'm quite capable, you know,' she says.

'I would never doubt that.' He lifts the bags and shuffles them into place. Once they all are all inside, Dylan swivels and says, 'I thought we might just head into town first, get a coffee and run through the schedule. Today's pretty easy, so we've got plenty of time. It's probably good just to have a look at the maps and get an idea of how it'll go.'

'I hope it's not going to be this bloody hot every day,' says Cole, blotchy and beaded.

'That's one thing I can't control.'

# Twelve

The road is a straight, wide platinum band heading east towards the delta where the Duncan River enters Admiralty Sound. Through the Dry season, river and ocean integrate in a gentle marriage, but in full spate, as Wet season rain deluges a plateau the size of a country, monsoonal waters aggressively penetrate the sound's salty potage.

'This is pretty much the eastern edge of the Duncan River floodplain,' explains Dylan. The hour on the road has been punctuated by more replies from Kate in the back seat than Cole in the front, where he sits, jaw set, staring out of his side window. So Dylan has adjusted the rear-view mirror so that he can catch a glimpse of Kate when she speaks.

'In a good Wet, this all goes under,' he says. 'The average January rainfall in Carter's Ford is around 150 millimetres. The record's over 460. When Cyclone Sylvia came through three years ago, they got 240 mills in twenty-four hours up on the plateau. Winds over 300 kilometres an hour.'

'I sort of remember that.' She returns his glance. 'Have you been here in the Wet?' Making conversation.

'It's fantastic. In the build-up – from about November – you get a real tension. Big lightning storms in the evenings. The whole place feels edgy. The people, too. Then the rain starts to come and everyone breathes a sigh of relief. This country's deceptive. The ground's rock-hard now, but within a few minutes of a downpour, it's turned to slime, then brown porridge.' She nods encouragement. 'And then, after the Wet, the grasses come up. It's lush and green – completely transformed from what you see now. I love it.'

'Well, good on you,' says Cole under his breath, looking at a deserted, featureless, useless landscape.

They pass burnt stretches with singed birds' nests in bushes that have curled into bowers. Termite mounds are mud-sculpted by white ants who have hauled up the beige earth from below.

They stop just before the Willywilly Bridge, Dylan pulling the LandCruiser to one side and suggesting they walk across for a look. Cole is first out, surprising them by striding ahead down the middle of the highway, for his first real view of the Duncan River. The bridge is twenty metres above the brown riverbed, where there are still pools of water and somewhere under the surface, the river runs, in a fashion.

'I've stood on this bridge with the water just below the road level and felt it shaking with the force,' says Dylan. 'And then it went under. In fact, nearly twenty kilometres of the highway went under water.'

'That's a lot of water,' says Cole, suddenly animated. A lot of water going to waste, he thinks. Using it for the city is too obvious. 'So who lives around here?'

'There's a roadhouse the other side, and they've got a caravan park. Cattle stations back on to the river, and stretch pretty well up to the Sound. Johnny Burleigh's got the land behind us, to the west. In fact, he owns most of the land on the north side of the road we've been driving up. Only a young bloke and I'm not sure where the money's coming from. We've got a lunch meeting with him in Nine Mile. I think you'll find him worth talking to, though there's only this last property that borders the area we're looking at. If the cut-off's the river, he may not be eligible for a solar plant, but I thought there was no harm in meeting him…'

He looks for response but there is none. 'Then there are seven major Aboriginal language groups in this area. Originally they had specific rights to certain places, but now they've all come together in the valley, in many respects. They are still separate tribes, of course, but they share some cultural practices and beliefs.'

'And stories?' asks Kate.

'Sure. Some are particular to tribes or individuals, of course. They own them. But a few are broad. For example, they all have stories with mythic beings in the form of rainbow serpents. There are differing names for them, but there's what you might call a universal theme. Then, even within that, there are specific stories. One tribal group believes the Duncan River was created by a rainbow serpent that was speared by a mythic being who was fishing in the same pool using poison from the majarla tree. It's the freshwater mangrove. *Barringtonia acutangula*.'

'Enough of the mumbo-jumbo,' Cole suddenly snaps. 'How many people are there, then. In total, around this part of the river?'

Dylan feels slapped. 'Probably a hundred people, on a good day.'

'And what, precisely, is a good day?'

'When there isn't a funeral, when they're not off visiting, when it isn't Thursday.'

'Thursday?' whips back Cole.

'Pension day in town.'

'I see.'

'Ready to rock and roll?' Dylan turns to walk back across the bridge to the vehicle, but Cole ignores him, strolls out of earshot in the opposite direction, produces his smartphone from his pocket, launches its recording app and holds it to his mouth.

Kate falls in step beside Dylan. 'OK?'

'I'm a big boy.'

After a few steps, she adds, 'Dylan, there's just one thing. I think I should say it. Although everyone's committed to the power project, when we start meeting people, we won't actually promise it. You know how things can change. Backfire. Better to call this "fact finding".'

It sends a shiver through him. 'There's some doubt? There has never been any doubt up to this minute. You were clear that it was a done deal – I thought this was just to confirm logistics.'

'I'm not saying it won't happen. Just that there are still a lot of processes after this.'

'And politicians don't necessarily do what they say?' He suddenly sees how much trust he has put in her. From his first email to a few moments ago, he has just sucked in whatever he's been told. How could he have been so naïve. He knows better than that. For goodness sake, he knows better than that. And now, with his reputation on the line, the goalposts have been shifted.

'Hold on. I'm not saying that. Just under-promise and over-deliver.'

And Dylan looks into her face and sees some sort of turmoil in there, too.

'Sure,' he says.

'It'll all work out.'

'Sure,' he says. 'Sure.'

Two pink and grey galahs tumble past, silly as wheels, madly shrieking at one another. *Cacatua roseicapilla* making a scene. They land on the branch of a river gum and hang upside down, beaking at one another, screeching like nails drawn down a blackboard. A mob of sulphur-crested cockatoos walks bandy-legged in the bed, mumbling coarsely to one another. Little corellas chorus in the trees. Separate tribes of *Cacatua* all come together in the valley.

Nine Mile has a wide main street that ends abruptly at the tidal mudflats that are crazed into exactly-fitting pieces in the Dry and like dark pus in the Wet.

White four-wheel drives are lined up outside the supermarket and oversized women in big blouses lug out box after box, sweating acrid crescent moons under their armpits. Men stand under the awning in blue shirts, hats tilted back, beery pregnancies slung over plaited kangaroo belts, squinting through gluey pterygiums. They talk cattle, beef prices, the politics of agriculture, and weather. Dark kids with yellow-white teeth ride cobbled-up bicycles in circles around a dog scratching at the scabs on its back, until it slinks off under a mango tree speckled with hard, green, unripe fruit. Old men sit in circles in the shade, surrounded by litter. They shout to another man, sitting alone over the road on the low school wall. He ignores them. A young Aboriginal woman pushes her baby in a pram, with carefully rigged shade over it. The police paddy wagon rattles past, driven by a young cop in khaki and blade sunglasses, with another on lookout.

Dylan swings the Toyota into the car park of the Admiralty Sound Hotel, which has been tizzed up by the new city owner. She's smart and sassy, with hide like a bull and a personality that pushes all over you. Chrissie's already got the place mostly booked out with mine workers and the pilots who fly tourist seaplanes. All on contract. Dylan checks his watch. Noon. She'll be there, ready to show them every room, for sure.

Johnny Burleigh looks manicured, moisturised and massaged. Fresh as a daisy. The cells of his skin are plump, his hair has a quality cut and is lightly gelled. He has the respect of cattlemen and the business world, a firm but ethical philosophy, and an attractiveness to women of which he is largely unaware.

'Good to see you again, Dylan. How've you been?' Johnny's handshake is a reaffirmation of respect. 'Pleased to meet you both,' he adds, not quite replicating it. 'So, you're going to put a nice new solar plant in for me,' he gently baits. 'That's very kind of the government.'

'It may not be quite that simple,' shoots Cole, momentarily undermined by the rapport between the other two men. Fighting for ground. 'He might have misled you.'

Johnny Burleigh runs some solar, but relies on diesel generators for his latest project.

'We're a cattle station first and foremost, but I've put in sweet potatoes along the river block and irrigated them. Just an experiment – a toe in the water – but it's going OK. I reticulate all through the Dry. Plenty of water here. The crop only takes as much water as passes under the Willywilly Bridge in seven seconds in the Wet.' Cole digs a bit, trying to flush out Burleigh's connections, but he's cool and collected, and giving nothing away. Burleigh swings the conversation onto Dylan. 'This man's done some good things up here. It's important to have people like Dylan – a sort of conduit between us and the city. Particularly for the Indigenous people. You're lucky to have him as your entree into this place. It can be, well, not so easy up here.' He turns to Dylan. 'I didn't want to embarrass you, but it needed to be said.'

Kate hears a compliment, Cole a warning.

When Chrissie Borthwick insists on showing them all the rooms, Cole says he's got other things to do, and when they get back to the vehicle, he's dictating voice-to-text into his smartphone.

'We'll fuel up and head east,' says Dylan.

'Anything I can do to help?' Kate has jumped from the vehicle, now parked at a bowser.

'You could just hold this nozzle for me, if you like. It's a bit greasy, though. I'll get paper towel.'

'No problem.'

'I've just got to make a couple of last phone calls. You lose mobile coverage pretty quickly outside town.'

The phone barely rings before it's answered. 'Uncle Vincent, it's Dylan.'

'M'boy. You on the road? How are they?'

'Fine, Uncle. We're in Nine Mile. We've just had lunch with Johnny and now I'm taking them to the art centre. We stopped and had a look at Willywilly. It all seems to be OK.'

'Well, we're expectin' you.' Vincent knows that's the one thing Dylan wants to be sure of; he understands the Aboriginal reputation for sudden absence. 'I'm not goin' walkabout and I'm not goin' t'a funeral. HA! I'm not even goin' fishing.' He roars with laughter at his own joke.

'Funny bastard.'

'You gotta mirror that end of the phone, boy?'

Then Dylan rings his mother, but there's no reply, so he leaves a message.


'Everything alright?' Kate has rattled the fuel pump's handpiece back into its holster.

'Yes and no,' he says with more frankness than he had expected.

'Tell me both.'

'Vincent's ready and waiting – and in good form, by the sound of him.'

'And "no"?'

'Oh, it's just that my dad hasn't been well and I'm a bit worried. I only heard this morning. I just rang my folks again, but there's no reply.'

'I'm sorry. It's come at a bad time.'

# Thirteen

'Do excuse us. There's been a hullabaloo.' Jo Fortescue is flushed and her short, light floral dress is stuck to her. 'But then, there *always* seems to be a hullabaloo of one sort or another.'

She wipes her hands on the cheeks of her backside, and holds the right one out. It is stringy and taut.

'Jo Fortescue,' she says first to Kate and then Cole, engaging them with bright eyes. With her left hand, she offers each a business card: 'Curator and coordinator, Nine Mile Art Centre, home of the Ngalgardi community.'

'And you,' she says, turning to Dylan, 'it's lovely to see *you* again.' She lifts long fingers to hold either side of Dylan's face and kisses him on each cheek. There are soft scoops of blonde vermicelli under each arm.

'You too,' he says into her ear.

'As you see, a lot of funding has gone into this new art centre.' Jo Fortescue begins her tour and presentation. 'The artists themselves saved nearly half a million dollars and that was matched by private industry and the state and federal governments. After some persuasion.

'We've finished stage one, and stage two will be completed through this next Wet season. It's not a bad time to build, as you can sometimes get the men more easily then. But we'll see. These builders are coming from Queensland – you can barely get anyone within the state, as they're all in mining now.'

She has led them through the artists' working areas, where two old Ngalgardi women in knitted beanies sit on the paint-dotted concrete floor, one in plastic sunglasses with bright pink rims, the other in an old No 23 footy shirt, and they stand now in the main gallery.

'But the costs have blown out so much that we haven't been able to replace the old diesel generator. It costs a fortune to run – and it's dirty, of course – and it isn't that reliable. There's nothing worse than losing the power when you've got a gallery full of people.'

'Is that what happened this morning? The "hullabaloo"?' Dylan hopes for something to push the point home.

'Oh no, no, NO!' Jo is dying to tell the story. 'No – we had some important art dealers from Melbourne in on a buying trip, and they were all standing round in their finery, and everyone was being very considered and intellectual – very *Melbourne* – and all my girls and the men were standing in the background not quite sure what to do, when this enormous snake suddenly appeared. I don't know whether it came in the back door, or it was already hiding in here. And I don't just mean enormous…I mean this thing was *huge*…'

By now women have shuffled in from the little office and from the painting area, clustering behind Jo. 'I'll say he was a big 'un,' murmurs the woman in the dark glasses looking down at the floor, just loud enough for others to hear. 'I've seen some big 'uns, but that was a *muddafucker*.' The last word is breathed gently – more air than vocal chords. Some of the Ngalgardi women titter at the innuendo. 'And she's seen some big 'uns,' one of them says under her breath.

'You can just imagine it...' continues Jo, looking at Dylan, 'everyone started running round screaming and making a terrible fuss. And that was just my mob.'

'But you obviously got it out...' Kate looks around edgily.

'There's a snake man in town,' says Jo. 'But before we could call him, Sylvester hit it with a shovel. We've just cleaned it up.'

Jo Fortescue had been a mess when she left Melbourne and moved to Nine Mile. A master's degree in fine arts had led to curatorial work at the art gallery. She met and fell in love with Thomas, but three years later discovered that not only had he also been with his childhood sweetheart all along, but she had borne him a child during those years. The pain was unspeakable. She felt cleaved. She howled from some primal, almost-forgotten part of the species. She didn't even recognise it as a sound she could make and it scared her.

All she could do was leave Melbourne.

Jo knows there wasn't any real competition for the position of facilitator at Ngalgardi community's then-simple Nine Mile arts set-up. She had the most important qualification – she wanted to live in the remote Aboriginal community off the side of a tough outback town, scorched half the year, drowned and steamy the rest, and earn very little money. She was a shoe-in.

She first met Dylan when he bought a small, inexpensive but striking painting by one of the young artists. An ancestor image. Jo told him then that Vivienne Yalani's work was a good investment. She was emerging, was committed to a career, and prices throughout the Indigenous field were showing substantial gains.

It was what most buyers wanted to hear.

Dylan was gracious. 'I'm sure that's all true,' he said. 'But that's not why I bought it.' He just wanted to hang it in his office at the Scimitar Project and bring the country in.

Jo smiled. 'So you bought it for the right reasons.'

She knew what was inside him, and knew even more the day that Vivienne's niece died.

Dylan pieced together the Scimitar Project's financial support for the new arts centre, despite Eric Garson's reluctance. 'It's out of our patch. Is there a point?'

Dylan found a good enough reason and they chipped in. He made some calls which helped to move the state government into position, then the federal government fell into line.

'Without you, I don't think it would have happened,' said Jo, who had just prepared them a dinner of crayfish and chilled a Kiwi sauvignon blanc to celebrate the final funding being signed off.

'Sure it would. I didn't really do anything.'

'You did. You *did*,' she said.

They slept together, just that once, in warm air and the atmosphere of celebration, and breakfasted like friends.

A week later she opened a handwritten letter from Dylan. He said he was caught up in the work and that he hadn't much to offer. He didn't say he was terrified, but she knew that was what he meant. She knew he was bailing.

She told herself she hadn't had any expectations, knowing it was a lie. She tore the letter into small squares and let them flutter into the bin. It was like playing a wedding video backwards – he took off the ring, backed down the aisle, jumped in a car and vanished. Like the old joke about a country and western song in reverse.

'A hullabaloo, alright,' she says. 'I'm afraid the Melbourne buyers were a bit put off, but they're staying at the Admiralty Sound Hotel and they'll be back tomorrow. I think we'll do alright with them.'

She catches her breath. 'Just give me a minute and I'll show you around the gallery – and, Dylan, Vivienne's just back from the outcamp. She's got some very interesting new work. I think she'll show you.'

Jo steps back into the glass-fronted office and Kate notices her leaning over a big Aboriginal woman who is staring at a pile of paperwork on the table. One teaching, one learning, both respectful.

The gallery, off to the left, is spacious and carefully lit, with tall white walls, unobvious air conditioning, three hundred paintings hung and some carvings and weavings on white plinths.

'We have sixty or so artists working at the centre, and eight senior painters. Three tribes come together on this country. The paintings are hung in clan groups,' Jo explains. 'That's a slightly different approach and has been important, culturally. In everyday life, there are certain restrictions on who may speak to whom; even who may look at whom. This is reflected in the hanging of works – an unusual curatorial approach, I think. Generally we would be more inclined towards subject, style or chronology. The curator often imposes visually – that's their work, in a sense, to create a bigger artwork from the component pieces.

'But I digress...'

Kate follows as Jo tells what she can of the stories revealed through images. Cole hangs back, scribbling in a small notebook words which Dylan suspects have nothing to do with the conversation.

Creators and ancestors. Instructive tales. Moralistic themes. Spiritual symbols and metaphors. Haunting images from the half-forgotten. Animal allegories. Stories across time.

'The image of the snake, for example, is regularly incorporated, as you see,' says Jo. 'Serpents often rape the earth and the female principle.'

As she weaves words in the air, two Aboriginal women drift in from the work area and shuffle closer. One, in a loose, wattle-yellow singlet, casts her eyes up towards Dylan, and when he smiles a little, she nods.

The woman from the office edges out from behind the glass and joins them.

Near the end of the last wall, a striking group of images hangs together. Snakes curl, their innards shown in X-ray. Other animals dot about the canvasses. A quoll? The horseshoe shapes of waterholes.

'Vivienne Yalani's work,' says Jo, 'and we are fortunate

to have the artist with us.' She smiles towards the woman in the yellow singlet, who shrugs and turns away a little. 'This is Vivienne, one of our rising stars.'

Dylan cringes, predicting Vivienne's shy reaction.

But, to his surprise, she steps forward, breaking long-standing cultural mores and, looking around the group, greets each visitor with a reserved smile.

It is something he hadn't expected.

Things changed for Vivienne when her niece suicided. They had just found the twelve-year-old hanging in a tree when Dylan, Vincent alongside, pulled up for a funding meeting. The two men knew this wasn't the usual hullabaloo. A woman ran in circles screeching and stirring a pall of cinnamon dust. Little kids sat owl-eyed. The dogs stood to attention.

Jo, with Vivienne behind her, was struggling to get a big aluminium stepladder out of the centre's side door. It clanked against the steel doorframe.

'Let me help.' Dylan had run up, feeling the tremor.

Jo's face was painted with a numb horror. 'It's Catrina. One of the little girls. Hanging. Out the back, in the bush.'

'My niece.' It was all Vivienne said, and in her face Dylan saw not horror, but a more terrible resignation.

He ran full-pelt with the stepladder, Jo beside him, Vincent in a stiff sprint behind. Youngsters clustered under a colourful veil hanging in the bloodwood. Catrina had put on one of her mother's long dresses, and as she hung, it covered her hands and feet.

'Oh-no-no-no...' Vincent chanted through dragged breath as he helped Dylan open the steps.

'Get the kids away. Get them away,' Dylan urged Jo.

'They'll watch,' was all she said.

And he climbed the shiny steps until he was level with Catrina's beautiful face and open eyes. There was cloth in the tree, where she had sat before swinging out. The nylon cord had made a carmine stripe around her throat.

There was no easy way. As he slit the line, she fell untidily in the dirt; an overweighted doll.

Vincent dropped to his knees, leaning over her, trying to enshroud her head with his bulk. 'Child,' he cried, and Vivienne knelt too, her arms encircling his shoulders. 'I'll get something,' Dylan said, and looked at Vivienne for approval.

Woman had started to gather, wailing. The men kept their distance.

At the vehicle, Dylan unbelted his swag and pulled a sheet from it. Vincent and Vivienne eased their hold on Catrina and Dylan carefully wrapped her in the sheet. They all looked at the cotton bundle on the red earth.

Jo returned from the building. 'I've called the ambulance. The police will come.' She looked down, too. 'Perhaps we could take her inside.' And Dylan pushed his hands under the neck and knees, knuckles grinding against the dirt, and lifted Catrina's light, shrouded body and walked with a funereal gait across the bleached, open ground, in through the side doors, and laid her on a workbench which Jo had swept everything from. It lay clean against the paint stains. Dylan went outside.

He knelt in the sand, way off, surrounded by wattle, and wished he could vomit out all the feeling, too. First it was only white froth, then viscous, green bile. His body had always done this, rather than cry. The contractions still ran up him, ending in gobs of steamy air, even when his system was dry.

He felt a hand in the middle of his back, gently rubbing, and Vincent's other soft hand supporting his forehead. 'S'orright son. Let it out.' He cooed. 'Having a child is like having your heart walking round outside your body. And they are all our children.'

Later the other kids told how they'd sensed Catrina walking down a tunnel and no-one had been able to stop her.

Vivienne Yalani used her grief, rather than letting it use her up. She took up brushes and tried to paint it out of her.

Dylan gave up fishing. The feeling of the weight on the line made bile well up in him.

But it went on and on. Catrina's death was in the early part of a suicide cluster. More than twenty youngsters killed themselves in the small community and nearby Nine Mile that year. Generally they hanged themselves. When they'd done it, the tree was cut down. Both places were forested with stumps.

Jo's delivery to Cole and Kate is practised. 'A priority of the art centre is to better inform the people who are on their way up the Duncan River valley to look at Indigenous rock art sites.' She looks from one to the other. 'The thirst for cultural knowledge is there. This is about getting authenticity into the experience. What you see here is uncompromisingly scrupulous work; this mob is integrity personified.'

She pauses and changes tack. 'It's very important to control the environment in the gallery. First the weather up here is hot as Hades, then it's steamy. We had to put in dehumidifiers as well as the air conditioning and the fuel bill is horrendous. When the generator breaks down, we have to wait days for an engineer to come and fix it. We've even had to fly one in. You have to bear in mind what these paintings are worth. We'll turn over about $4 million this year, through the gallery and online sales.'

Cole sees that although the community has been able to hook into mining companies' social conscience slush funds, and swung a bit of government funding, it's basically a small business on its own. After all, they needed Ward's connections to pull it off – clearly they didn't have their own. It heartens him.

As they walk towards the vehicle, Cole strides ahead, opens the rear nearside passenger door and gets in. Kate glances sideways and Dylan shrugs. He's happy not to sit shoulder to shoulder with Cole and his notebook jottings. But it surprises Dylan even more than Cole immediately plugs earbuds into his smartphone and tilts the cream fedora so that it hides his eyes and shows the complete fore-aft crease across the crown.

'Front seat?' he says to Kate.

'Why not,' she replies, though it's both what she wants and the last thing she needs. For she realises she hasn't really thought about her part in this whole dishonesty, just the practicalities – how to pull it off and look good doing it. But now it's facing her square-on.

As they swing out of Nine Mile Arts Centre, Jo is on the front step with the women. They wave because she's told them to, but her hand held palm-up to Dylan is intimate.

'She's impressive.' Kate is fishing.

'Yes.'

'She thinks you are too.'

'We've just known each other a while.'

'I see that.'

'These gigs are isolating. I've seen a bit of it. Generally there's a three or four-year cycle. However well you settle, however much the community embraces you, it's a very different lifestyle and culture.'

'Sometimes we need someone to rely on,' says Kate.

Dylan leans forward over the wheel, looks right and left down the road, then pulls out to the east, happy to be distracted.


Soon the bitumen gives way to gravel and they plunge into the dirt of the Duncan River valley itself.

Black wattle has popped up in disturbed areas along the roadside, and there's *Eucalyptus miniata*; tall trees in the open woodland landscape, nearly finished with their orange flowers. Kapok bush sprouts across the landscape; *Cochlospermum fraseri* with its fluffy flowers. Dylan slows the vehicle and they dip into a dry creek crossing which still has small pools of water and is lined with pandanus screw palms and ghost gums. *Eucalyptus bella,* timeless and sentinel.

Dylan names them all, and most with their botanical titles too.

'Native hibiscus, the adopted symbol of the stolen generations of Aborigines.' He wishes he could see *Eucalyptus polycarpa* differently. Near them, the extended family of bloodwoods.

Passing one pool, he points to a foot-sized Johnson freshwater crocodile, suspended on the surface, snout in the air and legs dangling into a greenish abyss. *Crocodylus johnsoni* flat out like a lizard drinking.

The pure voices and varied tunes of pied butcher birds. Black-faced cuckoo-shrikes scuttle up through one tree then peel off to the next.

From the back seat there is the muted, indecipherable chink-chink-chink of Cole's music. Mozart or Madonna? Dylan wonders.

The broad, open floor of the Duncan River valley peels away left and right to a quivering horizon. The country is so wide and open that Kate can see the gentle curve of the naked earth. In the centre of such vastness, she might expect to feel exposed; out of context. But there is none of that. Kate feels unexpectedly part of the landscape and drifts into a private odyssey. 'It's so beautiful,' she says, the words spilling off the end of those thoughts.

'It just carries you with it, doesn't it, Kate.' It's as if Dylan has been thinking in parallel and come to the same point of wanting to speak it. Analogous patterns crossing. Many different paths leading to the same Elysian fields.

Jack Cole has slumped to his right on the back seat, hands knitted together and resting above the slight rise of his bulging shirt, hat askew, fast asleep. With an epiglottal spasm, he seems to throw up the tonsils he has nearly swallowed. He inhales again with a gulp, snores and swallows again, with a fish-out-of-water sound, then exhales in a surprisingly peaceful sigh.

'It's so nice when they're tucked up and fast asleep.' Dylan fills the beckoning space.

The Scimitar Range curves to the south, broadening and pointing towards the desert, but from the ground its walls simply rise in buttresses the colour of pumice. Three hundred and fifty million years ago, it was reef and under the ocean.

The road heads into a cut through the range. For a moment there is shade, but then they burst out again into all-round light and the dusty ribbon ahead. Half an hour later, they rise steadily into the Prince Oswald Range, and Dylan pulls over to the right at the top, so that they can see the view back down to the valley. Its floor is already several hundred metres below, and they are surrounded by boabs and kapok with furry green seed pods and sprays of yellow flowers. They hear the slow, crawling roar of a vehicle coming up the other side of the range, its sound suddenly bursting through the pass. A white LandCruiser troop carrier appears, slewed over and taking the bend almost too fast. It veers past, sucking hot air into its snorkel and corkscrewing smoke out the back, a black hand held out the window nearest them, thumbs-up, faces lost in the shade inside.

Dylan acknowledges with his right hand, held up, palm out, open-cupped at belt height. Kate is intrigued by this understated, private greeting.

Dylan spreads a map across the bonnet and points. 'This is where we passed through the bottom of the Scimitar Range. You can see how it sticks into the Duncan River valley – we were on a spur. And now we are here, at the bottom of the Prince Oswald Range, which forms the north edge of the valley. We'll head south-east to Daydawn Biosphere Reserve, down into the town of Carter's Ford itself and then back through the centre of the valley. The southern part of the valley is pretty well uninhabited these days – the pastoral leases have mainly been taken over by the cattle stations, which are further north. They muster cattle out of the Oswalds and take them to fatten on the southern river pastures before shipping.

'For now, it's about an hour further east to Mt Goode Station – here – where we'll be for the night. I'll tell you about Pullet Ingham when we get closer.'

It always seems ridiculous using a vehicle's indicator in the middle of nowhere, but Dylan habitually does, and still wonders why. He swings in past the Mt Goode sign, stops at a booth, picks up a microphone and calls the station, listening for the crackling replies. It's three-quarters of an hour up the drive and Ingham Pullet likes visitors to radio ahead.

Dylan is soon back in the driver seat. 'Pullet says he's putting the champagne and sav blanc on ice and "there's-beer-for-those-as-wants-it". He's rolling out the red carpet.'

'Elucidate on this Mr Ingham.' Cole is suddenly alert and prompting. 'For a start, what's his *actual* first name?' Cole's pen is poised over his notepad.

'I don't know,' says Dylan. 'It's like that up here. A nickname's often more important than what you were born with. I should think Pullet barely remembers his first name, but it'd be his proper surname. Ingham's a brand of chicken, you see. And a pullet's a female chicken before laying…'

'He's out here on his own?' asks Kate, thinking she's changing the subject.

'He was for a long time. That's where the other meaning of Pullet comes in…'

# Fourteen

Before Pullet Ingham took over Mt Goode Station seventeen years ago, Limpy Peters had battled on for almost two decades, just like Big Edwin Mumbles before him, who arrived in 1950. But earlier, it had taken Thomas Cusworth, the original settler, just four good years to realise he'd never be able to walk fattened cattle west through the Prince Oswald Range to the meatworks and coastal trader ships in any sort of condition. The country between him and trading the stock was simply too tough. He couldn't beat 2,400 million years of geology. Eventually, deflated and bankrupt, he dug a trench, sat on the lip at one end, repeated what he could remember of the Lord's Prayer and shot himself dead, rolling forward and in, just as he'd planned, to save anyone else a job.

Pullet sees a beauty in history.

'He said to me once that in their defeat he saw a kind of romance,' says Dylan, as they rumble up a corrugated track as wide as a grader blade but with only a vague memory of its smoothing cut. 'I think he only ever wanted to live out here and get by.'

'And how does he do that?' asks Cole pointedly.

'He does well enough with tourists – he's a good homestead cook. From the end of May until the beginning of August, I guess, he'd average half a dozen guests a night. I think he can take sixteen when he's full and they're paying a hundred and something bucks a night each, so he probably does enough during the Dry to get him through the Wet. But the fuel bill for all these guys is horrendous. You'll hear about that, and about his old generator.' Trust me, he thinks, you'll hear about that.

The sky over the airstrip turns gold as egg yolk and the sphere of the sun is bent elliptical, its base drawn to earth.

Pullet Ingham greets them with an orphan kangaroo under one arm and a backpacker under the other. He introduces the joey and the slender girl evaporates, past the frangipani trees and in through the kitchen's back door.

Pullet has a stubby, taut form that makes him look shorter than he is, a good eye and steady finger behind a rifle, and patience. He spent years in the inland deserts, living out of a canvas swag and shooting roos into a freezer container which was trucked out to a pet food company. He lived on roo meat, made every bullet count.

He loved the roos. That was the contradiction. He loved them and he hunted them and that connected him to them.

He tore out bits from magazines and books and kept them stuffed together in a folder under the driver's seat. In one he'd read that the kangaroo has the most efficient animal movement on earth. In another how their tails levered, pumping their lungs. In a third, that pregnant females could postpone the foetus's growth until the season was good. Incredible, he reckoned. He'd read it but could barely believe it. Pullet saw poetry in their movement – their flow – and loved their pretty faces and soft ears. He liked shooting them clean, like it was a favour. Better him than some dud shot.

He set dingo traps, partly to pit himself against something even smarter than the roos, partly because he liked moving out of the savannah plains and up into the rocky jump-ups to the caves they favoured, and partly because he liked scalping them and tucking their neat little cut-off ears into bows to take into town for the bounty.

But then Pullet got tired of the constant metallic smell of blood and spent bullets and moved north for work on stations. He did a bit of fencing and got the hang of cattle work but didn't like it much. They weren't like the roos and dingoes; meat manufacturing and a bolt through the brain at the meatworks. That's all it was.

When his mother died, the solicitors sent him the cheque from the sale of the family home and he bought Mt Goode Station cheap as chips because it was a dud, and that suited him just fine.

The station's Cyclone gate has been stuck open for years and there's no wire in the fence. A fissured concrete path leads to the homestead between oleanders and poincianas brought here in the early days and which have grown into monsters.

Between the garden and the airstrip there are sheds and an old Galion road grader, swamped by long, button-headed grasses. The 1970 GN A550's a dinosaur resting. There are two disused fuel pumps with glass bulbs and impellers painted like the poles outside an old-fashioned barber shop. A sign reads 'Welcome to Mt Goode Domestic Airport'. And, in smaller, peeling paint, 'First class departure lounge temporarily unavailable.'

Pullet shakes hands with Dylan, nods to Kate and closes in on Cole.

'I'll take yer down the genny shed now,' he says in the dying light, squinting hard, but not into the sun. 'It's blokes like me who are battlin'. We're the ones as-has been here for years without any help. See, you can get as much funding as you want if you're an Aboriginal corporation or a govie conservation agency. Different set of rules. Just stick a hand out. So I'm glad to see yer. Just a long time coming.'

'Not just now.' Cole is curt. 'Show me a room, I've got some things to do.' He looks at his watch. Four forty-five. 'We'll meet at five forty-five. Here at the gate.'

Pullet Ingham falls into line. 'Five forty-five it is.'

———

The homestead that Thomas Cusworth started building in 1935 now stands at the back of the sprawl of Mt Goode's buildings. He made it like a cave, cutting bush poles then laying solid stringers with a tin roof on top. Mixing and pouring a middle-finger's depth of concrete brought in on the backs of donkeys. Looking for coolness. When the concrete was set, he stripped down the tin from underneath and used it for verandahs, enjoying the sets of matching waves. Big Edwin Mumbles added more haphazard outhouses, ringers' quarters, stores and sheds, all hauled on donkeys. 'Those taxis that belong to Jesus', the Aborigines called them. Then Limpy Peters put up the generator shed in 1975, and built the front homestead and guest quarters.

When Pullet took over Mt Goode, it was already ramshackle and lost somewhere in the tropical jungle of its three and a half hectares of gardens. All he had to do was cheer it up and keep patching the holes.

Pullet leads them to two buildings, separate and side by side. Each has a pair of bedrooms, a lounge area with couches and books between them and a breezeway all the way round. Two metres wide and with painted concrete floors, this passageway has flywire in place of glass and the slightest stir of breeze circles the rooms through the open bedroom windows which look into it.

'Take whichever bedroom you like,' says Pullet, showing Cole to the first building. 'You're on your own in there.'

'I'll write up my notes on the laptop and see you in an hour,' calls Kate.

Pullet leads Dylan and Kate to the second building – 'Bedroom on the right's coolest, for the lady. Dunnies and showers outside' – then they go back to the vehicle, deliver Cole's bags and drag their own through the groomed dirt.

Cole pulls off his rank shirt, closes the bedroom's door and louvred window shutters, turns on every light and opens the tan Chiarugi leather briefcase. He lays Professor Pearson's map, with its red waterline, across the double bed. From Nine Mile, he traces their route east through the southern tip of the Scimitars and the pass in the Prince Oswald Range.

The Oswalds look like the fingers of half a dozen hands spread out. He finds the turn-off to Mt Goode Station and follows the wriggling line north to the homestead. Professor Pearson's tide clearly goes a couple of kilometres past the homestead. All this will be underwater, thinks Cole, and no great loss.

Dylan stretches out on the bed, fingers linked behind his head, glad to be alone. He hears Kate head out to the corrugated tin showers. Soon after, she's moving around in the lounge area. He springs from the bed, straightens his shirt and smoothes his hair.

'How are you feeling?'

'Tired, but good,' she smiles. 'All that driving.'

'It's a big stretch, leaving the city in the morning and being here by teatime.'

'It feels like a long way. I feel quite blown-out.'

'A stroll might help. Would you like to see the old homestead? It's just over the back.'

'Sure,' she smiles. 'Perhaps we should ask Mr Cole – Jack – too.'

When Dylan calls to Cole, he gets the feeling the lack of reply is deliberate.

They pass a small, square meat store, long replaced by fuel-guzzling freezers, its mesh walls holed. A water tank sits up on a wonky platform, pipes not connected. Outside the original homestead there's a chair that was once packing cases, an adze that cleaned bush poles and an axe struck into a hacked block. Rusted stirrups and horseshoes parade along a windowsill, and a Tom Thumb full cheek bit and some spirited stockhorse's Dutch gag hang either side of a toothy dingo trap.

It all sits under a separate, more highly-slung tropical roof, which covers the lot and overhangs into the greenery. There are only gutters over the doorways.

'Mind your head,' warns Dylan, 'this one's low,' and they duck through the front door and into the breezeway. Before them is a plaque, painted freehand, announcing this as a heritage site and giving a brief tribute to Thomas Cusworth, who is credited with vision, fortitude, resourcefulness and creativity. Walls are two hand-spans thick, made from hunks of local stone. The lino-floored breezeways are like bowling alleys, and there are black and white photographs and paintings done over the years by guests. Triumphs of enthusiasm over talent. They are mottled with gecko dung and few hang straight.

The six bedrooms are as dark and cool as the far recesses of Thomas Cusworth's mind.

'What's with the girl?' Kate asks quietly.

'I don't quite understand that one,' Dylan replies. 'But then, I don't need to.'

Pullet Ingham has sucked back a few beers to replace his fluids, line his stomach, and prepare for another great moment in Mt Goode Station's history. It is a lineage he loves and a legacy of which he considers himself the guardian. He, Pullet Ingham, walks in the footsteps of the pioneers and, as he often says, embraces the history of those who were here before them and adds modern enlightenment to it. He casts himself in the role and dresses from the RM Williams catalogue. It's what makes him tick. It gives him status and a story. And when he gets going on it, he can talk a glass eye to sleep.

'That old flathead Ford in the corner did the work for Limpy Peters, but this Perkins generator's been as long as I have and it's on its last legs,' Pullet says. 'You couldn't jump over the diesel invoices and you can't even get fuel in here for four months of the year.'

'But you're closed to visitors then,' says Cole abruptly.

'I'm still here. I've got to survive.' Pullet refuses to get ruffled. 'I've done the research. I reckon we'll need twenty-eight 75-watt solar photovoltaic modules. Here, I've written it out.' He hands each of them a printed sheet. 'The 2.1kW array feeds power into forty-eight batteries with 566 amp-hour cells that will hold 54 kilowatt-hours of energy. A 3kVA sine-wave inverter converts the additional low-voltage DC electricity to 240 volt AC. When it needs back-up, the system is charged from an 8.5kVA diesel generator, thanks to the inverter.'

Pullet is charged by his own enthusiasm. 'Over a complete year, I reckon it'll give seventy per cent of our power needs.' He pauses. 'I've done my homework on it.'

Dinner is chicken breast with a parmesan crust, chunky potatoes roasted in olive oil, a sizeable bowl of salad and another of beetroot and orange. The backpacker stays in the kitchen and Pullet plays host, thickening his accent.

'Tell me about the guests who come,' says Cole, his sudden interest sucking in Pullet.

'We get a lot through word-of-mouth recommendations and repeat business,' Pullet struts.

'But who are they?'

'Internationals, Sydney and Melbourne. A lot with their own businesses. One chap with an air conditioner firm; makes a fortune. A picture-framer who has a black Hummer with all the fruit – he showed me the picture in his wallet. Successful types.'

Cole couldn't be less interested in them. 'Anyone well-known?' he insists.

'We're all famous to our friends.'

I thought so, Cole reflects silently and with pleasure.


'I'll leave the generator on all night,' says Pullet, wishing them goodnight, 'despite the cost. But just look out when you're moving around the place – the snakes have just finished hibernating and we generally see a few now. We had a brown snake over two metres long last week – took one of the Jack Russell pups and hardly a mouthful for him. Gotta be careful with snakes about.'

# Fifteen

In the first drift of morning, Dylan sits out at one of the two tables under umbrellas, barefoot in jeans, a searing blue shirt untucked and partially unbuttoned. Spikes of his fair hair aim at all points of the compass. He was up early, walked over to the kitchen and boiled the kettle to make tea, and sits with a white china mug of it close to him, and another behind that. He wriggles his toes into the dirt, liking the give in it.

He is surrounded by silky lavender-oil light and the thin sounds of morning, occasional sharp bird calls adding to the overture of daybreak.

Dylan plays with the mug handle, swigs at the cooling tea, and curls and cants his shoulders forward in turn so that the shoulder blades crack. He stretches his chin up and lets his body slump straight with his arms hooked over the back of the chair.

'Morning yoga?' Kate has been watching him for a moment through the flywire, and now walks out to join him.

'Not exactly,' he smiles. 'Tea?'

'Point me in the direction.'

'I'll make you one. I'd give you this, but it's got sugar. I always make myself two mugs.'

'No – that's good. I take *one*.'

He slides the mug towards her, turning the handle so that it faces her. 'No-one else seems to take sugar anymore.'

'Remember the old days when everyone seemed to take three?'

'Whatever happened to that?'

A yellow-tinted honeyeater clucks at the morning and its rufous-throated brother joins in. Pardalotes dart through bushes and a friarbird bobs devotions at the water bowl.

'I like the history of this place, and Pullet taking it on. He's a good sort. When you think of the people we've met already...' Dylan's chit-chat mirrors that of the birds.

'The women at Ngalgardi are making a difference.' Kate worms under his candour.

'I hope this doesn't all come to nothing.'

'I told you, the Minister's committed. But it has to be reported back. That's all. That's the process.' The greater lie is still behind it.

'But you can already see that the impact would be significant...'

'I think you're meant to be working.' Cole, who has come out unnoticed, is happy to add to the rub between them.

'We are.' Kate is pointlessly defensive.

'Mmm. We wouldn't want Mr Ward here earning the taxpayers' "hard-earned" under false pretences.' The exercise of morning combat.

'That'll never be an issue,' says Dylan, rising to the bait.

'Good-o,' chirps Cole, contented just like that.

—

Pullet Ingham has just placed enough well-cooked bacon in the middle of the breakfast table to feed a small army. Aiming to kill the pig. Enough muesli to drown in, if a strong current pulled you down.

'What do you think of it?' He spits the night's agitations straight at Cole. 'The funding? For the solar?' Puts the acid on him.

'The final decision's up to the government.' Cole despises desperation but he plays the diplomat. 'I'm just fact-finding, so I can't say.' The last words are emphatic.

'Well, if you could put in a good word...' Pullet trails off.

After Dylan has dialled, the phone rings and rings before he hears Vincent.

'Uncle? It's Dylan. Yes, we'll be there in three days. Yes, we'll do the day on the river and camp at the gorge. I'll bring the supplies.'

Vincent hears tension.

'I'm alright,' says Dylan. 'Just a bit bugged by a few things this morning.'

'Don't let them get under your skin, boy.'

Dylan doesn't know why he feels disappointed in Kate. 'Cole's just a prick,' he says, sensing someone and turning to meet Cole's smug gaze.

'Anyway, I'll see you, Uncle.' He fumbles the phone down.

'No need to say anything,' says Cole. 'I'm a big boy. I'm not here to be Mr Popular, just do a job. You might remember that yourself.'

'You can bank on professionalism.' Dylan stands his ground.

Cole lifts his eyebrows and smiles too sweetly. 'Really?' He's seen Dylan's eyes on the nice Ms Kennedy.

Dylan pushes past him and, as he serves the last of the plunger coffee, he spreads the map on the table, holding the corners down with salt and pepper shakers and two empty water glasses. Kate and Cole position themselves to see.

'Yesterday…here to here to here to here,' he says, running a forefinger over the paper. 'Today, we take this shortcut, east of the main track we came in on yesterday. We get back to the road about twenty kilometres along from where we turned in, then about ten kays further east, we'll stop in to have a look at Henry Gorge before turning down to Daydawn Biosphere Reserve. The length of their driveway is about another hour and a half. So, only about three hours' driving, that's all.'

'So, what are we waiting for?' says Cole abruptly.

'Whaddya think?' whispers Pullet to Dylan as he walks beside him to the vehicle. 'Do you think I've got it?'

'I wouldn't know, mate,' says Dylan. 'They're looking at the whole valley, so it's a pretty big plan. They say they're "fact finding". But thanks for the hospitality.'

'Good to have company at this end of the season,' he says. 'Warming up now. Just about ready to pull down the shutters for the year.'

'At least you've got some company for the Wet. She staying around?' Dylan nods towards the slim girl looking out from behind flywire.

'Dunno,' says Pullet. 'She doesn't say much.'

'What's the story there?' It's Cole's turn to ask when the barefoot girl tucks herself under the swing of Pullet's arm as he waves them off. Her silk slip suggests a body lithe as a roo's and catches in the soft fur of her lap.

'Geology, history, meteorology, botany, fauna I'm here to help you with,' says Dylan. 'But that one's none of my business.'

The morning is young but the heat has already matured. In the side mirrors, Kate watches the curling plumes of dust. Cole looks out of the back window briefly, then tilts his hat forward and pretends to sleep.

They skirt the airfield and pick up a little-used track, which swings misleadingly to the north and east before settling southward. 'Getting away from homesteads is the trickiest part,' Dylan making conversation. 'All tracks lead there, but it's a different story coming away. It's easy to end up back at the front door.' They run parallel to a ridge with inky, tumbling blocks. 'Some is mined for kitchen counter tops,' Dylan explains. 'They sell it as "black granite", but it could be anything from dolerite, like this, to charnockite.'

They pass dry gullies, one so deeply cut that it looks like it's been blasted. 'There must have been a lot of water,' says Kate.

'And it all turns up together.' Dylan points to a log twice the length of the vehicle and half its girth wedged in a tree eight metres up. 'That'd weigh a tonne at least.'

'From the water?'

'That was the level. Imagine the force.'

'Incredible,' she says.

Peaceful doves pick at seeds showered into the sand. Morning tea for *Geopelia striata*.

By the time they get to Henry Gorge, they could fry eggs on the rocks. The heat that is muscling upwards arm-wrestles the massive weight of the sun's rays pushing down. With hats, water bottles and bathers, Dylan leads them down a snaking path on stony ground, then the land peels away into the gorge. They peer into the elliptical bowl far below. Its striated walls are more grey than brown. Upstream, a canyon cascades scree from ridges set against the sky. To their right, the bowl narrows to a spout over which the Wet's flood jets.

Dylan points to the far wall. The rock looks soft as marzipan, from dull silver to charcoal, with layers of beige or chocolate. Water chafe has left long, horizontal overhangs, maybe threefists deep, and a python's body, more than six metres long, is wedged along one. The widest part of its body is as thick as two thighs strapped together.

'Good God,' breathes Kate.

The snake's body protrudes from the overhang and then drops in five muscular ringlets towards the water, where it is latched onto the face of a drowned calf. It has already lifted the animal's deadweight a metre; only the hind-quarters are still in the water.

'That's extraordinary.' Even Cole is mesmerised. 'What happens next?'

'A snake that strong can get it up to the ledge,' says Dylan. 'It can't swallow it where it is. It wants to wedge it and then ingest.'

'It *can't* swallow that.'

'Believe me, it can. It'll unhinge its jaw and ingest the body over several hours. It won't need to eat again for months. A year, perhaps.'

'Bullshit.' Cole is emphatic. 'It'll never go inside that snake's body. Anyone can see that.' He breaks away, wiping himself with a handkerchief as rivulets pour off his short sideburns, and turns back towards the path.

Dylan and Kate look back towards the still scene. 'It's just resting now,' says Dylan.

'I don't doubt you,' she replies.

The path ends on a ledge, and Dylan leads off to the left. 'We climb from here.' He zig-zags down and across over the red blocks, skirting spinifex. Kate follows tentatively and Cole, eyes on her smooth legs, scrambles stiffly behind. There is no best way and Dylan just works systematically down and across, following the sandy ledges and looking for gullies and smooth rocks to step down to the next level. He regularly checks over his shoulder, and waits for them to almost catch up. 'All OK?'

'Fine,' says Kate, but nothing from further back.

Then Dylan hears a rumble and turns to see Cole skidding down a scree slope, grasping at the sharp grasses. Their eyes meet as Cole skis, and Dylan sees his fear. He also sees Cole's furious indignation at the moment's candour. He starts out towards Cole, still careful to place his own boots safely, but Kate is closer. By the time she clambers down to him, Cole has stopped sliding, but one shin is already bleeding where it has ragged along a rock.

'Are you OK?' She bends to him and his eyes delve. Furtive. He is buoyed by young, plump cells and tautness.

'Just slipped.'

'You're bleeding.'

'It's nothing,' Cole says, instantly strengthened by her proximity.

But she takes a tissue from her pocket and dabs at the red trickle.

Cole inhales the heady scent of perfume and sweat mixed. Dylan sees she knows it and doesn't pull back.

'Is it clean? I'll dress it when we get back up, if it's just a small cut. I've got a first-aid kit with me now, if it needs it.' Dylan knows to keep his distance.

Cole ignores it, but Kate looks towards Dylan, 'I think it will be OK.'

'Let's get going.' Cole bustles to his feet, bravado restored by a stolen glimpse down Kate's neckline.

At the bottom of the gorge, Dylan steps into an abrasion of rough sand and lets his daypack slide off, showing the wet shield on his back. He lifts his hat and sweeps a finger backwards over his head, blading sweat off. And then, for a slivered moment, he feels alone and bewitched by the place. The intensity of an experience, the reaction and emotion it creates, is not commensurate with the span of it.

Dylan turns as Kate skips off the last rock into gorge gravel, too, and sees Cole close behind her, puce and blowing. He stamps up and stands too-close. 'What now we're down here?'

'A swim. And just to see it.'

'Is that all this is about?' sizzles Cole. 'To see it?' It is said wars and deaths could have been averted if protagonists had just drunk a glass of cold water. For just this moment, the heat and the exposure get the better of Cole. Usually he'd force the issue, make them turn back, but he just seems to lose traction, and slumps into solid rock shade, sweating and glaring.

'Should we go back?' Dylan asks Kate, low-voiced.

She doesn't look at Cole. 'Let's swim. A quick dip.'

'Just a quick one, then.'

'Sure.' Her whispered intimacy confuses him.

The python's as still as plastic. Now they are close, the real size of it is formidable. Catatonic and big-eyed, solid as a punch bag. Cole is transfixed. He squints and scrutinises for any sign of movement, but it is just absorbing the steer's weight. One long, tensed muscle, frozen in pulsing heat. Man and reptile seem to meditate on encumbrances.

Behind chest-high rocks, Kate slips her things off and pulls the bathers on, then slings forwards, dropping her bra and pulling the top up. Dylan glimpses the movement and is briefly sidetracked.

He swaps moleskins for board shorts under his shirt tails.

They sit in frigid and slightly green water, then slide forward together over flat rocks covered in black algae. It clouds up above their white legs, which are yellowed and distorted by the water.

'Yuck,' she says.

'It won't hurt.'

But she imagines disease and leaches.

'Come on, let's swim out.'

Suddenly she looks horrified. 'What about crocodiles? Are there crocodiles?' She almost shrieks.

'Not here.'

She's wide-eyed and questioning.

'Not here,' he says again. 'Trust me.'

'I do,' she says, feeling the scarcity of that. The two words seem to echo. It is a moment when even Kate is puzzled by the speed of the change. She is baffled by the sense of being in country that is so completely new, inside as much as out. If she'd read it a month ago, she wouldn't have believed it. If a friend had told her, she would have silently snorted. We are what we are – how can we so quickly become something so completely different?

How can there be even the possibility that change can happen so fast? So massively that it can start to change your chemistry? She wonders if she was primed for it (and she doesn't discount her biological clock). Was something inside her looking for an excuse? Was she just waiting for it to happen and Dylan crossed her path at the right moment?

If she looks directly for an answer, it moves from view. But it's there, all around her, in her peripheral vision; encircling, complete, unavoidable.

Dylan takes the lead through the shallow water, lying flat forwards, legs drifting behind, pulling himself forward by gripping the slippery rocks. Like a newt with functioning forelegs only. With the weightlessness of a roo, scooting across a surface of scrub, dropping its legs in for propulsion. Flying over the jumbled rock landscape.

'Cold patches,' she gasps from behind. A jigsaw of temperature.

And then the water turns to ink and he launches himself

off the last reachable rock and over the chasm of it, gliding between navy below and air-force blue above.

She launches out too, and has the same feeling of being between two masses. Water below, air above. Being wedged. The compatible volumes of opposite but equal forces.

'Let's head away from that thing.' The python makes her nervous and she doesn't like the stewy suggestion of decomposition.

'Round the corner,' he breathes back, and rolls into a crawl, breathing to the right and seeing the chasm's side flash slowly past, frame by frame.

They tread water together in the deepest, narrowest cut of it. The eye of a needle. Then her toes touch a rock and she stands on it and lets her arms drift out as she lays her head back, hair drifting, to scan up and around in big arcs.

He sculls vertical nearby until she says, 'there's room for two', then fishes with his toes for the hard edge. Still lying back in the water, away from her, he fans for support, trying to keep some sort of balance. He starts to topple away and she reaches for his hands and draws him in. Their skin is close, only a pillow of chill between. A zephyr pushes through the gorge, and the ruffled surface laps at them.

She looks down into the water and sees him slim yet warped by refraction, blue boardies ballooning, and her own body, never quite perfect.

'Cold?'

'Not really.'

'Want to go back?'

'Not yet. I'll probably never be here again.'

'You can't be sure about that.'

'This isn't what my life is like,' she snorts, fighting for her old self.

'So, what is it like?'

'What it is like? My life? City. Work. I don't know – stress. Certainly not like being out here.'

'Does it have to be?'

'What do you mean? It's the way it is.' She is fumbling for explanation. 'It's what I am; what I come from. I don't have that "freedom gene".'

Dylan sees defensiveness, confusion and vulnerability and switches it from her to him. 'I feel I'm letting you down. Something's brewing.'

'With him?' she says. It doesn't need his reply, and he doesn't look for it. 'You probably don't deal with guys like Cole. I do, every day. They're all about ego, but they get things done. You have to respect them for that.'

Dylan remains silent.

'I've got no doubt he'll have a go about something or other before the trip's out. He has to. It's the law of the jungle for him. But it'll be alright.'

But while part of Kate relishes being out of sight of Cole, part fears it. She feels unguarded. Open to Dylan's interpretation.

'Come on,' she says, 'Now I'm getting cold. Let's go back.' The idea sends movement through her body and she drifts forwards towards him, brushing against his chest.

'Sorry,' he says.

She just smiles and plunges back into the dark water, wondering what she's playing at.

There is something about the python's forbearance and inaction that has started to rile Cole. The thing has a firm grip on its prey; why doesn't it finish it off? The idea of this slow, considered process gets under his skin.

He's cooled down, but still feels rattled, then sees the two heads reappear round the point, frog-kicking steadily side by side.

'We need to get a few things straight,' he says, squared up to Dylan, who's buttoning his shirt. Cole suddenly chilled down to clinical.

'Problems?'

Cole gropes for something specific, outside his general but maturing detestation for Dylan and a niggling, growing competitiveness. He catches a glimpse of Kate behind the rock, head tilted back, straightening her wet hair.

'Coming in here was a complete waste of time. We're not on holiday you know. This place is irrelevant.' The fact that it may just be relevant to the water project adds to his private pleasure in his attack.

'I just thought a general appreciation of the area…'

'There's nothing "general" about this brief. You are not here to do "general".' Cole is grateful that Ward has given him a word to latch on to. 'Specific, Ward. Specific. We are here to do – specific. Take heed.'

Cole knows he's got little real ammunition. On the final blast, he turns and sets off back up to the rim.

# Sixteen

Daydawn Biosphere Reserve is the sequel to a life-changing moment. Tedd Bakker was born in Detroit, avoided the grind of the big American automotive giants – the fate of most – and fell into a job selling pharmaceuticals. He launched out on his own, got through the first year by the skin of his teeth and then made a mint. Bakker had the knack of flying by the seat of his pants through the day and sleeping soundly at night. People said he was lucky.

Through his twenties, he opened drugstores across the US, and he set up a shopping-centre management company in his thirties. He plunged money into property development and made a killing. He had an apartment in Manhattan, a house in Malibu, a more modest place on the beach in Hawaii and went skiing in Aspen every year. He purposely lost touch with his parents, his mother died, his Australian-born father went home, he never married and when he was forty-five he was stopped in his tracks. After the strange quivering in his chest, a claw clutched it. He sucked in not-enough air and saw the white shopping-centre floor coming at him. Most of all he remembers terror. He was going to die of a cataclysmic heart attack in the middle of Rainbow Gate West and that would be that. Tedd Bakker RIP; who the hell was he?

But Tedd Bakker didn't die. He lay in hospital, plumbed with a quadruple bypass and a new aortic valve, and visited only by the secretary who came for signatures. He went home to a paid nurse, feeling more vulnerable than he could ever have imagined a human to be. He lost his confidence and had an epiphany.

In Australia, Tedd Bakker found his father in a salty wheatbelt town, threw his arms around him, asked for forgiveness and wept for his mother. His sense of aloneness was mollified not as much by the proximity of the old man as by the Australian bush. He became intoxicated by hot-day eucalyptus scent, the rhythm of cicadas, shimmer, seething ant mounds, chimerical water on salt lakes, the company of salmon gums. Dramatic days settling into static evenings and the sonorous warble of magpies. For the first and last time, Tedd Bakker fell in love.

'Bakker set up and ran Wildlife Australia with his own money,' explains Dylan. He bought two forest places in the hills, fenced out the cats, foxes and rabbits, baited anything trapped inside, and woylie and quenda soon thrived again. Their eyes became a galaxy by torchlight. Bakker added an old sheep spread where there was still some healthy scrub and a chance of saving the mallee fowl. He took up the lease on a headland with a soft coverlet of kwongan heath that fingered into a silty gulf. He had the neck of it fenced, put on staff, funded scientists and had biological surveys done.

'Bakker soon had a couple of dozen people working for him. That was when Wildlife Australia went public and started fundraising. It's been an interesting idea. They aimed squarely at the top end of town.' Their fundraisers were intimate dinner parties with celebrity chefs or on a private tennis court in an exclusive suburb. French champagne and canapés, Maseratis and Benzes in the driveway and six-figure cheques being written out. 'They didn't target businesses, just individuals with a lot of money. Hook them in, give them a sense of ownership. Win their hearts.'

When Jack Cole's not interested in something, he just shuts down. But when he is, he runs on all eight cylinders. And now he fires terse questions at Dylan about Bakker and Wildlife Australia's supporters. He jots in his book. He wants names.

'I'm sure they'll give you more detail,' Dylan says.

'Get good notes on this one,' Cole says to Kate.

The 3,100 square kilometres of Daydawn is still a pastoral lease. Minimum cattle numbers must be maintained and they are surrounded by Brahman stock. A bull eyes them. Mothers and calves have appealing blackened eyes and their mottled grey hides match the slick bark of the boab around them. Dylan pauses by a stand of the bulbous trees. If eight men stretched out their arms and held hands, they might just reach around the biggest. From the top, branches etch lacy against the sky. Young trees sprout around it like carrots.

'How old do you think the big one is?' asks Kate.

'Over a thousand years. How does the saying go? If humans lived as long as trees, the world'd be a different place.'

The land around them is clear to the horizon, just a few straggly shrubs sticking up. To Cole and Kate, it looks like all the rest, but to Dylan it looks trashed and eaten up.

Twenty minutes further on, they slow at a gate. Kate opens her door and skis her left boot over the bulldust. 'I'll get it.'

'It's a heavy one,' says Dylan. 'Lift the D.'

'DAYDAWN BIOSPHERE RESERVE.' And beneath, 'The conservation of Australia by Australians.'

The gates' five rolled hollow-steel horizontals are the size of Kate's forearm. It takes both hands to lift the hot cast-iron capital letter and with it comes a solid steel post bigger than her wrist. Her palms feel branded. She swings the gates open and Dylan drives through, watching in the mirror as she closes them, realises she's the wrong side, and slips through.

'Either side of us you see the essence of wildlife conservation work in Australia,' he says when she's back in. 'If you build a fox-proof, cat-proof, rabbit-proof fence, clear the ferals, stop grazing, protect the waterways and target the most noxious weeds, it's amazing how some areas can come back.'

For Dylan, passing through the fence is like driving into paradise. The land is alive; soft with cushiony grasses, short trees bursting with seed, tiny animal tracks in the sand around the spinifex.

Sanctuary manager Dr Pru Bearer joins them at one of the restaurant's long tables, and a girl in sandals, shorts and a khaki shirt with an embroidered Wildlife Australia logo asks if they'd like anything. Pru orders a plunger of coffee and a big pot of tea. 'And see if we've still got some of cook's biscuits in the jar out the back, would you?'

Pru gets glasses, and a jug of water from the fridge. She is tall, in her mid-thirties, calm yet purposeful. 'You've been over at Mt Goode, I hear?'

'Just for the night,' says Dylan.

'How's it looking that side of the road?'

'Pretty good,' says Dylan. 'Pullet says they haven't had the usual wildfires.'

'That's right,' says Pru, with the slightest smile. 'We've had some success with that.'

'Success?' Cole doesn't like being cast as an onlooker and unwittingly takes the bait.

'We suggested a meeting of all the landholders this end of the Kimberley, proposing a coordinated firebreak pattern. To our surprise, they all turned up, and agreed.'

'Surprise?'

'We're *greenies*, Mr Cole. Surely you can see that?'

'Meaning?'

'Meaning we smart-arsed city girls come up here with our fancy PhDs, new four-wheel drives and bright ideas and can't always expect the reception we'd like from people who've worked this landscape all their lives and been part of the generations that have brought it to the place it is now.'

'And where is that *place*?' persists Cole.

'At best, in terms of both biodiversity and sustainability, under pressure. At worst, seriously overgrazed, eroded, weedy and subject to critical fire regime changes. But all that can change again very quickly. You'll have noticed the difference after you came through the fence.' She walks to the wall, takes down a plaque and brings it over. 'We're rather proud. This year's review of protected areas in Australia included Daydawn in the top ten. It was judged the best non-government reserve.'

She calls Suzy Gift, the wilderness camp manager, on the two-way. 'Suzy'll show you to your tented cabins. We'll give you a chance to clean up, then I thought I'd show you some of the sanctuary and finish up on the lookout at sunset.'

Jack Cole's demeanour shifts when Suzy Gift bounces up in a T-shirt with a row of northern quolls hand-painted across her ample front. She has a gregarious smile that he mistakes for personal interest.

'Pleased to meet you.' She holds out a hand with a Buddhist thread bracelet around the wrist. Love herself and those around her.

'Jack Cole.' He projects charm. Dylan catches the glint and is intrigued by the manufacture and power of it.

'I'm really sorry about it, but we're chock-a-block...' Pru is saying to Dylan. 'If it's any consolation, you'll be the first to sleep in that part of the new staff quarters.'

'I'd be happy in the swag,' says Dylan truthfully. 'The staff quarters are more than fine, thanks.' He nods towards the receding figures of Suzy Gift and Jack Cole, Chiarugi briefcase in hand, Kate following behind. 'As long as they're comfortable, we'll all be happy.'

———

Behind the scenes, Daydawn is a hive of activity. Pru shows him the new laboratories, study rooms and lecture theatre.

'Volunteers have done all the work. And Jim. He heard what we were doing, rode his bicycle twenty-odd days across the Top End from Queensland to come and see and is still here. He'll turn his hand to anything. He's done most of the cabinetry – taught himself on the run. And we've got quite a few PhD and Master's students here at the moment, helping with the finch survey. We're aiming to tag a thousand birds. They've been out mist netting for the past couple of days and first indications are that the numbers are improving faster than we'd projected. But the Gouldian's got a long way to go.'

The Gouldian finch looks like it rolled in a rainbow. Like some divine creator opened their paintbox and dipped into every brilliant colour. Indulged themselves with *Erythrura gouldiae*. Scarlet face and head, black bib, olive back, turquoise at the base of the thin tail. Yolk-yellow undercarriage. A bright purple chest in the male, muted to lilac in the female.

Fifty years ago, kaleidoscopic flocks clouded waterholes across northern Australia, but the last couple of thousand Gouldians are vulnerable and in scattered communities. Most in the Kimberley; small pockets in the Northern Territory; a bare memory in Queensland. There are no colonies of more than 250 and Daydawn is its best chance of surviving in the wild.

Sometimes Dr Pru Bearer thinks she's died and gone to heaven. After years of study and theory, here is somewhere to put it all into practice. 'This is one of the most important places I can think of,' she shouts as the beige Troopie claws a rubbly hill. In the passenger seat, Cole's left fist grips the handhold by his head. Dylan and Kate, legs spread, brace themselves on the facing bench seats in the back. Dylan wedges a boot against the esky to stop it sliding.

'Wildlife Australia has thirteen properties and we're negotiating for three more. But Daydawn is iconic, and it is one of only two where supporters can stay and see the work firsthand. The others are true sanctuaries, with only scientific staff. Closed to the public. So this and Mount Binary – the other place – are our interface with sponsors. We have twelve tented cabins with ensuites, allow sixty campers, and have no plans to expand. Having guests but limiting their numbers is part of the sustainability plan. People get very enthusiastic and that's important, emotionally and financially.'

'And who exactly are the key stakeholders?' asks Cole.

'Mainly individuals with a conscience, I suppose you'd say. Successful people, certainly. We have just received a million dollars from a supporter in northern England. He has an acute interest in the Gouldian finch and has donated the funds purely for the work on it. We'll put in a second fox- and cat-proof fence around their most popular breeding sites.'

'Who is he?' Cole persists.

'I'd better check he hasn't asked for anonymity before I say anything,' says Pru. 'A lot of our supporters prefer to be invisible. We rely on personal, ethical decisions. It's proving a better basis than corporate philanthropy. Share prices fluctuate, company boards and priorities change. There isn't much continuity in that model – not as much as in committed and enthusiastic individuals.'

'And wealthy.'

'Wealthy helps, but so do the mums and dads chipping in. So does local support.'

'Local support?'

'The response from the land managers around us has been surprisingly good. Mind you, that's not down to me. There's nothing like a local putting in a good word for you.'

'Who's that?'

'A station owner further east. A good cattleman and a conservationist. He certainly helped to break the ice.'

'Billy Parkes?' asks Dylan.

'Yes, Billy, on Erindale Station. You know him? Comes from a cattle background but has an open mind and some good ideas. He's made a real go of the place on his own. He lost his brother a few years back, I'm told. But a good family man, too.'

'Yes,' says Dylan. 'That's Billy. He's a good friend of mine.'


The champagne's middle-of-the-road and not cold enough, the cheese lumps are sweaty and Cole has run out of both conversation and interest in the view from the lookout. The sky turns the tone of ooze from a wound. Cole turns his back and considers the people with a finger in the pie. He needs details. Needs someone to spill the beans. It won't be Pru, but it might just be Suzy. The idea cheers him.

'I've arranged for you all to see Emerald Gorge tomorrow,' says Pru, quieter in the half-dark. 'You'll have to do it in pairs, one in the morning, one in the afternoon. We restrict access to two people, so they get the gorge to themselves. There's a canoe at the top, where you park, and one further down. You walk over a rockfall to it. Kate and Dylan in the morning. And I've suggested that Suzy take you, Jack, in the afternoon – when she's got less on. You've been before, haven't you Dylan? You can explain the place to Kate.'

Pru pauses and smiles pointedly. 'But there's no such thing as a free lunch.' She has opened another bottle and does the rounds into crackly plastic beakers. Kate already feels light-headed. 'Jim'll also take you through the power plant and show you our plans for the future. At the moment we're still burning fossil fuels, I'm ashamed to say. Fifty thousand species a year becoming extinct, mostly due to environmental change imposed by us – the whole ethic of trucking in fuel and burning it out here keeps me awake at night. And we had to step up to a 170kVa generator three years ago. You have to bear in mind that there might be a hundred guests and thirty people working here when we're full. But we've costed $500,000 to replace the diesel generators with solar, then extra for a wind turbine as a booster and perhaps for night running. The Sustainable Energy Development Office is ready with a subsidy and there's a donor's pledge of $200,000.'

Cole'd trade his mother for that name.

—

Kate is happy to have a few minutes alone in her safari tent. She feels jangled up. She kicks off her suede boots and likes the waffling of the hessian matting on her bare feet. It lets them breathe. She unzips the safari tent's flyscreen and steps over boards to its bathroom, then takes everything off and hangs it behind the door, underwear hooked on top like froth. A thin trickle of warm water runs over her and she drops her head forward so that the shower hits the back of her neck. She looks down at her body, curving like landscape. The lie in her now seems so viscous that the water can't dilute it. She lathers, likes the silky feel of her hands, and watches it wash off, sudsy, into the tray. But she still feels sticky inside. The polarity of two stories feels like it's started to tease her into two parts. A loose end of thread being yanked so that it unravels a seam. The parts are separating so fast there's already a sliver of light between them.

When Jack Cole asked her to be at his room in twenty minutes to do some work, it had sounded more like an instruction. But now he runs the plastic zip up to let her in and produces a bottle from his second suitcase. 'A very decent Bordeaux. I bumped into the winemaker while I was in the Maldives recently. There was a French gastronomy dinner – a fourteen-seat restaurant on the ocean floor, would you believe? Exclusive. Anyway, he gave me the inside run on the 2003. It was 52°C in the vineyard and French people were dying from the heat, but some of the vines' roots went down fifteen metres into cold clay. It was the earliest harvest in Bordeaux since 1893 and produced a wine of extraordinary density. Rare as hen's teeth.' He pulls the cork without a second thought.

None of it impresses Kate, but she notices the small curls of hair rippling out of his loose singlet, set by dampness. Dark hair fans up from his chest and out across his shoulders. He exudes machismo.

'The Maldives?' she says, by way of changing the subject.

'I was with *someone*, but I can't say who. What happens on a trip stays on a trip. That's right, isn't it?'

But Kate's not taking the bait.

Dylan sits at the bar, more relaxed after phoning and hearing that Mitchell's much improved. He sips a beer and chats with guests. The couple in matching khaki shorts and short-sleeved shirts have come from Germany just to see the place – 'and zis *finch*' – and the other two are from Sydney.

'Hard to believe a snake could lift a dead calf out of the water,' says the Sydneysider, doubting Dylan's story.

'I agree,' says Kate, arriving behind him just then. 'I wouldn't have believed it if I hadn't seen it for myself.'

Dylan introduces her, and asks what she'd like to drink.

'Just a light beer, thanks.' Glad to wash the dust away.

At last Dylan lies in his room, alone but wishing he wasn't. Looking forward to the pre-dawn walk he's arranged with Kate, hoping to see Gouldian finches, and feeling like an over-excited teenager. Drenched by emotion in the amazing night. The softly breathing wind, insect noise and moop-moop of a barking owl.

In her tented cabin, up on its stilts, Kate stretches out under the fan.

Cole finishes off the second bottle of Bordeaux alone and sits hunched forward over a map, slapping at insects. He knows he's close to the only viable dam site in the valley and he feels bottled up.

# Seventeen

'Kate...Kate...*Kate*...' It's 4.30am and Dylan is urging quietly in the nacre sheen before dawn. As agreed.

'Uhu.'

'Do you still want to go?' Long before the first rays come, thin and sharp as packet spaghetti.

'Sure,' she whispers. 'Give me a sec. Come on up.'

He silently treads four dark steps and stands on the landing outside the tent. 'Won't be a minute.' Through mesh panels he can see her moving inside. She turns her back, pulls on a pair of linen pants under her short nightdress, crosses her arms and strips it over her head. Leans away and slips on a bra. Swings into a clean shirt. Knows he's watching and doesn't shy.

She purposefully bends, gathers hair in her right hand and slides a scrunchy from her left wrist onto the bunch.

'Do I need boots?'

'Boots'd be good.'

She undoes the zip just enough to squeeze through. Mastered it, to keep the insects out.

'Good morning,' he says.

'Good morning,' she says softly back. 'Sorry. I was awake most of the night, then dropped off to sleep a couple of hours ago.'

She sits on the top step and pulls on Explorer socks and laces her boots. 'Are we late?'

'No', he says, 'this is fine.'

A tenebrous path around white river gums. Two sandy ruts. He hadn't even been sure she'd come on an early bird walk and now, shielded by the white bodies of *Eucalyptus papuana* and out of earshot, he says, 'I'm so glad you're here,' and she smiles back. She reaches out and touches his forearm. 'I feel guilty,' he adds. 'I should've asked Cole.'

'He wouldn't have come, I'm sure. I wouldn't give it another thought. If he gets into a canoe today, I'll be surprised.'

Finches, fantails and flycatchers. Old-world warblers and flowerpeckers. Pardalotes. Chats and cuckoo-shrikes. Honeyeaters and magpie larks. Around them, and through the binoculars Dylan has brought each, the air is cosmopolitan. Zebra finches meep in the busy morning. Cascade past. Rainbow bee-eaters' wings purr overhead; the colourful fans of *Merops ornatus*, surging light behind.

Then Dylan points, crouches, steadies and raises his binoculars. 'There. About ten metres. In that bush. A purple-crowned fairy wren.'

'Where?' she whispers.

He folds his right shoulder around her back, leans in and points. Their cheeks almost touch and he can smell her hair. 'There.' Almost inaudible. 'In the top of that little shrub.'

She struggles to see anything. Finds it hard to keep the binoculars steady.

'There...' he says again, aiming them for her.

'Got it,' Kate sighs. 'Yes, got it. It's *stunning*.'

'Very rare,' he says. 'We're being treated.'


They cut away from the path and onto stonier ground. Kate falls in behind Dylan as he picks through rock and grass. 'There's an old water tank up there. Sometimes it drips, but even when it doesn't, condensation gathers on it. The birds like it in the mornings.'

'How many times have you been up here?'

'A few.'

Kate feels odd inside. Wishes it were his first and doesn't know why.

They settle away from the tank, mostly hidden behind the yellow of native hibiscus. Beside it, gorgeous *Grevillea refracta*, flowering freely. A sandpaper fig, fronds coarse as its name. *Ficus opposita* and *Eucalyptus Corymbia cadophora* – the twin-leafed bloodwood, with colossal leaves opposite one another.

Dylan whispers the names of each plant.

He unshoulders his black daypack and takes out a stainless steel flask of tea and two tin pannikin mugs. There's milk in a small plastic container and sugar in a well-used zip-top plastic bag. Kate notices a name written on the front in permanent marker. 'Carnegie.' She picks it up to look at it. 'If you name them, they seem to last longer,' Dylan explains a little self-consciously. 'It's probably a bit odd…but the fewer plastic bags in the world, the better…'

'But, "Carnegie" as in…?'

'Oh,' says Dylan. 'One of my heroes. David Carnegie. He was only twenty-five and newly arrived from England when he led an expedition up here, to Halls Creek. More than 4,500 kilometres and over a year. In 1896, from memory. Imagine being able to arrive here – like being on another planet – and do that, at that age. Remarkable. It's difficult enough when you know precisely where you're going – with a four-wheel drive, roads and tracks, communications…'

Dylan smiles and pauses. 'Sorry – over-enthusiastic. I'd tell you the rest, but I might sound like a raving lunatic.'

'No,' she says. 'Tell me. I like your enthusiasm. That earnestness of yours.'

'Sometimes I wonder if it sounds a bit pathetic.'

'Not pathetic…more passionate.'

They hold one another's gaze, then she smiles, breaking the spell.

'Well,' he says, encouraged, 'Carnegie was awarded a medal by the Royal Geographic Society and then given a big government appointment in Nigeria, of all places. Assistant, resident and magistrate, I think. He was out chasing a bandit when he was shot with a poisoned arrow. Died in minutes. Twenty-nine years old.' Dylan pauses. 'Come to think of it, commemorating him with a named plastic bag might just be irreverent.'

'Being remembered any-old-how is something.'

'True.'

And now she teases him, 'Have you named any other bags, then?' Raising her eyebrows comically.

'Giles. Parker King. Battye, Forrest, Hann. Loads of them. Remind me to bore you some more one day.'

'I will.'

'Let me bore you?'

'No, remind you,' she says. 'In future.'

They talk in murmurs, sipping hot tea with sugar, light growing around them. But now their attention is drawn away from words.

'Look,' Dylan says softly.

Gouldian finches come scudding in with the zebra finches. They dart into the water pipe in heterochromatic flashes of brilliance. Dominated at different angles by brilliant yellow, the green of their backs, purple chests or turquoise trim.

'Imagine,' he says. 'This is just how Gould himself saw them.'

'Another hero?'

British ornithological artist John Gould described the finch during an antipodean expedition in 1844, thinking of his wife, Elizabeth, and first calling it the Lady Gouldian. Australian birds taken back to Victorian Britain became all the rage in a cage. Gouldians outshone the zebra finch and budgerigar, and across the wide, brown continent they were doomed to decline. Aviary-trade trappers harvested them up to the 1980s. European settlement expanded through the savannah woodlands of the north, bringing grazing and feral animals.

'But their numbers were devastated by burning,' Dylan tells Kate. 'It was more intense and widespread than Aboriginal burning and destroyed the native grasses the birds depend on. Food shortage made them vulnerable to a parasite called the air-sac mite. Nasty little critter. Their waterholes were trashed by cattle and buffalo, and then came cats and foxes. Daydawn's their best chance.'

'Some have black heads, not red,' Kate speaks quietly. 'Different types?'

'Just a colour morph. They are both *Erythrura gouldiae.* The same weaver–finch family, *Estrildidae.* A sub-family of the passerines – perching songbirds.'

'Quite the expert.'

'I love 'em. All these little birds. I go spotlighting – shooting foxes.' The notion of Dylan with a rifle in his hands surprises her. 'I don't like doing it, but I hate their killing more. You look for their green eyes in the grass. Hit them with the .223 Luger and there's no question.' A tail, a nose and not even a surprised expression in between.

He changes the subject. 'I've got a couple of Gouldians at home, Tommy and Mabel.'

She guesses there's a story, and urges him.


Jimmy Skinner was born on a cattle station and Mabel Scarletfinch came from the Nine Mile community. Both from the same Aboriginal clan. They met on Langgi Langgi Station, backing on to the north-western boundary of Mt Goode. Him fencing, her cooking. They lived at Paradise Outcamp for a while, after Jimmy dreamed his stories and started painting.

'Jimmy Skinner's art was, quite literally, visionary,' explains Dylan. 'Those artists at Nine Mile have a very different future because of his dreams and what he did with them. He was in his late fifties when he died – a decade longer than most, but still too young. Mabel passed within months.'

Jimmy Skinner's and Mabel Scarletfinch's ragged old hats hang on Dylan's office wall, and move with him. Vincent Yimi was a good mate and passed them on to continue that sort of powerful friendship. A bloodline. 'And I reckon they'd have given you the time of day.'

———

After muesli, juice and weak coffee, Kate lies on her bed, almost-nude in swelling heat, frosted by the oscillating fan, and feels suspended. The morning's highlights are like bright plasticine folded into a soft, psychedelic ball. The radiant hues of birds, conversation, histories – complexities and simplicities – in one easy, supple conglomerate. Contradictions becoming compatible.

And in her swirling state, Kate remembers an exhibition of John Lennon's self-portraits that she saw in Sydney years before. Most were the simple oval black line of his face on the paper with two small circles for his famous spectacles, and a dot in each for eyes. The mouth was a line, but sometimes smiling, and the hair was drawn straight down from a centre parting. How brilliant, she thought, to see yourself that simply.

She wished she did. But she knows there's the Kate that the world sees, and the one inside. We are all like that, she's always thought. We all play roles; keep parts private. We are all basically alone, inside. The real us.

But now the two seem more the same shape.

# Eighteen

The Duncan River through Emerald Gorge is vitreous as Dylan and Kate walk high up on its flat sheet-rock sides, under the milky-blue cupola of mid-morning. There is the sense of the river moving gently westward and tell-tale signs of power unleashed in the Wet – boulders the size of vehicles tumbled to spheres, more big tree-trunks high up.

'It's awesome – whether it was 1,700 million years of water erosion or a Dreamtime serpent,' says Dylan. 'I came here with Vincent. He believes that water formed this land – that everything on it lives within the cycle of returning water.'

———

Dylan and Vincent were going to Nine Mile and Dylan had suggested they set out a day early as they had time. Stay over and have a look around Daydawn. 'You should see what's going on there.' Vincent had said he'd think about it and let him know, and Dylan knew that meant private permissions. 'I never been there,' said Vincent after a while. 'Know about it but never been there. Think it would be good to see now.'

Vincent had hated the canoe. 'Worse than Nelson's boat.' Dylan had tried sitting in the rear and easing it out backwards so the elder could step into the front. He braced the paddle like an islands outrigger. But the old boy banged his bunion on the top edge, lurched in and straight out the other side, slipped on the wet rocks, windmilled his arms and ended arse-first in the drink.

'Two left feet,' gibed Dylan.

Yimi snarled as he watched green slime swirl around his knobbly toes.

'Hold on. Let's try this.' Dylan was out over the side, twisted the canoe through one-eighty degrees and hauled it backwards. Stood wide-legged on the tops of dry rocks, and helped the old man up, then took his arm as he stepped into the front. Dylan lifted the stern and pushed forward, careful not to let the hull twist as the boat floated. When Vincent was right in, he thrust forward, hull surfing on a smooth cushion. He held the gunwales, paddle already stowed, dragging the toes of his back foot across the surface and swinging in. Dylan kept the tubby boat straight with easy j-strokes, first taking the weight of the water with the paddle at right-angles, then twisting the paddle shaft as it passed him, turning the whole thing into a trailing rudder. Feeling it all with his soft left hand, supporting it with his loose right. Keeping it smooth. The plunk and shoosh was a poem of short verses and even cadence.

With ancles crossed, Vincent sat in the front, slightly to one side and giving the canoe a permanent lean, which Dylan accounted for with his own weight. The old man's paddle sat across his lap like a shotgun, his thick fingers knitted and hanging between spread knees. As they entered the gorge, he looked either side and tilted his head courteously, as if greeting a crowd in recognition not simply of a memory installed, but one instilled through generations. Something intrinsically inside that had a separate life, and yet was his life. The rock galleries were past libraries and future stories, and the crevices in them hid spirit faces that he acknowledged. Cadjeputs caught his eye; *Melaleuca leucadendra* with nectar-laden flowers and honeyeaters visiting, and gleaning insects in their papery bark like beads of sweat.

Dylan heard murmurs but said nothing. Vague incantations like conversation. He looked down, minded his own business, concentrated on his rhythm and tried to make the garish plastic boat as good as invisible.

'Pretty, ain't it?' Vincent suddenly blurted, as if back from some other place and looking at something obvious. Some fairground thing.

'Thought you were communing.'

'What d'ya mean?'

'You know what I mean.'

'Maybe I do.'

'None of my business?'

'I wouldn't say that. You're here and feel it, so that makes some of it your business.'

'Some of it?'

'Not all of it.'

Dylan dropped his head again and saw the gunk in the bottom of the canoe drying.

'That all you got to say on the matter?' snorted Vincent.

'You teasing me?'
'Sure am.'

——

After walking beside the river for twenty-five minutes, Kate and Dylan come to the first canoe, and paddle a kilometre under shading ramparts to a tumble of rocks blocking the river.

They swim in the deep water, relieved to be cool, then scamper over the rock bar and into a second canoe. The mirror image of Emerald Gorge distorts into epic triangles. 'This place represents hope for me,' Dylan says from the back as they settle into a-stroke-a-second in the deepest, tightest neck of it. 'They were going to build a dam right here in the fifties, when there was some wild idea about piping water all the way to the city. Then in the nineties they wanted to do it to irrigate cotton. A wall thirty metres tall would make a reservoir from here to Carter's Ford. You might remember the campaign against it.'

After a few more strokes, he continues, almost as if he is talking to himself. 'The future of freshwater is the future story of the planet. Of the human race. There are more than 40,000 big dams in the world that are taller than four-storey buildings – 19,000 in China and 300 of them at least 150 metres tall. There's tension between China and India over the Brahmaputra; between Ethiopia and Egypt along the Nile; between Israel, Jordan and Palestine over the River Jordan. Turkey's plans to dam the Euphrates brought it to the brink of war with Syria.'

She sees the irony in him saying all this to her. The terrible incongruity of it. She feels pinpricks. She is surprised that part of her even wants to tell him what's really going on. But she simply says, 'Thousands have lived without love, not one without water.'

'What's that?' he asks.

'Something we had to learn at school. I'd forgotten it until now. Auden, I think.'

'Very apt.'

They let the silence close in again, and they tilt their heads back to look up the walls to the slot of sapphire above.

They haul up on a sandy beach for the morning tea that's been packed for them, and lounge on comfortable natural rock benches. There is just the sound of bird calls, the lap of water as zephyrs corrugate the surface, and the deep, mufflerless buzz of faraway insects travelling in straight lines.

They touch the precious feeling of simply being human.

'Elevenses,' says Dylan, unwrapping Anzac biscuits and fruit. 'Perfect.'

At the end of the second stretch, they pull their boots back on and stride across the tops of the smoothed rocks to see that the Duncan River continues through spectacular country.

'We could haul the canoe over the rocks and go on,' says Dylan.

'We might never come back,' says Kate, wanting only to be here like this, with him – but another part of her wishing she'd never see this place. Feeling the good and terribly bad in her.

She glances across and sees Dylan. She sees him strong in this clear light. Yes, strong, she thinks. That's the word. How could she have ever thought otherwise? She sees him now, in profile, like a painting – the bold colours and lines of a Gauguin. And she sees the landscape around him as an elaborate frame. One of those big, gold, carved picture frames that are as much an artwork as the painting itself. The two combine; complement one another. And seeing him in this landscape – in this gorge – in this frame, completes him. It displays him.

The two have combined, here, in this moment, to make the complete picture of Dylan. It is tactile, three-dimensional, full.

'Come on,' he says. 'We'd better head back then.'

And they turn for home, silent in the gorge and the sharing of it.

The canoe moves slowly through the water, and for a split second she thinks of telling him. She thinks of just blurting it out. 'This could all be gone. It could be underwater.' The two parts of her wrestle and she swirls inside like the water spinning off the paddle tips.

*Pull yourself together.* She says it so loud inside her head that she thinks he might hear it. It's like a slap. *What the hell do you think you're doing? You're thinking like a teenager. This isn't some little game. Pull yourself together.* At this, Kate reaches inside to the softer heart of her and encompasses it in an uncompromising embrace, until it is completely covered, silenced.

——

That afternoon, Cole can't get over the waste. Blind Freddie could see Emerald Gorge is a natural dam site. All that potential going down the drain. It's criminal, he thinks. Simple as that. The state's minerals seem virtually inexhaustible and China's crying out for them. The city's population of two million needs doubling to fully exploit them, and that means water. Cole shudders to think of the environmental protection studies they'd have to do on this joint. My God, if they *were* in China, they'd mobilise a million people to build a pipeline quick-smart.

In the front of the canoe, Suzy's hair falls onto her brown back from under a straw hat with a pink ribbon round the crown. Cole watches the stretch of her muscles under her bathers' criss-cross straps and looks forward to her getting wet. He keeps the paddling rhythm but eases on the pressure, so he's just going through the motions. She doesn't seem to notice. It's a good plan, he thinks.

After Jim has shown Dylan and Kate the generator room, he pulls out construction plans for the solar units. 'Has to be to Cyclone Category B specs. Concrete in the footings. A lot of earthworks, so I suggested it was cheaper to buy an excavator. I thought that it can't be that hard. I've been getting the hang of it.'

Kate heads back to her room, saying she should write up notes on the laptop but looking for space, tormented by the lie. She sets up a green director's chair and square jarrah table at the far end of the verandah. A stream runs through the flaky river paperbarks.

She spreads out a map, pens and some of the white sheets from the ream she has brought. With a licked forefinger, she leafs through her notebook. On one hand, the number of generators and replacement projections. On the other, the number of residents. Thoughts of displacement. My God, she thinks, what am I in the middle of?

She feels far removed from the colours and temperatures of the life she is used to, and the ease of her usual thinking. It was only the day before yesterday that she stepped onto a plane. She has never known such distance.

She gives up on the table, and lies on her bed with the fan going, feeling the all-consuming tide of slumber coming. Her limbs tingle with it.


Kate drifts into a sleep in which she is suspended, surrounded by water. She twists in all directions, but it is all the steel-blue water; below and above, too. She remembers hearing that you should breathe out and follow the bubbles to the surface and so she leaks air, but the bubbles just eddy around her and she swirls madly, still surrounded by them, then realises that her lungs are empty and gasps for air, but takes in only the deep blue of the water. She strokes out madly, reaching upwards knowing it could be downwards. She feels the panic of being engulfed and overwhelmed. Of being buried alive in water.

And she wakes completely terrified and gasping for air, which she bites down in big parcels, with the retching sound of someone vomiting.

# Nineteen

Jack and Kate are still packing their stuff after breakfast the next morning while Dylan puts ice into coolboxes for the overnight run to Barker River Station.

'Just thought I'd call by to say cheerio,' says Pru, head around the back of the vehicle. 'I hope it's been useful.'

'Thanks, Pru. You've all been a great help,' says Dylan. 'No Suzy?'

'She says goodbye.' Pru seems uneasy.

'Everything OK?'

'Fine.'

'Doesn't sound "fine".'

'Really, it's all OK. I'll tell you about it sometime, maybe. Not now.'

Dylan rapidly pulls threads together. 'What happened yesterday? Suzy took Cole up Emerald Gorge.'

'There's no problem.'

'If something's upset Suzy, I want to know. I'm responsible, Pru.'

'I really shouldn't have let on,' says Pru. 'I don't want anything said. Organisations like us rely on high-level support. From what Suzy says, things were difficult, but I've given her a couple of days off and she'll be fine. It'll wash through.'

'What the hell did he do?' Dylan is furious.

'He didn't do anything.'

'Well, what did he try to do?'

'In retrospect, perhaps I shouldn't have sent Suzy up Emerald alone with Mr Cole, but one just expects that someone representing the Minister…well, one just *expects*.'

Dylan is flushed.

'He tried it on and she got upset. He was, well, *forceful* – but nothing really *happened*, in the physical sense, if you know what I mean…'

'Jesus Christ,' says Dylan. 'That's it…'

'No. I know your heart's in these projects. Just think it through.'

Dylan slams the esky lid shut and turns away, fists clenched, but Pru catches him by the crook of one arm and spins him.

'Please, Dylan.' He sees her calmness. 'She handled it. I need you not to say anything, and so does this place. It's not that we can't live without their solar power plant, or that we couldn't raise the money for it ourselves. Of course we could. But men like Jack Cole specialise in politics and revenge, and organisations like us don't need someone like that out to get us.'

Pru sees the resistance in him.

'Suzy agrees,' she snaps. 'It's a tough old world. You just have to get on with the good stuff.' Pru is not going to take no for an answer.

'Now,' she says. 'Give Kate our regards. We hope we see her again.' She gives a no-compromise smile.

Dylan needs somewhere to let the heat in him defuse and follows a path that plunges in among trees. It is almost instantly still and dark, bleaching sunlight restrained around the edges. Protected from glare, the spongy litter absorbs the jarring in him and there is the homey scent of organic moisture.

He feels the calming ambience of good company. Grevillea and beefwood, corkwood and common hakea. A coolamon – stinkwood, nicknamed for its pungency on the fire. *Gyrocarpus americanus*'s seeds flying like helicopters. Acacia and wild mango. *Irvingia gabonensis* with a fibre so hardy that even termites find it difficult to swallow. The tangle of creepers.

Grey pebbles draw his eye, and there are two small twig hedges in parallel vertical lines as long as his forearm, bent in and meeting at the top. The sight dilutes his anger. When he's sure the bowerbird isn't near, he edges forward for a closer look at the sticks and the stones that trickle through the middle and form a doormat either side. And then he notices a different colour amongst them. *Chlamydera nuchalis*, the hoarder. There are half a dozen pieces of green glass – shards of a bottle, worn smooth in a creek bed. There is the ring-pull from a can, several beer-bottle tops, wood screws, a bolt and two nuts, a bit of light chain, a few unused rivets and an empty .22 shell.

'Males are such collectors, aren't they...'

Suzy is behind him.

Dylan rises from his crouch. 'Hi. How are you?'

'I just saw Pru. We're worried about how you might react.'

He says nothing.

'It wasn't such a big deal,' she continues. 'Just awkward. He's a prick, but there are plenty of those around.'

'I feel like stopping somewhere down the road, throwing him out and leaving him.' Dylan is only half-joking.

'Not very helpful for any of us. Pru says you feel responsible. Well, you are. You're responsible for bringing him here. We all need to be "on the map" with government, and this helps to do that. It was good to bring them here and now you've still got to make it work for us. That's your responsibility.' She smiles at him, laying down the law. 'I've got over it, so do the same.'

Dylan can't find words.

'If you need some inspiration for that, just take another look at that nest. Do you know how many bowerbirds there are left, and can you possibly imagine how few live somewhere uninterrupted, like this? Well, it just isn't that many. If you need something to get your head straight, focus on that. And now we'd all like you to put Mr Cole in that vehicle and go and impress upon him the importance of government support for everyone in the bush.'

Her smile is resolute now.

'And look out for Kate.'

'I will,' says Dylan '…to all that.'

Suzy is wearing knee-length shorts, sparkly thongs and a white T-shirt. 'Thanks.' As she steps forward and lifts her arms to embrace him, the sleeves ride up and he sees finger-spaced bruises on each bicep.

———

Cole and Kate are waiting by the vehicle.

'I thought you said eight o'clock,' snaps Cole.

Dylan curbs his reaction. 'I got caught up. Let's get going.' He reaches into the back of the vehicle and eases his Akubra Rough Rider hat on. Avoiding eyes. The sun is already trying to burn the backs of his calves through his moleskins.

Cole has climbed into the back seat, leaving his door open, but Kate comes round behind the vehicle where Dylan is stowing their bags and lifting the last coolbox from the shade under the vehicle. 'Everything OK?' Reading body language. She stands, waiting for an answer.

'Yeah. Everything's fine, thanks. Let's get going.'

He slams the swing door shut and doesn't meet her puzzled scrutiny.

The atmosphere is strained and Dylan wishes he'd handled things outside differently. He has left Kate winded and now they're in the vehicle with Cole. He pushes the CD player's button on, glances at her and smiles. But she looks away, jaw set.

Dylan checks in the rear-view mirror, sees Cole already tucked under his fedora, and then takes a chance, reaching across and touching her hand. Kate looks towards him questioningly, and he keeps a warm, steady gaze. Gradually the muscles in her face relax and she responds. 'What?' she mouths silently. 'Not now,' he tells her with his eyes and an almost imperceptible shake of his head. She shows her understanding, and then they are just caught in one another's stare, as the vehicle heads along the straight track.

'We'll camp at Adanson Gorge tonight,' says Dylan, pouring tea from the billy can into mugs, to go with the light fruit cake he's cut on the tailgate for morning tea. 'It's too much of a stretch to Barker River Station in one day, and Adanson's a pretty spot. This way we'll get time to look around on the way. Sleep out and get a feel for the place.'

'Sounds good,' says Kate.

Cole shudders at the thought of camping. He has no idea what people see in this godforsaken country. It's not a place for humans, he thinks. He takes two pieces of cake, compressing them in his left hand. 'It'd better be cooler than this.' He turns away from the tea, gets back into the vehicle, sitting part-sideways with the door open, and draws his right sleeve over his face, leaving it wringing wet.

Dylan takes guilty pleasure in Cole's florid face.

# Twenty

Kate is first into the gorge's pool and she glides, absorbing a day in landscape. From ravines to ranges, the treed veins of underground creek systems to glittering showers of quartz, the country has been laid out before her and quietly interpreted by Dylan. She feels saturated by it.

She twists over, lies back and floats, ears just under, hair wafting like weed in the dark water. She looks up at the walls, with their delicate ferns, and feels icy and warmer currents drifting. In the far left corner, a waterfall drops six storeys. It is misty, but pounds the surface to a milky froth. When she looks directly up, droplets fall at her, beginning far above. There is no sense of their movement; they just sparkle as they get bigger. She squints as they land pin-sharp on her face.

Then she shivers. It is such a big convulsion that it sends out ripples. She rolls over on to her front and breast-strokes, occasionally putting her head right under and enjoying the glide of a big kick.

'When you get cold, head to the right,' Dylan had said as she left to walk up to the pool. 'And look up when you do it.'

'Why?' she asked.

'You'll see.'

As she veers over, the water warms, and she sees that one corner has a low rock wall under the surface. She shimmies over it into a tepid bath, deep enough to cover her when she lies back, and with a soft, round-stone bottom. She quickly feels its silky heat start to enter her and realises how cold she's got, but can't remember ever feeling more relaxed and happy.

Then she remembers the last of Dylan's words and looks up. Above her, faint on the wall, is a gallery of rock art. Wallabies, she thinks, and a fish and a long crocodile. Higher to the right, a maroon-coloured figure with a lizard body and two sets each of front and rear legs, and a head with dark eyes and no mouth, and a great frill around its head. Perhaps one image over another and perhaps many years apart. She notices another figure higher up, also lizard-like, with long, curved claws, a fat tail and straight line marks down its body. This time with jug-ears.

But the whole centrepiece of the wall is taken up with circles four and five metres apart, joined by straight lines, some of them seeming to come off a coloured-in ellipse. It looks almost like a constellation. Some believe that a sandstone shrike-thrush once broke its beak on a rock and painted with the blood from it. That was how this started.

Kate swims towards the gorge wall and pulls herself out on flat rocks that become slippery as soon as they are wet. She has the sense of being somewhere long-used and notices something high up and moving. Two empty white snake skins hang off a branch and blow in air imperceptibly moving. A pair of delicate wind socks. The mouth and eye holes are clearly visible, giving them a ghostly appearance and the sense of previous life.

'I thought you might be getting webbed fingers.' Dylan is clattering the dinner underway. He has pulled down the big plate-and-mesh barbecue from the roof rack, unwrapped it from its corrugated cardboard, gathered snappy gum and let its flames die down. The perfect cooking coals of *Eucalyptus brevifolia*. He has prepared vegetables to go with the vacuum-packed chicken breasts and steak, which he's had in Mt Goode's and Daydawn's fridges during the nights and kept chilled by day. Onions, tomatoes and capsicum for the grill. Fine-sliced potatoes to cook in olive oil on the plate. And he has halved an iceberg lettuce, impressed with the staying power of its stout heart.

Now he places on the camp table an entrée platter with olives, goat's cheese from a jar, bell peppers and dry biscuits. 'What would you like to drink?'

'Another cold beer. A very cold beer,' cuts in Cole, appearing from behind a tree, still pulling up his zip, suddenly seeming cheerful. 'Thank Christ that heat's died down a bit.'

'You should try a swim,' suggests Kate.

'I might in a minute. In fact,' he says, taking the beer from Dylan, 'I might just take this up there now.' He pauses. 'Come to that, I might need more than one.'

Dylan offers nothing in return. 'Dinner in about forty-five minutes.'

'That'll be fine,' says Cole amiably, and he heads off up the path, whistling. *If I Were a Rich Man...*

'He's in a good mood,' says Kate. 'We want that.'

Dylan says nothing.

'So, what happened this morning?'

'It's all good now,' he says.

'What happened?'

'It's OK. It's passed.' Some of him wants to warn her, but it might make the next days impossible, and he fears losing them. Another part of him says that if Cole did chance his arm, Kate could handle him. But most of him just wants to keep watch over her and prove he won't let her down.

'Well, if there's anything I should know...'

'No, it's all good. Have something to nibble on. And how about some white wine? Do you like it here?'

'It is unbelievable. You've brought me to a place I could never have dreamed of.'

Dylan has put up two small dome tents, without their flysheets, for Kate and Cole. He's rolled out a canvas swag in each. 'If you feel like dragging them outside, feel free. I've got mosquito nets, if you'd like me to hang those up. Whatever's most comfortable. I just thought you might like some privacy.' Cole surprises him with a warm reply. 'Thanks,' he says. 'The tent's good. I've got some paperwork. That'll keep the insects away when I've got the light on, I guess.' Cole has cooled off in the pool and drowned himself in boutique beers. He's the best part of the way through a decent bottle of Margaret River cab sav and considering the next. He sits back, mellow, full of good food, and loosens the top of his shorts.

'I think I'll use a tent, too,' says Kate. 'I'd like to see the stars, but I just hate the idea of snakes...'

Dylan is dismissive. 'They won't bother you. I've spent hundreds of nights in a swag.'

'Don't they come in looking for warmth?' chips in Cole. 'I heard that at school. Some old story about a snake curling up on a bloke's chest.'

'Where was school?' asks Dylan, expecting Cole to back off.

'Wheatbelt,' he replies, almost without thinking.

Dylan and Kate are surprised.

'Hated it,' says Cole. 'A dump.'

'No ties there?' asks Dylan.

'None at all,' says Cole. 'Now, what have we got in that box of wines?'

'Just about anything you fancy,' says Dylan.

'Good,' he says. 'I feel like another drink.'

———

Jack Cole was born into a droughty farm in the wheatbelt. His father Mervin looked down at the screaming baby and merely said, 'In seasons like this, a man's just happy to get his seed back.'

Little Jack hated the bleaching light and a landscape coloured only by blond wheat and the resilient red of the thin and hopelessly under-nourishing ground. He hated the town edged by salmon gums, which had only one real road and a rail line through it. The wide, gridded back-block streets of timber weatherboard cottages. The retold family history of moral men and women in Welsh valleys infuriated him. He detested hearing about the gritty forebears who emigrated to Western Australia. They called it honest work and seemed to rejoice in it, but he thought they slaved too hard for too little, and he resented that stupidity. He learnt to sidestep chores with a locked bathroom door.

He was disdainful of teachers in the small town school. 'Could you pay a little attention?' said Mrs Giles. 'I'm paying as little attention as I can,' he replied.

He didn't attract friends, but demanded notice. His particular joy came from picking on the boy next door – Perfect Peter, he called him – whom his mother called 'little darling' and who willingly helped Mervyn in the shed. Jack honed his ability to manipulate Peter and destroy his confidence at will. It amused him.

He became dismissive of his father and shouted at his mother, and in his teenage years, there was always the threat of his fists. He shrugged off his mother's attempts to touch him. Started to think that bullets'd bounce off him.

He was rat-cunning rather than smart; won a scholarship and got out of there as soon as he could. And he never looked back. His first break came in the Hills. He'd talked big money off backers and paid councillors' campaign costs even before he hassled a block of land of a near-broke orchardist. The subdivision was bulldozed through. They were heady, pre-loan days and he sold blocks for cash and stuffed the notes into laundry bags in the boot of his old Merc.

It gave him seed money and he worked on contacts. He pulled strings for his next piece of land, down on the sand plain. It was cleared and prepared, and sprayed with green papier-mâché filled with grass seed. Within a couple of weeks, the dunes looked like bowling greens and the brochure looked lush. The blocks sold like hot cakes.

He deepened his grip in the business community, scouted out the vulnerable and hooked himself into the political scene. Cole hoarded information, stored favours, made deals, and started putting together contacts and getting into mineral resources. But property deals were what he loved.

Cole eases into the solitude of his tent with a bottle of Aussie shiraz that's jam-packed with fruit. Raspberry and blackberry on the palate. Apricot nose. Thick as tractor oil.

With the battery lantern on, he half-heartedly jots notes, but his mind is elsewhere. The wheatbelt, he thinks. His childhood. What was all that about? Those people; even now he can't bring himself to use the word 'family'. He remembers becoming convinced he was adopted. He can't recall how he came up with the idea, but he remembers thinking he'd found the solution to the puzzle. He never asked his parents, so they'd never had the opportunity to deny it.

Cole pulls a bottle of XO brandy from his leather holdall and sucks straight from it. The voices by the fire rise and fall; the lilt of humans communicating, just like the harmonies of his parents in his childhood. Muted through the fibro walls, they were choral.

The XO swirls around Cole's brain like some golden cloud, sending sparky lightning through lobes, cerebellum and pons. And in a familiar moment that never comes sober, he craves company. More specifically, he craves female company and dreams of a girl the colour of pearl.

The fire dying down, Dylan and Kate have pulled their camp chairs closer and are chatting.

'Get three fresh glasses and we can share a nightcap,' blusters in Cole. 'What are you two on about?' A blunt intrusion.

'Dylan's father has been poorly. Something similar to Michael Mooney, I think.' Kate immediately wishes she hadn't said it.

'Mooney's sick?' One of Cole's eyebrows lifts, hawky in the firelight.

'My dad just had a heart flutter,' Dylan pushes in, sensing her need for a distraction. 'But he's fine now.'

'And Mooney has a dicky heart?'

'I've spoken out of turn,' says Kate. 'I'll get the glasses.'

Cole knows when to accept a gift, and that's what all information about a man's weaknesses is, he thinks. He files it for the future. 'Is the old man having the op?' he asks Dylan. 'Amazing how fast they get them back on their feet. Even towns that get a bypass seem to survive these days.' Snorts at his joke.

'No,' says Dylan. 'He doesn't need that. He's just been very het-up lately about a development behind their place.'

'Which development?' asks Cole.

'Tuart Crest.'

———

Property development is Jack Cole's infatuation and excitement. His hunt. Sometimes he can hardly believe how easy he finds it and the extraordinary money it generates.

Development is the contribution of men of action and that's precisely why all his companies incorporate that word. Action Developments, Action Real Estate, Action Nominees, Action Securities. And there are more, in that deliberately complex web to which he is the only key.

Even compared with his first break in the Hills, when he'd fleeced a near-bankrupt orchardist, Tuart Crest has been easy. The land had been in the same family for four generations, and he'd watched the last old couple falter. The son was in England, lecturing at a regional university, recently married and with a new kid. He'd be dying for the money. The daughter was a single mum in a rented Sydney apartment. Desperate, no doubt.

But the old couple were haunted by the generations before them and had refused to sell. Cole had kept calling, cajoling and offering gentle support through a difficult decision. When they said they wouldn't have anywhere to go, he returned with brochures for Action Retirement Villages that gave them 'lifestyle options'.

Soon they dreaded seeing the black Range Rover swoop in, and once dropped to their knees and cowered under window-height, nose to nose, until, after ringing the bell, walking round the house and looking into every window, he finally relented, leaving a charming Action Greeting Card.

And then Cole became impatient. He turned up the heat. He took them newspaper clippings about land shortages and reports about house prices rocketing. He drew graphs with 'Under 30s' written across the bottom and 'House supply' up the side, and no scales for either, and showed them how it was only 'Supply' that could maintain 'Affordability'. He told them that they, personally, were ruining the chances of young people buying their own home. With textas on a clean sheet, he drew another wild graph to prove the hopelessness of the renting cycle.

On the next visit, he brought a printout from Action Real Estate with a list of names. He said they were young couples hoping to buy and they only stood a chance with his economical building techniques.

The couple teetered, but then New Year came and the old woman made a resolution that she would stay in her own home. When the ABC talkback show host asked people to share their resolutions, she rang in and told him. And when he asked why and she explained, he sounded gobsmacked, on air.

But deep in the dark of a windy night, contorted by thoughts of it all, she felt a tingling start in her toes and move in a wave up her body, until her heart felt floppy, unruly and too big for her chest. She died, breathless, in the room next to her snoring and mostly-deaf husband.

After the funeral, when the son and daughter had left again, Cole listened patiently to the old man's childhood and war stories, and soon convinced him that it was only his wife that had stood in the way of their friendship and a comfortable, cared-for life. He persuaded him that, for tax reasons, he was better off not getting a lump sum, but instead exchanging the property for sheltered accommodation and live-in fees.

It was a masterstroke. The land would barely cost Cole a cent.

The deal was signed and watertight before anyone else was aware of it. Cole knew that neither son nor daughter had the finances to drag him through court, and if they did, it'd take years and he'd just keep throwing money at it. With what he'd make out of the development, it just didn't matter.

Cole helped the old man move into an Action Retirement Village, enjoyed lifting the few boxes of personal possessions into the back of the Range Rover. It was the physical moment when the deal felt done. He had a sense of achievement.

The thin old boy seemed to vanish into the front leather seat.


Locals made as much noise as they could about Tuart Crest, but Cole had funded enough of the councillors' campaigns to have the voting numbers. He rang around and reminded them of their obligations.


Dylan talks on about his parents' distress and the day he walked through to the cleared land. 'They only left one tuart tree,' he says. 'It's obscene.' He knows Cole won't like hearing it.

Cole weighs it up. A stoush'd perk things up, but there's still a fair way to go. He's focused on bigger outcomes. The moment for indulgences will come, he tells himself, and it is only then that it occurs to him that Dylan reminds him of the Peter Perfect of his childhood.

'That'll do me,' is all he says. 'Time to turn in.' Soon they hear him rustle into his swag and, within minutes, snoring. The sleep of the righteous.


'I suppose I should go to bed, too,' says Kate. 'I'm zonked. And another big day tomorrow.'

'Nah, easy one,' says Dylan. 'Just up to Barker River Station. We'll be there by lunchtime, so we can look around.

But I want to get away at sparrow's the next day...it's a long way north to Warramorra, at the top of the peninsula. Vincent and Henny are meeting us there.'

Dylan puts the billy on the embers to make a sweet tea, and adds a few sticks for more light. Kate slides back in her chair until her body is almost straight, ankles and arms crossed. Time stretches out with her.

They have each stepped away from the fire with a small mug of water and cleaned their teeth, spitting into bushes, Dylan covering the white paste with dirt. He has shovelled in the edges of the fire to neaten it and rolled out his soft, faded swag nearby.

'Good night then,' she says, and it seems an expectant moment.

Neither seems to know quite what to do.

Dylan holds her in his gaze. 'It's been just a wonderful day.'

# Twenty-one

Barker River's a full-on cattle station and Peter Goodson plays the grumpy old bastard. Legs bowed, indigo eyes dodging under his brim, he leads the visitors to three of the new homestay rooms while rolling a cigarette.

'They've all got thunderboxes,' referring to the ensuites his boy Nick and daughter-in-law Janet dug in over. 'I dunno,' he adds, 'in the old days we all used to eat inside and shit outside. Now everyone wants to eat outside and shit inside. Doesn't make sense.' Shakes his head. 'Disgusting, shitting in yer bedroom.'

Peter Goodson treats his place the way he always has. He overgrazes it, pulls off big numbers of bulls in the dry season, fattens yearlings down on the southern boundary by the river and isn't apparently open to questioning, education or a change of opinion. And yet Dylan likes him. He reckons Goodson's wrong, but at least he's straight as a die.

'Hope you'll be comfortable, Mr Cole.' Goodson surprises Dylan by turning on the charm. The cunning old bastard's done his homework. 'Because I'm gonna bend yer ear later.'

'I look forward to it,' says Cole, enjoying the prospect of a bit of straightforward argy-bargy.

The yard is full of peahens and two of their more elaborate male mates rustling their petticoats. Knee-high wallabies scatter from the shade. A Shetland pony is parked up head-first under a fig tree, looking like he's just walked into it and stalled. A light truck is loaded with sacks of phosphorous and protein for the cattle and Uramol dry feed supplement. Big licks of it to go out in big, bald tyres.

Homemade pie, chunky-cut vegetables, bottles of red and stocky conversation. 'The facts are simple,' says Nick. 'The grid covers less than eighty per cent of Australia, and diesel electricity costs three to ten times more than city electricity. It'd be three years before we'd be in front, even if we had the 120,000-grand for solar.'

'We're not all Aboriginal corporations,' slips in the old man.

'Meaning?' Cole seizing the lead.

'They get the handouts and we work our arses off and then go into more debt.'

Dylan cuts in. 'Yeah, well you know how level the playing field is across the board, Peter.'

'Just a point of view,' says Goodson, surprising Cole by deferring to Dylan.

'But I understand your feelings,' Dylan adds.

'The fact is,' continues Nick Goodson, 'that many Aboriginal communities now have sustainable technology but pastoral properties are struggling to afford it.'

'But there are subsidies...' adds Kate.

'A lot of us are just getting by,' Nick turns quietly to her. 'Most of us are up to our throats in debt.' She senses him holding back desperation.

'I've been getting the low-down from a mate in the Northern Territory,' says Nick, enthused, making it worse. 'He's got a 12kVa system – eighty panels, sixty watts each – and reckons seventy per cent of their power comes from the sun. A regulator charges the batteries and the 240 comes out of an inverter. The diesel generators are just for back-up. Reckons it's better than the town systems – no surging.'

'It'd be godsend,' says Janet, who's slid in along the bench. 'Just knowing the freezers and fridges wouldn't go off. That's such a nightmare.'

For a moment, Cole is glad the whole solar power story is sort of true. 'You've argued your case well,' he says, reaching for the shiraz.


The station's ringers are up well before dawn the next day. They've just mustered 3,000 head of cattle and are moving them south. Before the light's full, they mill around the yards, backing up trucks, starting the loading. Cattle race gates clang. There is the pungency of salty hide and hot meat.

Not much later, after silent mugs of tea at the homestead table, Goodson pulls on his dogger boots, then loads his big first-aid kit, water bottle and swag, which is faded to a creamy green and strapped with wide leather belts.

'G'day and it's been a pleasure,' he says, shaking hands with each guest. 'Hope you can do something for us, Mr Cole,' he adds, pushing on his hat, stepping onto the lush lawn and dismissing them. 'See you again, Dylan,' he adds, without looking back.

'He likes you,' says Nick, unseen behind Dylan and ready to follow his father.

'Is that "liking someone"?' asks Kate.

'Oh yes,' says Nick. 'That's liking someone.'

Nick Goodson fans out three white A4 envelopes. 'I've itemised some of the things we talked about last night. Bullet points. I'd appreciate it if you could give them some consideration. 'And we are really grateful for your effort in coming. Give my regards to the folk up the peninsula, Dylan.' They shake warmly.

'Nick's obviously got a bit of running on the place. The next generation.' They're passing out of the homestead gateway and Cole doesn't waste time. 'Educated?'

'He boarded at one of the private schools in the city, then went on to uni. Did commerce, I think.'

'You can see that in him.'

'But it'll be hard to shift Pete's ideas. He's old-school and a tough campaigner. He's locked up in all those bad habits that grow up over generations – not that it's his fault. Ideas just change as we learn more. But Nick's got good concepts, I think, and he's mates with Billy Parkes, who's out further east – Pru mentioned him. That'll be inspiring him. I think that's where the idea for the new homestay rooms came from. Billy has been clever with his diversification of Erindale. He's away at a biodiversity conference at the moment, or he'd have come over to meet us, though his place is 200 kays outside the valley.'

Good, thinks Cole. Parkes sounds smart and energetic. Better that he's not part of things in the Duncan River basin.

'Nick's just the sort of young bloke the pastoralists and graziers need on their committees.' Cole continues laying bait.

'You're right, but I think he's got his hands too full to get tied up with that at the moment. I think they'll just be busy trying to keep their heads above water.'

Cole thinks so, too.

# Twenty-two

There are six seasons for the Aboriginal people of the peninsula, who live alongside fertile waters where the Duncan River's final delta pours into the Indian Ocean. The Wet comes from mid-December to January, with the end of the Wet in February. This is followed by king tide season to mid-May, with the ocean rising and falling by up to ten metres. Then the south-east wind brings mosquitoes. In the old days, the people used to move back to the sandhills to live.

Then the cold season, a time of honey collection, with the pandanus screw palm's nuts ripening red and ready to eat. The knock-'em-down winds follow, then the warming up season in August and September, after the spear wattle and paperbarks have flowered. Lastly, married turtle time, when the turtles are mating.

The peninsula has a pulse.

———

The old people of Warramorra crushed bunyjoord creeper tubers and made up a brew to stun fish trapped in reef holes as the tide fell. They circled in the receding broth, then floated like croutons. 'I was a little kid when I saw people doing it,' Uncle Vincent told Dylan once, sitting there. 'Pa took me to Warramorra beach. He put this stuff in and the fish came up. We weren't from here – we were river people – but he knew how to do it.'

'The boys here still know the trick, but they prefer spears,' Dylan tells Kate and Cole as they cover the last few kilometres of red road to Warramorra. 'The young blokes go fishing every day, but now they take tourists for $30 each and make 300 bucks too. They think it's pretty funny.' The old men do culture tours, stomping round a familiar block, pointing out the obvious. It couldn't have happened eighteen years ago, Dylan says. 'Perhaps it couldn't have happened ten years ago.' Aboriginal people being sought out just because they're Aboriginal. 'It's like Uncle Vincent says, they're being paid to be listened to, but for the last century they've been talking and no-one heard.

'And there's the shift on the Indigenous side, too. Twenty years ago, culture and stories weren't readily shared with whitefellas. Then a book of desert women's stories came out – about fifteen years ago – and the introduction said it was time to share their stories. It was the first tangible thing I saw of the shift about to take place. Aboriginal communities have found a way to communicate and some of us have found a way to listen. Somewhere from that, comes trading – cultural, economic. If a community doesn't have anything to trade, it faces extinction.' Thinking aloud. 'Sorry,' he says. 'Lecture over.'

The women at Five Turtles Point got into tourism when their kids were young. They didn't want them going in to town when they were teenagers, looking for work, getting into trouble. They wanted incomes and interesting people at the Warramorra community. *Get the world to come here*, they said.

'When you stay here, you mix with the community,' explains Deejay Munumurra leading the visitors across watered lawns with a practised spiel. Deejay's a young bloke, but an elder in the peninsula's big Munumurra family group and president of Warramorra Corporation.

He shows them three self-contained cabins, four double rooms and a bunkhouse. All air-conditioned. 'There's twenty-four guest beds – we don't want to ruin the country by having too many visitors.'

'How many people are there here? How many involved in tourism?' Kate is taking notes.

'Sixty people live here, ten work directly in tourism, but the whole community is involved.' A careful answer. Then Deejay adds, more casually, 'We've just been real busy. We have big groups of students from America – about 200 a year. They come over as part of their college cultural studies course. They're fantastic – our kids love having them here – but it's a fair bit of work.'

'Some were here last time I came through,' says Dylan.

'Yeah. Well, it's regular now.'

It had been stinking hot and Dylan saw kids pour out of four-wheel drive buses on the beach at the end of a daytrip. They helter-skeltered into the ocean. Then, *Shark!* American kids ran from the water as the Aboriginal boys charged in with spears to shoo the hammerhead off. Then, brown bodies beaded with saltwater, they peered into the turquoise water, stalking like herons.

The dream of more than a decade ago is here, working.

Not long after they met at the Scimitar Project, Vincent brought Dylan here to go mud-crabbing. 'Bit out of your country?' asked Dylan.

'There's always been cousins here,' said Vincent. 'Yimis been here. You can still feel the Duncan River. Everything washes out here, see. The goodness of the country's the lifeblood of the peninsula. Little stuff feeds on it, bigger stuff feeds on that, and the really big stuff feeds on that.'

'Pretty simple,' says Dylan.

'Gotta remember it,' grins Vincent. 'Life's pretty simple. It's us-as makes it complicated.'

Mud crabs, monster fish and green, hawksbill, loggerhead, flatback and leatherback turtles. Occasionally, maybe, an Olive Ridley, too. Some drag up the beach to lay eggs, leaving tell-tale tractor marks and the indentations of their nests. Dugong, dolphins, sharks and whales. Estuarine crocodiles patrol the coast; *Crocodylus porosus*, biggest of the reptiles, with 150 million years here and a brain the size of a walnut, needing the Duncan River's fresh water to reproduce. A white-bellied sea eagle wheels out from the mangroves. One of oldest genera of birds, *Haliaeetus leucogaster* has a snake in its beak, looped like a shepherd's crook.

'Busy as hell out there,' says Vincent. 'Needs traffic lights.'

Deejay Munumurra shows them to rooms. 'When you've put your things down, Dylan might take you up to the church,' he says. 'Explain that part of the history.'

'Is Brother Ted out on the point?' asks Dylan.

'No. He's in Rome, on business.'

It's a still day and folk amble around the grassy heart of Warramorra, which looks like an old village green. St Peter's Church was built in 1934 by Aboriginal people, from mangrove poles under a paperbark wood roof, and the doors and windows of it are thrown wide.

'The Roman Catholic mission is part and parcel of the place,' Dylan explains. 'Aboriginal kids were brought here. Adults, too. From different places and all put together, regardless of tribe. Today that might look appalling, but the other side of it is that Christianity brought Western education. It's a tricky thing to judge from our vantage point now.'

'Best thing that ever happened to them.' Cole has been showing no interest in the place, but now he swings and goes for the jugular. 'Turned them into something.'

Dylan bristles. 'I think they already were something.'

'Primitives running round the bush in bloody loin cloths?'

Dylan feels bait being laid, but takes it and swallows down hard. 'It's a longstanding culture; a complex society.' Fumbling for a hook.

'Bullshit. They go on about being here for tens of thousands of years, but they did damn all with the place. And look at them now. Drunks, bludgers, rorters, child abusers. Hopeless. Heading for extinction.'

'Sweeping statements,' Dylan spits, wrong-footed by ferociousness so easily unleashed. 'That's all people like you are capable of.'

'*People like me*?' Cole cuts in, voice frigid, glare calculating. 'Now we're getting to it.'

It's like a bucket of ice water over Dylan. He knew he was being led, and now he's there – away from the issue and onto something personal.

'And what *are* people like me?' Cole squares up to him.

'I don't think this is helpful.' Kate walks forcefully between them, facing Dylan first. 'You're here to facilitate, not agitate. Just get on with that.' She glances back at Cole and sees the smirk.

Dylan feels attacked all-round. Cole's brutality, and the blistering speed and violence of it, has dazed him. He doesn't see Kate's intervention as a defence.

But it seems to have cheered Cole up. 'I'll leave you two it,' he suddenly says, turning and striding off towards his room, whistling.

'Come on,' she says. 'Show me Brother Ted's place.'

Brother Ted lives in a tin shack out on the end of the peninsula.

'Alone?' asks Kate.

'A contemplative monk. There to pray. He says he's like a radio transmitter.'

His big canvas tent has a metal-framed bed and a chair; a table for his writing materials and a stand-up shelf for his books. 'Strange he should be here, alone,' says Kate.

'And Ted's such a gregarious guy. Young, too,' adds Dylan, cooled and relieved that things were hauled onto a new course. 'He's up-to-date – knowledgeable, contemporary. And he's obviously highly thought of in the Vatican. They call him back about twice a year. He describes the camp here as his "contemplative office". Says he comes to work here, like other blokes go offshore to do a "swing". He says it's "intense" work – not because of the actual depth of the contemplation and prayer, but just because he's camping.'

She looks puzzled.

'Camping's often *in tents*,' explains Dylan, grimacing at the weakness of the joke.

But Kate turns to face him. Looks directly at him. 'I'm sorry about that, back there. Sorry I stepped in.'

'I can look after myself, you know.'

'I know. I've never doubted that. It's just that men like Cole rely on random acts of violence. It's their way of keeping the upper hand. Hit when it's not warranted, and hit hard. It keeps people around them nervous. Scared.'

'I'm not scared of him.'

'I know. I can see that.'

'I know some people think I'm a pushover – weak – but I'm not.'

She's wide-eyed. 'What a funny thing to say.'

'What?'

'That. That some people think you're weak.'

'You know – touchy-feely guys. Not into footy, boozing, fast cars. It's the stereotype. Embroidered jackets, blathering on about sustainability, concerned about things. I know how it looks. How it goes. I get it. I'm sure you think that... thought that.'

And Kate knows that she did think something like that in the beginning. A first email, a first meeting, a first judgement. But not now. 'Actually, I think you are one of the strongest people I've ever met.' She is surprised to hear herself say it. 'You've worked out what you believe and you stand by it. You certainly are one of the most honest people I've ever met.

Probably *the* most honest. And you've worked out who you can trust, and people trust you.'

'And I trust you,' he says to Kate. 'I know you're caught in the middle. I know you live in that government world. But I see what's inside you. Right inside you. I see it when you meet people. How you connect with them. I saw it straight away at the art centre. Whether you'd like to admit it or not, you care.'

She feels a shot of something into her veins. Some wayward chemical injected. A surge that feels like panic. She'd like to gasp for more air. She'd like to turn, so he's not looking straight at the person squirming inside her.

A basketball's springy plunk reverberates off bitumen. A lanky boy bounces it half a dozen times, then shoots at a wonky and net-less hoop. His wrist flops forward and he squints at the ball as it drifts against the cobalt sky. It doesn't touch the backboard, but drops cleanly in and hits the bitumen again, louder.

'Nice shot,' says Kate, just loud enough for him to hear. He ignores her, but a girl who has been twisting in silent dance on the court, looks up from her daydream and grins.

Other teenagers sit on a bench, knees wide, heads down, caps turned backwards. One has a Chicago Bulls singlet and they all have loose, shiny black pants. They seem encouraged, and two boys ease up and walk languidly towards the hoop. The other reaches forward and grabs the toes of his Dunlop Volleys, stretching his calf muscles before he, too, gets up.

The boy with the ball throws it flat and hard to one of the others, who bounces it twice and then lobs it high to one of the others. Then they are all standing at four-points-of-a-square, passing the ball between them with ever more inventive and elaborate moves.

Then the boy dribbles the ball in, fast and aggressive, pushes through the others, and lobs an uncanny, looping ball into the net.

'What you runnin' on bro?' another asks. 'Better get you a dope test.'

'No need,' says the girl, with a lopsided smile. 'We know he'd pass.'

'They're good.'

'Yeah, naturals,' says Dylan. 'Basketball's been a big gig in the communities for a long time. Way back, one of the first league teams was all-Aboriginal.'

'So why do they want to look like Americans?' cuts in Cole. 'A Black Power thing?'

Dylan is guarded now. 'They all see the TV, the music clips, hear the rap. It's probably just a fashion thing – most oldies despair at the younger generation's clothes at some point, I guess.' He wants to tell Cole that if your story's one of disenfranchisement, the US black movement must offer hope.

They watch the boys break into two-on-twos and one runs at the basket and launches himself through the defenders, grabbing the hoop, slam-dunking. Showing off. Doing a boy thing.

'A lot of the boys are turning back to Aussie Rules. They like the look of footy money,' adds Dylan. 'But the basketball court's somewhere to hang out. A focal point. An old-fashioned village square, I suppose.'

They chat in the shop and Cole buys a Coke and waits for the few cents to come back from the dollar coins he's handed over. 'Change comes from within,' grins the old-timer behind the counter. 'Nice try,' growls Cole, holding out his hand.

And then a hand slaps Dylan on the back. 'Hello, Uncle,' he says, without turning.

Uncle Vincent, Henny just behind him, pushes his silver Elvis sunglasses back on his head and greets Cole and Kate with a handshake and shrewd eyes full of trachoma. His face glistens with his usual oily sweat as he takes a measure of them. Henny shakes hands respectfully, uncharacteristically wordless.

'We've got a couple of hours free now,' Dylan says, 'and then Deejay's hosting dinner in the main refectory. He wants to run through a Powerpoint presentation – history of the place, developments, projected outcomes. He'll have power provision, usage and costs.'

'He seems cluey.' Cole casts new bait.

'Deejay's on top of things – we did a lot together when I was with the Scimitar Project. We put funds into cultural components of the tourism development – training and so on. He also represents the Warramorra Peninsula Indigenous Tourism Operators on state forums.'

'Tell 'em about the morning,' cuts in Vincent suddenly, drowning in all this city-speak.

'And in the morning the young lads are taking us mud-crabbing and spearfishing – those that want to go.'

'Young boys being paid to go fishing and old men being paid to tell stories. Cultural tourism happening.' They have eaten and Deejay Munumurra has shown his Powerpoint – a mixture of feel-good footage and one-liners, simplified spreadsheets and projections graphs. A bit of video of mud-crabbing trips, kayaking excursions and fishing trips mixed in.

To Cole, it doesn't add up to much more than froth and bubble – people talking themselves up. But Munumurra's someone to watch. Cole reckons first you dream it, then you talk it, and then it's reality. Simple as that.

'Aboriginal land rights have played a part in this,' Deejay says, off the cuff now. 'The "first point of contact" was forced. Business, developers and land managers suddenly had to consult traditional owners and communities. But I'd like to read you a quote from last year's state mining conference...' He digs through papers and finds a sheet. 'One of the speakers said: "A river starts with a trickle. If you have one conversation with an Aboriginal person it will undermine a dozen conceptions." I treasure that. Behind it comes the shift. One word's written more than any others in the visitors' book: "shared." The place is shared; it's a shared experience. It's our way.'

# Twenty-three

It's a funny convoy. Out front is a knocked-up Warramorra community four-wheel drive, full of young black blokes showing the shortcut to Mt Jane Station, at the bottom east end of the peninsula. Then Vincent's dilapidated dual cab straying around the sand track, radiating Henny's rap music. And in the swirling wake, a flashy LandCruiser, windows shut and air-con on.

Monaro McDay flicks the MIG welder's rod, strikes an arc and backs it in to about three millimetres from steel sheets. The metal mounts up under the rod's tip and he starts moving it, keeping a pool behind the arc, feeding in the electrode. Holding it steady. He lays down a neat-enough bead, then lifts his dark mask and turns to find the slag hammer, but instead sees vehicles arriving. A hubbub. He flips the MIG's isolator and by the time he's taken his gauntlets and leather apron off, they are all stranded in the broad, open sand patch in front of the homestead, blinking in the sunlight. The

Warramorra boys from the Troopie are already skylarking, happy to be back at the cattle station.

'Oi,' calls Monaro, industrial cut-through in the timbre of his voice.

'Boss,' they yell out, and tumble to the shed. 'How yu bin, Boss?'

Monaro's father George walked cattle in here in the 1940s, married a Warramorra woman and had three boys, the first two dying in childhood, one from dysentery, one just from the effects of diarrhoea. As a teenager, this one surviving boy dropped his Christian name, Xavier, in favour of the iconic V8 Holden he dreamed of owning and now has, shiny black and under a cotton cover in the other shed.

Fair, hard-arsed and funny as hell, Monaro has stocked up the station and is running it smart. Most of the community lads have worked for him.


'He makes a decent living, has some tourist accommodation and is pretty good at hooking into the grant system...' Dylan had said on the way down.

'He's half Aboriginal?' Kate treading carefully.

'Which half?' Cole stirring the pot.

Dylan ignores him. 'Reckons the incentives are there to use. He has a lot of the young guys in for mustering and casual work, and for work experience. He takes responsibility.'


At the beginning of the Dry season, Monaro McDay had some of the boys down from Five Turtles to make what he calls the Taj Mahal of stables and horse yards. Paid them hourly for a long, slow job. They built a huge tack room, tie-up and wash-down area, a round yard and a separate breaking yard, and then a lot of stables and small home paddocks.

'He didn't really need any of it,' explains Dylan. 'Monaro likes to get groups of the young guys down to work with horses. Sends them out to muster a few brumbies, then helps them break and educate them. He does it to give them some excitement and put them in touch with another part of their history.' The old Aboriginal stockmen were skilled and respected, but got thrown off when they got equal pay in the sixties. Even Mt Jane couldn't afford them. 'Those old boys are something to be proud of.'

Monaro has had old pictures of the local stockmen printed up and hung them around the social room at the stables. Black and white, ragged edged, you can't miss the glint of dignity.

Monaro McDay doesn't wait for things to happen, he just gets them done. And, he reckoned, considering solar panels had been around since his old man set up here, the time had come. He put in fifty-six photovoltaics over three years, still with the genny to back them up, but only occasionally with its six flap windows propped up and fumes pouring from its big exhaust pipe. The place runs pretty much on the sun.

Peacocks rustle across the reticulated lawn, their gigantic petticoats folded back, as Ree McDay brings out double-handled, bucket-sized pots of tea, trays full of mismatched mugs and basins of sugar. Two of the community boys jump up to help her and carry plates of warm biscuits and homemade lemonade, ice blocks percussing in the tall glass jugs. They all sit on benches down long tables in the shade of the trees that George McDay planted.

Now, outside the red high-tide line on his map, Cole becomes effusive, egged on by McDay's no-nonsense toughness. Monaro is telling him that he should come up for a muster, and Jack says he might just do that.

Kate and Dylan exchange a glance, and Vincent sees it between them.

They leave the Warramorra boys there to muck around the stables and camp overnight. Monaro has a killer beast hanging in the meat room and promises a cook-up.

'And some singing,' chimes up one.

'And singing,' agrees Monaro, always happy to crank up his Fender and sing, in a raw voice, his own songs of musters and cattle drives, and Dreamtime spirits.

Cole shakes hands with Monaro and jumps into the front passenger seat, still chatting through the window he winds down when Dylan turns the key.

When Uncle Vincent finally coaxes Henny out of the mob, the LandCruiser is way ahead, its dust almost settled.

'We've lost 'em,' shouts Henny over the diesel engine and washboard rattle.

'I know where Carter's Ford is,' assures Vincent.

Kate shifts in the back seat so she's sitting sideways, staring out of the window, just watching the country. Staring out of the same little spot in the glass, she sees landscape file past. A blur of low trees, rocky hillocks and grasses. She likes the blur. It's what she needs now. It gives the impression of being endless and seems to connect the billions of years of the life of the planet with her own fleeting life.

The span of one existence is from the beginning of your everything to the end of it. An exhaustive entirety. But even epic moments for one human being don't measure on the planetary timescale.

The view becomes a smudge of tawny, gold and ochre.

'Kate,' calls back Cole. 'We'll spend a couple of hours going through some things this evening.' A glance at the Rolex Oyster. 'It's two o'clock now...there around four...say we clean up and schedule 5pm to 7pm, then have dinner together.'

Making it clear that Dylan is not included.

'I'll tell the Minister you need "overtime".' Letting her know who's in charge.

Dylan thinks back to Suzy – wants to warn Kate – but when he manages to catch her eye in the rear-view mirror, her resolute confidence reassures him.

On the sign which says WELCOME TO CARTER'S FORD, someone has now scrawled YOU'RE in front. 'We'll do a lap before checking in at the hotel,' says Dylan. 'See a bit of the place.'

Australia's greatest wild waterway, the Duncan River, and this natural crossing of it, spawned and shaped the settlement. Originally there were two tribal groups, edging either bank, but desert migration, marriage, ritual trading and totemic affiliations brought others to the valley. Drawn, too, by bush foods and medicines. There has always been fishing with traps, nets (even those still made from rolled and soaked grasses), lines and using bush poison. Majarla trees cut into logs; then they'd all sit round the edge of a pool, pounding the bark off and making a soapy lather. Its red stain spread over the surface, and eventually the fish came up, just floating there dead. More than this, the Duncan River was induced and produced by the Dreaming, and in it lives an intricate cast of mythic beings; water snakes, living rainbow serpents.

The river is crucial for ceremonies linked to death and mourning, and its rainbow serpents intrinsic to the reproduction of water; indispensable in the lives of animals, birds and plants. Children still learn on family fishing trips, and social security payments are supplemented with fish, eels, prawns and mussels. Ancient and modern. Practical and spiritual. For traditional Indigenous people, it's all one and Dylan tries to catch the power of it in words.

Just as tribal clans had gravitated to the natural crossing of the Duncan River, the first white settlers found they could get supply trains across it for most of the year. Always a place at a crossroads.

There are a few messy locals outside the hotel. You're welcome to Carter's Ford, alright, Cole thinks. A hotbed of Indigenous drug taking, glue sniffing, petrol abuse and alcoholism. They even scull mouthwash, for Chrissake. A breeding ground for domestic violence, suicide, child sex and incest. *How do you know when it's time for bed in Carter's Ford? The big hand touches the little hand…*as the local saying goes.

It sucks up government money that doesn't make a jot of difference. Give them new houses and they pull them apart and burn them. Give them new vehicles and they're abandoned when the first tank of fuel runs out. Or so the stories go.

The place is a disaster, Cole reckons, and a lake on its doorstep'd clean it up.

'I'm not glossing over the problems,' Dylan is saying, pulling into the hotel. 'I'm just saying that there are plenty of people here just looking after their families, bringing up their children and trying to give them a future – despite generational disenfranchisement.' He turns the engine off.

'Look at Vincent Yimi. People like that are doing all they can to improve things. Make a better future.'

'So, what makes him tick?' asks Kate. 'What motivates him?'

'I can't speak for him on that – but he might tell you himself, if he trusts you.' He pauses and turns to her. 'His trust is a big thing to earn.'

But Cole isn't listening anymore. Since they drove into reception range, his smartphone has flooded with messages, emails and missed calls. He's bent forward over it, stroking through them, tapping out answers with his thumbs, increasingly agitated. Fired up. And then he comes to one that he can't answer on the run. 'Hell.' He spits it.

'Problem?' asks Dylan, looking back at him in the mirror.

Cole doesn't even raise his eyes.

# Twenty-four

'Something's come up that I have to deal with in person,' Cole announces that evening. 'My assistant has a light plane lined up to take me back to Shoal Bay in the morning, so I can catch an early flight down to the city.' It has all been scheduled so that he can be with his lawyers for the afternoon, going through legal contracts that have just been delivered, out of the blue, to his office. Only his autograph can clinch a land deal he's been pushing through for a year and he doesn't want a moment's delay in finalising it. It's a slippery one and could too easily steal away from his grasp. 'I'll be back late afternoon the next day.' To Kate and Dylan, there is no explanation and apology. 'I'll be away a night. I'm sure you two can amuse yourselves.' With big financial fish to fry, he really doesn't care what they do.

Kate settles to spend the evening in her room going through work emails. Dylan talks for half an hour to his mother and then to Mitchell, who sounds stronger and says 'everything's calmed down.' Then he knocks on Kate's door, apologises for interrupting her, and says he's got some ideas for tomorrow.

'I was just going to hang around here tomorrow,' she says. 'To be honest, I could do with a breather from our Mr Cole. I probably shouldn't say that. But it's a bit tense in the car.'

'I hope that's not my fault,' Dylan says earnestly. 'I'm doing my best…'

'No, it's not your fault. We're just a funny old crew.'

But what she doesn't tell him is that most of the tension is that of a hidden deceit, and it is deep within her. Spumy chat about sustainable power belies the darker depths of the dam project. But she knows it is there, and the dichotomy stirs conflicts within her. Isn't a bit of dishonesty a normal part of everyday life? Little white lies. Doesn't it keep society going? Prevent personal hurt and lubricate business – and government, for that matter? Wouldn't you lie to save someone's feelings, or a deal? But now she is starting to see an honesty the existence of which she had never even imagined. A sort of calm, penetrating, all-pervading, drenching, relentless, brutal honesty. The sort of honesty that makes the cells of your body fit together. It feels totally natural and, she is surprised to think, if you lived within it, it'd be the most comfortable coat to wear. But to take it on and off, get wrapped up in it when it suits and take it off and hang it up when it is inconvenient…well, that must be damaging, confusing, dangerous. And she feels the possibility of all of these now, and she sees two paths ahead.

'His absence doesn't really throw out our plans much,' Dylan is saying. 'We can work around it. He'll be back for the community meeting. It's 7pm, so that doesn't need changing, thankfully. We've got a lot of people organised to come. I was going to show you Minjubal country before that, but we can do that afterwards. Uncle Vincent's flexible. He won't mind.'

'Well, I've got plenty of emails to keep me busy tomorrow, to be honest,' Kate says, drawn back to the self she has known best, but hearing the words as if they are spoken out loud by a stranger. 'Though that's the last thing I want to do.' And then, mostly to herself, she adds, 'It suddenly all seems such...dross.'

'We're just keeping ourselves busy until we die,' Dylan says.

'That's a rather cynical view, isn't it?'

'If you like. Anything urgent?'

'No. Just the usual stuff.'

'Well,' he says, 'if it can wait, I've got another idea...'

'What is it?'

'A surprise.'

'Oh?'

'No – it's a surprise...'

'Aaargh,' she says, and play-punches him on the bicep. It pulls them both up, as if it's the most intimate physical moment each has ever experienced.


When Dylan suggested it, Vincent said yeah, he'd like to join them for breakfast the next morning, and the three of them now sit out early on a verandah by gaudy bougainvillea and under thin wisteria. Kate is picking through a bowl of fruit and Dylan is spreading Vegemite on his dry toast when Vincent, already on his third mug of sweet black tea, abruptly pushes his chair back and announces he's off to the buffet. He comes back with a plate piled high – a mountain of scrambled eggs, mushrooms that've been doing backstroke in butter, half-tomatoes grilled with a cheese-slice topping, four chipolatas and a pile of bacon.

'Getting value for my money,' chips Dylan.

'Killing the pig,' Vincent grins, folding a rasher with his knife, slipping it into his mouth and then whipping the empty fork from his mouth with a flourish, brandishing it best-parlour style. 'You seen The Simpsons on TV?' he says, mouth still half-full, but a hand in front of it. 'Seen that one where Homer's getting Bart to eat bad stuff? "Butter up that bacon boy" – "but Dad, my heart hurts," Bart says – "live under my roof, live by my rules."' Laughing like a pork chop. 'I s'pose you shouldn't laugh, with obesity and all that,' he says, 'but it's funny-as.'

They sit back and the morning and breakfasty scents fold together in one delicious, quiet moment.

'So, the surprise,' says Vincent abruptly. 'It's just a spot we're going to take you to. But it's a significant place. Not everyone gets to go there – not every white person, anyways. It's where three songlines cross.'

'I've heard of songlines. Wasn't there a book about them?' says Kate.

'Yeah, I heard-a that book, but haven't read it.'

'By an English writer,' says Dylan, and it sounds vaguely disapproving.

'That's alright. Everyone entitled to their say – their take on things.'

'But isn't this Aboriginal business?' asks Kate. 'I'd have thought you wouldn't like someone else writing a book about your business.'

'Nah,' says Vincent. 'It's not just Aboriginal business – it's human business. Henny, he plays the drums but he's not

African. The other boys play guitars but they're not Spanish. We're one big race – gotta get over all the small stuff. Take songlines,' he says. 'We call 'em songlines, but other people follow a path. A destiny. No big difference. We've all got beliefs of one sort or another – or, at least, the fortunate do. More than anything, I believe in belief.'

He smiles at the point.

'Anyways, this won't get the baby bathed. Let's get going, you slackers.' And Vincent dramatically scrapes back his chair, stands and hauls up the waistband of his sagging jeans with his thumbs, turns and starts to stomp off. 'I'll tell you about songlines down the track,' he says, businesslike, over his shoulder. Then he turns back, gently, to Kate. 'You'll need your toothbrush and any other lady-stuff for overnight.'

Dylan goes to the kitchen door and carries out an esky that the cook has loaded up from his fridges. He carries it round, puts it on the red dirt next to the tray of Vincent's dual cab, and reaches in to make space for it.

'Gotta bit of stuff in there,' says Vincent, coming towards him with a rolling gait, legs bowed, standing up the collar of his vivid blue workshirt and flattening its front down.

'It's a disgrace,' scolds Dylan. 'Needs a good clear-out. I'll do it for you.'

'Nah,' says Vincent. 'Nature abhors a void. Clean that lot out and more'll come. You mark my words.' And he reaches in and pushes stuff aside. 'There. It'll fit nicely, see.'

Dylan has already added his and Kate's swags to Vincent's. There's a cooking plate wrapped in newspapers, with an occy strap round it, a long fork and a couple of blackened stainless-steel billy cans – one big, the other huge. Water's in a jerry can and there's a cardboard box full of mismatched enamel plates, mugs, knives and forks – a jumble-sale of them, all chucked in together.

Kate comes down the stairs from her room and sees Dylan and Vincent working quietly together. There's a synchronicity that's so pleasant.

'We're taking your car then, Vincent?' she asks.

'Yeah, he wants to,' answers Dylan.

'It's better for us,' is all that Vincent will offer, ignoring the too-white gleam of the big, hired four-wheel drive next to them. 'You're in the front with me,' he says to Kate as she crosses the wide, parking area. 'I'm just making some room in the tray for *him*.'

'*You know how many whitefellas die every year like that? Well, I can tell you it's a damned lot...*' says Dylan, mimicking Henny.

'Alright. Alright,' says Uncle Vincent. 'Yer just a little tacker. You can ride in the cab. But in the back.'

As Vincent Yimi drives, hands hooked over the top of the wheel, craning forward as if he was seeing things in another way, another dimension, he says that songlines go straight through this country, across Plumtree Plains one way and right out past Langgi Langgi Station the other. 'From generation to generation, they stay the same.

'A straight line. Linking place to place. Linking this moment to the past.' He draws his right index finger horizontal through the air before him as if to emphasise it. Clarify and cement it.

His eyes are fixed on the horizon, and he speaks low and evenly, as if praying. 'Songlines connect us to all things. They're that important. There are creation songlines and songlines drawn on the country itself – the ones that take us from place to place. They bring us shelter, food and protection from harm, in both the physical and spirit worlds.

'And this place you're going to see, it's special because three songlines meet there. This is where they cross.' Vincent pauses, thinking for an example. 'You know when people sing really nice. Sometimes when there are three perfect voices in harmony, they fit so well together – resonate – that you think you can hear a fourth. And that one's the harmonic. It's like when two people really love each other – in a good way, love each other. They're more than just two individuals. If you add them up they seem to be more than two. Well, the same's true with songlines. When everything's done well and there's harmony, they are powerful for good.

'By singing songlines we can cross big distances. You sing the songs in sequence, see, and they show you the way. Rivers, rocks, hills, the sky, the stars. They're all in the songs. But the most important things to learn in the songs are the spiritual sites – significant ancestoral sites. That's why we gotta keep singing them. We elders gotta pass the songlines on, and we all got to keep singing the land, to keep the Dreaming of the ancestors alive. Then they can guide us through life.'

'I think I see,' says Kate.

'And it's not just us Aborigines,' says Uncle Vincent. 'I reckon it's everyone, in their way. We all gotta sing our own song. We all follow songlines, of sorts. And we can all hear when the song's no good. We know when we're singing with the wrong people or we're forcing ourselves to sing a part someone else has written. See, we can sing their song, and not our own, but it won't work forever. You gotta sing your own song. Follow your own songline. Harmony and dischord – well, that depends on who we meet on the journey. But we've got choices. Find harmony with yourself. We gotta aim for a sweet harmony.' And by now, Vincent's words are like a song, his voice low and steady, chanting, cooing.

He suddenly turns to look directly at her. 'You following your own songline, or singing someone else's, Kate?'

She meets his gaze but isn't sure what he knows, what he feels, what he guesses.

They drive on to a big area between rising rocks and punctuated with boab trees. Uncle Vincent explains that this is the spot where, last year, nearly 5,000 Kimberley Aborigines met and camped for two weeks to practise and reinvigorate law and culture. 'They came from all over,' he says. 'From saltwater country to desert and river people.' And here, under this tree, elders sat. 'Right here.' And little people, who are often seen in traditional Aboriginal life, told them this wasn't their area. 'Not their country.' So the elders embarked on a smoking ceremony. He tells Kate how, for those big gatherings, they might use leaves and branches from the konkerberry and wood from the majarla tree for smoke. 'Specially for ritual healing.'

Vincent stoops around with his rolling gait and tall, dusty Akubra, collecting spinifex and eucalypt branches. He calls to the spirits – a high, demanding, strident call. Seems to be talking directly to them. He lights the spinifex and summons them through it, one by one. Smoking them. A traditional ceremony.

He tells them that culture is strong here. Most boys still go through initiation.

Then he climbs the rocks and brings a small nub of dark spinifex wax, collected by ants and stuck to the rock. It is traditionally used to glue spearheads to shafts, patch cracks, cover wounds. He shows a sandpaper tree, with leaves like wet-and-dry. He points to a huge boab tree shattered to a stump by lightning.

'There are plenty of stories around here,' Uncle Vincent suddenly says, turning to Kate. 'Other stories that need to be told in their country. But it's too early in the season, after a big Wet, to get into that country.' He smiles at her. 'When you come back,' he says. 'And you will come back.'

'Will I?'

'Oh, yeah,' he says.

And then Vincent leads them to sit in the dirt, in the solid shade of the shattered boab. He looks at the ground and says to Kate, 'You want to know what's going on inside here?' He taps his own head. 'Well, it's the same as going on inside here,' and he taps his heart. 'Young-fella-Dylan says there's things you want to know, and I'm gonna tell you.' And he lets his head sink on his shoulders and talks in a low, slow voice, almost as if he's in a trance.

And he tells this story...

——

The boy was ten and a friend of Vivienne Yalani's twelve-year-old niece. He liked to hang around the Duncan River. It was where he was happiest. It felt like his place. Some old bloke gave him a four-foot throw-net to get the hang of and he'd learnt how to cast it. Then he'd found an old six-footer in a yard, not too bust-up, and his Aunty Cissy showed him how to fix the holes in it. It was a handful to begin with, that big net, but he carefully did just the same as he'd learned. He looped the end of its rope around his left wrist and gathered the line in coils in that hand until he was holding the top of the net. Then take hold of the middle of the net in his left hand and drape it over that hand too. Spread the net, pick up a loop of the line of lead weights around the net's edge and sit it on the fingers of his left hand. Another loop and another loop. Then he'd gather half of the remaining net and throw it, right hand over left, like a flock of little corellas rising. The delicate sequence culminating in this controlled explosion. It landed, almost every time, with the lead line in a big, neat circle, hitting the surface in one ring. It sank, catching everything on its slow, descending path to the bottom of the river. He sometimes wondered what it must look like from below – for some fish or yabbie or shrimp looking up, seeing a big, white cloud above it. Seeing it blanketing out the world. As the boy pulled in the net, nice and slowly, nice and steadily, letting the lead weights drag over the bottom until they all closed together. The terrible claustrophobia of entrapment; the being relentlessly pulled from its own element. From the river it knew to somewhere else. He thought he understood a feeling of such helplessness. Hopelessness.

To white people, he was Vincent's nephew, but under Aboriginal kinship he was his son. He was a good boy and everyone liked him. He was interested in his culture; good on the computer. He worked hard at school, adults thought he was kind and sensible, his friends thought he was cool. He hadn't argued with anyone, he didn't sniff or smoke, but one morning he hanged himself. He was one of four of Vincent's tribal sons and daughters who did it in a year. Four of the eight children in Duncan River valley in that year. Eight children in one high school.

'Fact is, a kid commits suicide almost every week in Western Australia. One in four young people'll have a depressive disorder by the end of their adolescence. Not just our kids – white kids, too. How do we elders – black and white – live with that?

'How do I live with knowing I didn't see it in my boy? Didn't help him enough?'

And then, right out of the blue, Vincent struggles to his feet, rolls around on his stiff legs, and announces: 'I'm off.'

'Off?'

'Yep, off out of it.'

'I thought we were camping here, Uncle.'

'We was. You are. I'm off.' He reaches into the tray. 'Here.' He lifts out a big, blue esky. 'Here's your tea. You got your swags. I'll pick you up in the morning.'

'We can't stay here without you.'

'What you scared of? Boogie-man?' HA! He laughs at that.

'No, but we need you here.'

'If you think I'm gonna babysit two grown adults when I've got things to do, you got another think coming.'

'What things?'

'Well, there's rumblings over the community meeting. People don't always like city folk coming up here having their say. Even if it's good news. They don't trust them. No-one gets something for nothing. They think there must be something going on in the background.' And then he lifts his voice. 'Is there something going on in the background?'

And he swings and looks directly into Dylan's eyes. The young man meets his stare. 'No, Uncle. There's nothing going on. It's just all good news.'

'Right, well if you say that – and I can see the truth in you, boy – then that's what I'll tell 'em. I believe you, they'll believe me, and they'll come.'

Vincent doesn't turn towards Kate. Only in his peripheral vision does he watch her looking at the ground.

'OK, but we should come too,' says Dylan. 'We can't camp here for the night. The two of us.'

'What – you need a chaperone?' says Vincent. He looks at Kate and chuckles, 'I think I can trust her.' Then back to Dylan, 'And you – you just be on best behaviour.'

Dylan turns to Kate to say, 'What do you think? Are you OK with this? Should we go back with him? Is it inappropriate?'

And she smiles and says, distracted, 'No – as long as it's OK to stay here, I'm happy to stay. I've never slept outside like this before. Under the stars.' She turns to Vincent, 'and especially here. I really do thank you, Vincent. As long as you say it's safe.' And then she hears herself say, 'I don't just mean snakes. I mean safe spiritually…' and thinks how uncharacteristic it sounds, even to her. Perhaps she has some strange notion of an ancestor looking into a dark corner of her heart.

'Yeah, you're safe from the spirits,' Uncle Vincent says. 'And as for him…' He glances with playful reproachful towards Dylan. 'Reckon you can trust him, at least spiritually.'

And with that, Vincent heaves his bulk into the driver's seat of the dual cab and cranks the engine. Over the rattly noise of it, he booms, 'don't do nothing I wouldn't do,' laughs like a donkey, and bolts off with a jerk of the clutch before Kate's even had time to answer.

'He's a lovely bloke until you get to know him...' says Dylan, watching him go.

Then he turns to Kate. 'I didn't know he was going to do this. It's not a set-up. I wouldn't do anything like that.'

———

The southern sky wheels over them in a slow arc, pinpricks of brilliance against velvetine. They sleep separate but close enough that they could reach out and touch fingertips. Close enough to talk in whispers.

'Are you awake?' And hers is such a low whisper.

There is almost no pause. 'Yes.' He's awake. He seems to be always awake. Someone once told him, 'You don't seem to sleep, just wait'. The truth is that he lies in the dark, comfortable, for hours (or maybe it's minutes, he thinks) and lets the night wash around him and through him, and it's as good as sleep. And, wherever he is – however tired, however relaxed – he'll get up three, probably four times, and maybe walk outside and see how the night weather is, and stand in the warm humidity of summer, or under cold clouds scudding past the neon moon in winter, and be glad he nightly sees this part of the cycle, too. Glad that he lives a full life – the light and the dark are all part of the same day, just calling on different senses to be seen.

'Do you know any of the stars?' she asks. 'Is that the Southern Cross down there, by my feet? I think it is.'

'Yes,' he says, 'that's the Southern Cross. To the south.' It will simply revolve around the feet pointing towards it. Circumpolar. 'It's properly called Crux, for the Latin cross,' he says. 'But I always think it looks more like an old-fashioned kite. You remember, like we made as children – brown paper, glue, two thin garden canes, a long tail and twisty newspaper bowties to make it fly.'

'We never did that. At least I didn't. I don't remember Andrew doing anything like that, either.'

'Andrew?'

'My brother. He's a lawyer now, in Scotland. I don't think he ever made a kite.'

'Pity,' he says. 'It was great fun. My dad was always doing stuff like that with me. He always had a project up his sleeve. On picnics, he'd get out a bow saw and some strong string and we'd cut green branches and make bows. He cut this sort of notch in the ends and bent them. They worked a treat.' He pauses, letting the stars take him back to early days, too. 'I'm sure it was all for me, but he loved it, too.'

'Sounds lovely,' she says.

'And I've looked up at the Southern Cross a few times with him.' Another pause. 'It's the smallest of the eighty-eight modern constellations.'

'Really?' Surprised by the sudden burst of science.

'Yep. You see the five stars in it. Well, the main three are – let me see – Acrux, Mimosa and Delta Crucis. I do know that they're all between ten and twenty million years old. The two pointers are Alpha Centauri and Beta Centauri.'

Dylan raises an arm and starts pointing around. 'Mars and Saturn to the west. Pluto.' He carefully points out the constellation of Orion, with his belt and dagger, and Lepus just above it. Taurus next to it.

'Like the horoscopes.'

'Yep, Taurus the bull. Then Aries,' he points, 'Pisces.'

'Your star sign?'

'No, I'm a Cancerian. Late June. But see there – Sagittarius, my favourite.'

'You have favourites?' She sounds dreamy, half-asleep now.

'Oh yes,' he says. 'Can I tell you the story about it?'

'Please do,' she says. So this is what it was like, a bedtime story.

'Not boring you?'

'No – it's lovely.'

'You see at the top there, well that's Lambda Sagitarii. And there are clusters, if you can see them. One of those is the closest and biggest in our galaxy. One has more than a hundred stars, two thousand light-years away, in curving chains and arcs. And Sagittarius is in a region of the Galactic Centre, thirty thousand light-years away. At the heart of that is a black hole three million times the size of our Sun. Imagine that.'

'I can't,' she says, but she sounds mostly asleep.

'But it's not all that that I really love. It's the stories of Sagittarius. It is the centaur of Babylonian mythology. The Milky Way – you see it – is at its widest, densest and brightest in Sagittarius. In various cultures it's seen as a bridge between Heaven and Earth. A river. The Chinese call it the River of Heaven. I can't remember their words for it. I remember that the Arabs call it Al Nahr – the river. In New Zealand, Maori call it the Long Fish…'

His lullaby voice has trailed off into a hush, and it seems that silent stories now tell themselves to the night in the echo of his words. He hears her breathing gently near him. He knows that he is falling in love with her – as she is now, this gentle person sleeping so elegantly, beautifully, in the night beside him. Here, under the River of Heaven.

Another time she wakes briefly and thinks its funny lying so close to a man like this. All alone, in a strangely romantic place, yet he hasn't tried it on. He's interested – she can surely sense that – but he hasn't made a move. He won't make a move. It seems so absolutely alien to everything – *every man* – she's ever known. She feels safe with him.

He hears her wake with a start. He hears her voice sound in the breath snatches.

'Are you alright?'

'Mmm,' she says. 'I had a dream. A nightmare.'

'What was it?'

'There must be snakes here. What if they come into our swags?'

'Was that the dream?' he asks.

'No, but it had a sort-of snake in it, and it made me think of that.'

'Don't worry about snakes,' he says. 'We'll be fine out here in the open tonight. But tell me about the dream. It might help.'

'It was just a sort-of snake shape,' she says again. 'Like a grey, shaded pencil shape, really. Like it was on paper. Not a real one. But not really a drawn one. It looked at me. It had bright, ruby eyes.'

'Too many stories,' he said.

'It didn't try to bite me,' she says, and he can sense that she is losing the image – that the dream is drifting away from her consciousness. 'It looked at me. It made me feel guilty.'

And he knows that she's actually asleep again; talking in her sleep.

And then she breathes sleep again, but with little jumps and starts as she dreams that her body turns to a sort-of milky turquoise mercury, from the bottom upwards. As if the feet, the legs, the torso, the arms just dissolve into liquid and stream away from her. As if some dam inside her is breached and everything she has been dissolves, and this liquid breaks through, and she flows like the water itself. She flows like the river.


At each waking, the constellations have moved. They judder across the sky; another step, another step at each waking. Crux spinning, Orion cartwheeling, the great planets cloaking themselves in night, to reveal themselves again a handspan away; the great magicians of the night sky. She wakes again, and her now conscious self has decided to tell Dylan about the dam, the water pipeline, the whole thing.

But she doesn't know the first words – how to start – and in those moments it all comes crashing in. The reality of the conversation, all her fears, the guilt, the repercussions – and the disloyalty, too. Doing the right thing, doing the wrong thing. It all makes her shudder.

'Are you cold? It's cooled down quite a bit,' he whispers.

'No,' she says, all the resolve gone from her at the sound of his voice.

'Perhaps someone walked over your grave.'

'Perhaps someone did.' And she turns away from him, and looks across the dark shapes of the rocks, the trees, the planet itself, and into the great, fleecy dark abyss curving beyond.

Yes, at each waking, the constellations have moved – the staccato night of drifty sleep and the moving sky. The night has cooled, but he senses her warmth so near to him.

'Dylan?' It is the tiniest whisper.

'Yes.'

But she pauses. Perhaps she just wanted to check he was still there. Perhaps she just wanted to say his name.

'Yes, Kate,' he repeats.

'It's funny isn't it. Being here like this. Where three songlines cross. Where two destinies cross.' She's silent for just a few seconds. 'Not "funny". That's the wrong word. A stupid word. I am just trying to say that – well – I think this is probably the most amazing night of my life.'

The most intense, gentle, spiritual, sublime night.

He doesn't need to answer.

———

In the morning, they move around the little campsite, consummated by the night. With a new synchronicity. Not needing to speak.

'Got over the nightmare?' he asks eventually.

'What nightmare?'

'You woke once with something in your head. If you've forgotten it, it's nothing.'

'Oh,' she says. 'Yes – whatever it was, it's not there now. Well, not consciously.'

And it seems that, just for this moment, in her being she's both more conscious and more unconscious – more simply living, feeling, moving – than she's ever been. As if you could ever explain that to anyone.


They have supped down their first mug of tea and Dylan is tending toast over the coals when he hears an engine. The unmistakeable rough-running of Vincent's four-wheel drive. The sound grows until it drowns the chatter of finches.

The window is wound down, and eventually Dylan can hear the high-treble sound of his cassette player, '...Just turn me loose, let me straddle my old saddle, underneath the western skies...'

And then Vincent singing along, '...and gaze at the moon till I lose my senses, I can't look at hobbles and I can't stand fences...*don't fence me in...*'


Vincent Yimi's capacity for imbibing tea is the stuff of legend. 'How do you take it?' Kate asks.

'Black and by the bucketful,' he replies. 'Sleep alright?' He says it matter-of-factly.

'Yes.' But there's hesitation in it.

'Something up?'

'I was a bit worried about snakes. I had a bad dream about one.'

'Generally they won't bother you, unless they have cause. Except with these two fellas once...' Vincent has dropped his voice to add to the drama, and Dylan catches the glint in his eye.

'What happened to them?'

'They was just two fellas camping in the bush. And one gets bit by a snake, see. Right there...' he points, '...on his arse. Serious bite, too. So the other bloke goes off and radios the Flying Doc and they say he has to cut the wound and suck the poison out. And when this fella gets back, his mate asks him what they said. *You're gonna die!*' Uncle Vincent Yimi roars at the old joke.

'I don't think they advise "cut-and-suck" any more,' says Dylan, playfully. 'It's all pressure wrapping and demobilisation.'

'Prob'ly,' says Vincent. 'But spoils a damned good story.'

'Well, there were no snakes last night,' says Dylan. 'Plenty of stars though. A big skyful. We kept waking and watching them.'

'Ancestors' campfires,' Vincent says, turning to Kate. 'That's what we think. They'd be looking down on you. They knew you were there – I told 'em. Sleeping in snatches makes you realise how big a day is...*what a difference a day makes...*'

'Look out, he's going to sing again...' warns Dylan, appearing from behind a bush with his toothbrush and a mug now empty of water.

'Hey, there's nothing wrong with my singing, cheeky young pup.'

Mock applause, 'We bring you *Vincent Yimi and the Heartbreakers*...and the crowd goes wild ...'

Vincent rounds on him in a slow, considered manner. 'Well, you *have* got up bushy-tailed this morning.' Fires a friendly warning shot. 'So, you want to chat or hear the news?'

'News, please.' Dylan knows when to back off.

'Well, it's all good.'

'The meeting?' asks Kate, and they both hear the shift in her voice, back to business.

'They're all coming. I reckon a hundred or so. They're all keen to hear now.'

'Not worried about the government thing?' asks Dylan.

'Tumblers and jugglers – always got to worry about them. But we'll all be there for the meeting.'

Jack Cole arrives at the community centre hall straight from the plane, pinstripe-trousered, sharp shoes shining, circles of sweat under the arms of his white business shirt, to a cacophony of scraping chairs. Mobs gather in corners, nodding, saying each other's names. Reaffirming connections. Tracing histories. Kids run around, boys with their arms stretched out, air-planing in wild arcs, or stopping, knees bent, stick in hand, to gun someone down. Girls skip, one with a pink ribbon, another singing a snatch of a pop song and dancing like in the video.

Henny and his mates stand by a wall, larking, checking out the girls who gather in tight, circling shoals, flashing glances from under long lashes, and giggling together. The young blokes from the cattle stations in scuffed boots with Cuban heels and two belts, one through denim loops, the other slung low under it. A fashion.

At tables to one side, station folk, local government types, and two people in khaki from a university, doing a cultural values study in the valley; a professor clad in new and neat khaki and his doctorate student. Next to them, at another table, two women and a young man, his rough blond hair pulled back into a high ponytail. The women are in identical light-blue shirts and cream moleskins – something like a uniform. The older woman has a big file open on the table in front of her, with half a ream of printed sheets fanned like a big deck of cards, and another closed next to it. The other woman – about Dylan's age – has a laptop open, its screen glowing. A little Aboriginal boy stands beside her, mouth gaping, mesmerised, watching, waiting, until he realises the computer's gameless and, clearly stumped by the pointlessness of that, bursts into action and returns to his run-around mates.

Dylan sees all this as he walks down the side of the hall to the front. As he passes the women, he notices that the laptop's screensaver matches that of the sticker on the front of the closed file next to it: *Wildlife Preservation Society of Australia.*

And, as he passes the back of the younger woman, whose hair is dyed more auburn than is natural and cut in a severe and business-like sharp-edged bob, he catches a familiar scent – a musky perfume which his senses know so well that it touches every nerve end and fires a little spark. It makes him look again at the back of her, but without recognition.

On the low stage, Vincent already sits next to Kate, who has her own laptop on her knees and is staring into it. Dylan stands off to the side.

Cole takes the three steps onto the platform and, without greeting, takes his place next to Kate. He stage-whispers 'go alright last night?' without looking sideways, and without that much interest; a random destabiliser. He barks 'table' to Dylan and, when a small, chipped white table has been carried up, Cole empties half the files from his briefcase and sets up.

When he's had the nod, Vincent eventually shouts above the din. 'Right, you mob. Quieten down.' And gradually they do. 'By way of introduction, this here is Mr Jack Cole, who's going to tell us about the government's plans to give us new power that means we won't have to buy diesel any more.' He points at Cole with a sharp finger, so there's no doubt. 'And this here is Kate, who's working alongside him.' And he points again. 'And this here is Dylan, who's showing them around our place.' A nod with the point. 'And you all know me.'

The khaki professor raises a hand.

'What's this?' Vincent looks affronted. 'We ain't started yet.'

'Professor George Sleeman,' he announces himself formally as he stands. 'I am conducting a cultural values study in this region.' He pauses. 'Just a matter of order, Mr Chairman,' he continues, 'I think for the sake of the Minutes perhaps you should state your own name and credentials.' The room erupts and as he sits under the weight of it, he murmurs with far less volume '...as a matter of record...'

'Why,' screeches a woman near him. 'That's old Vincent. He's a boss man. We all knows 'im, alright.'

And there's howling laughter. It eggs her on. 'In fact,' she says, 'he's related to most of us, and had relations with the rest.' There are whooping cheers. She circles, waving, then sits.

'Just settle down you lot. This is serious business.'

'Ooooh-eeeh,' comes a chorus and then, indeed, they do quieten down. Women slouch, looking elsewhere but letting it all go in. Passing children are grabbed by a thin bicep and unceremoniously grounded to the floor, where they instantly settle to more silent play, and men stand with hands in pockets, heads hung almost to their chests. Henny holds a flat hand in front of his mouth to whisper a joke to the mate beside him.

Cole stands, spreads his hands wide and leans forward to hold either side of the table, looks down at his papers, and then up at the crowd. He looks for all the world like a wartime prime minister about to address his cabinet, and he slowly draws himself up to his full height. 'Good evening… and thank you…Mr Chairman.' Cole is going to play this by the rules. Cool, calm, detailed, totally professional, in control.

He lays out the solar power plan in concise words – emphasising the government's commitment to community benefit, touching on the technical, outlining criteria, telling them there are information sheets with details on how to comment or apply. He does it all calmly, smoothly and (surprising to him) without interruption. Then he slides into a bit of feel-good government spin to wrap up, and Vincent is out of his seat to thank him and ask for questions.

Without standing, a woman screeches, 'What's the catch?'

Cole is unperturbed. 'Madam,' he says. 'This is simply exemplary, visionary government.' He likes that line.

Kate has not been called upon to speak, and is thankful. She has sat mostly with the laptop shut, her hands folded on it, looking at the back of the hall, just above the attendees' heads, their faces just out of focus.

'He's good,' Vincent whispers to Dylan as he steps from the stage.

'Oh yes,' replies Dylan. 'He's good.'

'All OK with little Katie?'

'I think so. She seems pretty quiet.'

Yimi doesn't answer.

'I guess she's just leaving it to him,' says Dylan, filling in the gap.

As Cole marches from the stage, he is greeted by a half-moon of people with specific questions. 'Do we qualify?' 'Are you coming out to my place?'

He calls Kate over with a glance, and she takes up station just beside him, handing out information sheets and taking details. He clearly loves it. It's like the media doorstop interviews the pollies face every day; attention that he envies.

'So, it's all good news.' The female voice behind him is instantly fused with the latent memory that the perfume excited, resolving it in one word.

Dylan spins on his heels, saying simultaneously, 'Jules.' She stands before him – the woman from the table, with harsh haircut and uniform, whom he had not recognised from behind.

'Hello, Dylan,' she says. 'I was looking forward to seeing you. I'm surprised you recognised me.' Aware of the changes in herself.

'Of course I recognised you.' And then he admits, 'I smelt it was you, actually.'

'*Sorry?*' A theatrical indignation.

'The perfume. You still use the same perfume.'

'You recognised my perfume? Isn't that funny,' she says. 'Yes – the same perfume. In some ways I haven't moved on,' she says, looking down at the blue shirt, the moleskins, the clean boots; aware of the haircut and plump face with its lines. 'You know, even back then when I didn't have a brass razoo – even when I was in jail, not exactly looking my best – I still used it. My one decadence. My weakness.' And then, jokily, 'Everyone needs a little weakness.'

Dylan says quietly, 'Can we talk about that?'

'Little weaknesses?' Jules is still in a light mood. 'My you *have* changed. Precisely what little weakness do you want to own up to? Let me see – you're a secret stockbroker...you've traded your mandolin for a tuba...you're playing in a pink shirt...'

'No, this is serious,' he says. 'It isn't easy for me. Could we go outside?'

Kate sees Dylan leave the room with a woman, a palm lightly touching her lower back as he holds the springless door with one hand and allows her through first. The familiarity of this small gesture is piercing.


They sit on a bench nearby. 'Obviously I didn't expect to see you,' he says, by way of an opener.

'Ah, well I knew I'd see you,' Jules says. 'I heard you were behind this little circus.'

'Just the tour guide,' he cuts in to correct. 'They're the big hitters.'

'The Wildlife Preservation Society of Australia has been funding some specific research projects at Daydawn Biosphere Reserve. The people there have been working with local stakeholders to get better outcomes by coordinating their fire regimes.'

He can't help himself. 'I never thought I'd hear you come out with a mouthful like that.'

'Like what?'

'You know precisely like what,' he laughs. 'If you say "going forward", I'll have to slap you.'

'Slap me? Interesting. So, my technique's become more subtle, and you've gone the other way...'

Dylan realises she's flirting with him.

'Jules.' He decides to just plunge into it, fixing her with a guileless gaze. Their eyes meet as if there have been no years, no time in between. It is the same complete connection. 'I'm sorry. I'm so sorry for what happened back then. It's hard to even find the words to express it all.'

She goes to cut in, but he gently raises his hand. The lightest halt.

'I bailed on you. I can't quite believe now what I did then. I convinced myself that doing a deal with the authorities was right because I'd be of more use if I didn't have a police record. But that wasn't the truth. I just completely let you down; you went to prison for six months and it was my fault. I was responsible. It is the most terrible thing I have ever done. I don't know what I was thinking. I am so, so ashamed...'

'Is that what you think?' Jules says, smiling gently, generously. 'Is that what you've been thinking all these years?'

But Dylan's eyes are moist and there are no more words in him.

'Well, I have never blamed you. I have never held you responsible for my actions, or the consequences I faced because of them. I was sad – grief-stricken – because you didn't come to visit me, or even make contact with me. You didn't respond to those two letters. So it wasn't the court case or jail that really hurt me, it was just the heart-break of losing you. That was worse than any of it.'

'You were thinking of that while you were in prison? Thinking of me like that? Not hating me?'

'Oh no, Dylan,' she says. 'I could never hate you. I loved you...'

He feels a jolt inside as he thinks of Kate.

'...but not as much as I love Lyn,' she quickly finishes.

'Lyn?'

'She was at the table with me. She handles all the admin for the preservation society. She's very good at all that – very professional. But we have been together for years – personally.' She pauses and laughs gently at the surprise on his face. 'I suppose, being a girl, I was always playing in a pink shirt... but now I'm *really* playing in a pink shirt.' She pauses and then adds, 'Perhaps I have you to thank for Lyn.'

It has a bittersweet sound.

'And the Wildlife Preservation Society took you on, even with a record.'

'Probably because of it – you did me a favour,' Jules says. 'It was a long time ago, and it's an honourable battle scar in the conservation world. "Prepared to go to jail for your convictions." I've done rather better because of it, actually, I think. Once you've matured enough so that these organisations know you've finished with the radical stuff and you're committed to working on systemic change, it becomes a useful little badge of honour to hang in the trophy cabinet. I went over to the east coast after prison – a fresh start. Started with volunteering in organisations, got on, got on. Then got a gig with the preservation society. Met Lyn. We've been there for years. Then, goodness, eventually made me chief executive and Lyn general manager. We're the perfect package...' she pauses pointedly, intimately, 'in every way.'

Then she adds, 'There's a lesson — love what you do, not what you did. Love what you are, rather than hating what you were.' She smiles again, reaches forwards and holds his face between her hands. Then she eases her face back so he is just in focus again. 'So, on every front, I should thank you.' And then she kisses him. He is so lost in the brief warmth of it, in the forgiveness and his release from the past that he doesn't hear Kate slam the community hall door behind her.

Kate is relieved to swing the security chain across the door of her hotel room and be alone.

She instinctively goes to the bathroom and turns on the shower taps — hot on full, just a smidgen of cold. She drops her clothes to the beige-tiled floor and turns to the basin, resting her hands either side and looking up into the mirror. Though it is quickly misting, she sees herself clearly. She is looking directly at herself, and she is confident about that. She straightens and sees herself naked and somehow taller. She can't have lost weight, she thinks, but it's a better look. Something about her posture gives a better shape to her.

She can see a new sense of life in herself — some vibrancy that had been eaten away. This would sound silly to anyone else, she thinks, but she remembers that she's young. She looks taller.

She looks at herself as she is gently obliterated by the milky steam, and even if she didn't believe in the naked truth, she would not be able to ignore the strange evidence that she's seen.

After showering, Kate puts on comfortable clothes, props herself on pillows on the bed, turns the TV on low and taps the keyboard of her laptop, writing up notes about the meeting. But her heart's not in it and her mind is elsewhere. She is rattled and that confuses her – it has never been her style.

She rings reception and someone brings a toasted club sandwich with a basket of chips, the torn-off sheet of paper towel in the bottom made almost transparent by fat. The squeezy bottle of tomato sauce has a crust round the top, but she's still glad she managed to sidestep Jack Cole's offer of dinner.

She suddenly feels too cooped up in her room and slips on thongs, picks up the key and steps outside. The air is warm, but cooling, and the night soft. It is still, but with the slightest movement of air the big river gums rustle. She crosses the deep, scratchy lawn, walking towards the river. Then she stumbles down the bank. Gravity scampers her down the last of the slope, through dust and into the river's gravel. It feels cooler and rougher between her toes. Now that she's right beside the Duncan River, out of the trees, the moon is big above and it is quite light. The surface of the river is streaked silver by thin currents which spin out to the sides. Broken-off branches pass, static in their motion. The water smells alive, musty, fresh, earthy, all at once, and she senses the power of it and loses herself in it. She wishes Dylan was there. It is an instinctive thought – a natural response to the space.

And then she remembers crocodiles.

And it is just at this moment that there is the slightest movement further down the bank.

Kate lets out a little gasp and takes a step backwards, away from the water.

'Mesmerising, int-it.' A voice off in the dark, some way upstream. The man's voice is so low, so drawled, so hypnotic that she doesn't recognise it. But she realises that there's been no other movement, so he must have been there for some time. 'Don't be scared,' he says, seeing her tense. 'It's Vincent Yimi.'

'I didn't expect anyone to be here,' she says, relieved.

They walk the few steps towards one another, then stand together. She can smell the pungency of him, he the unusual absence of her perfume.

'I just needed a few quiet moments,' she says. 'I just needed to get out of that hotel room. Away from all the stuff back there.'

'I was just thinking about the river – hearing it,' Vincent says. 'Thinking about us all going up it tomorrow. I came to tell the river about it.'

It seems a funny notion to her.

Silence again, then Vincent continues. 'You know about our Dreamtime snakes?' One rainbow serpent made the universe, another made the rivers. 'A Dreamtime snake is like our mother.' He pauses. 'So, I thought, seeing as tomorrow's going to be an interesting day for her, I'd come quietly and let her know. Prepare her.

'Always better to do that than to ask for forgiveness afterwards, I reckon. Better than jumping into things and getting them wrong.' She knows he is wearing his kind smile. 'Reconciliation, see, is a tricky old business. How can I put it to you?' he says, weighing his words.

Vincent lets the river push a little time past and draws in a stream of new air. 'I've read a lot about Nelson Mandela. He's the one I think of in all of this reconciliation stuff – what he did. That's what I want, his attitude. Forgive but don't forget, that's what he said.

'In their first government, anti-apartheid men sat alongside their old enemies. Inspiring. Through all that, Mandela was insistent about forgiveness.' Vincent talks like the streaming water before him. 'You know, he was sometimes asked whether he'd been forgiving too easily, after twenty-seven years in prison. He was always clear on it, though. I memorised something he said, "Courageous people do not fear forgiving, for the sake of peace".' Vincent repeats it, even slower, even lower. 'Courageous people do not fear forgiving, for the sake of peace.'

And the words do not roll away with the river. They seem to just hang in the air over it.

Vincent shakes his head slowly. 'Takes a lot of guts, and strength, to forgive someone. To accept them as they are...'

He pauses and turns towards her. 'See, the guts of it is that I reckon you haven't got real reconciliation until one person says they're sorry and the other says they forgive them.'

'Before that you still have an imbalance?' she says.

'Yep. An imbalance.'

'Still angry, but more empowered,' she says.

'Gotta have the heart to forgive.'

———

Kate is back alone in her room and feeling every nuance of her silence. Vincent's honesty bruises against her secret. Silence is deception. What am I, she asks herself?

She looks for distraction, flicks on the TV and it burbles companionably; first a mix of rural ads for sheep dip and sheds and then into the halfway point of some feel-good road-trip movie.

She crams the plastic kettle sideways into the bathroom sink and fills it through the spout, water spraying up over the mirror. She tears the top off a sachet of instant coffee and peels the foil cap off the little longlife milk carton ready to gurgle it into the mug, and when the kettle finally boils, she splashes hot water onto brown powder.

Coffee. At this time of night. Ridiculous, really, but it's an instinct.

The coffee's aroma bursts through the room and with it comes an instantly deafening echo. The words 'little heart-starter' flood her with repulsion. She feels hit.

Then, in one violent mash: A straight black skirt, dusty workboots, the orange stain of a takeaway lid, red charcoal in a fire, an ignorance of landscape, of setting, of context, opening a door into a golden room, a repulsive flash of memory from her internship, a polite new population in her life, jealousy and forgiveness, a new vocabulary, father John and mother Alison, Vincent and Dylan, Cole and Mooney, Mandela, father time and mother earth, the locked door of a childhood, steam climbing a reflection, the spray of water across a mirror. Everything smashes in with no conclusions. It is the most real moment of her life.

# Twenty-five

Dylan is eager to show Kate the Minjubal country from the Duncan River itself but, with Cole coming along, he has reservations. Still, he has made the preparations, and jeez, there was some dicking around last night. Henny reckoned he'd heard that the boat's outboard was stuffed, and they spent half the night tracking it down to check it.

'Where's Uncle? He'll know where it is,' asks Dylan.

'Gone off walkabout. Down the river, I reckon,' says Henny. 'Anyways, I wouldn't be surprised if it was at Nelson's.' They started there, but no-one was at the stilted house. They'd searched among the old engine blocks, salt-eaten trailer skeletons and motorcycles stripped to their guts – seats and tanks long gone – and found nothing.

Then they decided that the outboard Nelson had used to take them up the Duncan River was too small, anyway.

'Danny'll have a bigger one,' said Henny.

They went on to Danny's, where a dozen men were hanging out on the front verandah and none of them

– including Danny – had any clue about any outboard. But he reckoned Joseph'd have one.

Joseph's skin was so matt-dark that when he spoke to them under the moon in his front yard, they could only see his white teeth flashing. 'I had one you coulda used, but it's gone,' he said.

'Gone where, bro?' asked Henny.

'Just gone,' he said. Try Sprocket, he reckoned. Sprocket always had stuff.

And Sprocket crashed around in his shed and found an old Evinrude. 'Good as gold,' he promised. He took an hour to get it going, hooking it onto the bull-bar of his Toyota HJ40 and standing the prop leg in a fish-crate of water. The crappy two-stroke spluttered and then snarled into manic life, blue-grey smoke winding off into the dark as it over-revved and promptly died.

If there is a serpent spirit, thought Dylan, that should have woken it up.

'It'll be right as rain,' Sprocket promised cheerily.

———

A day on the river and an overnight camp in the river country with Vincent, Henny and Airplane would let Cole and Kate feel the connection these Minjubal people had to the land. A community that would really benefit from the solar package.

But this morning, standing in the hotel's reception, watching Vincent and Henny arguing over something-or-other outside as they stalk around the aluminium boat on its trailer, arms flailing and eyes bulging, Dylan can't believe he's set himself up for this when it's not strictly necessary.

It's pure, theatrical farce.

'Good morning.' Kate greets him from behind. 'I didn't see you at breakfast.' There is something pointed in her voice, but Dylan doesn't know what.

'I didn't sleep much,' he says, making it worse without realising it. 'And I was up early. I've been out and about.' After saying goodbye to Jules, Dylan had finished up inside the hall and then gone back to the hotel. The thought that something so disabling for so many years could be so easily dissolved had mixed with memories and rolled around the dark room, half in the hot air and half in dreams, until he'd seen the first splinter of light and gone out to find Henny. They picked up the boat, tested the motor again, fuelled it and, as a precaution, unbolted the LandCruiser's second battery and stowed it in the boat's stern. Just in case. Ice, food and water packed in the eskies. Bait, handlines, hooks. Made sure the mandolin was in. His mind was on lots of different things.

Then they picked up Vincent, who'd wanted to check the two young blokes had got it all organised right, which took another half-hour. Up and about, alright, Dylan thinks.

'How did you go last night?' he asks Kate, making conversation.

'Last night? Oh, I wrote up some notes, then got them to bring something to my room, actually. Jack suggested dinner, but I had a headache.' She gently spouts chilled air.

'Feeling better?' He's cautious, but warm.

'Eventually,' she confides, and her anger fractures into shards – glittering will-o'-the-wisps that try to fly away, but she pinches them out of the air and pulls them back inside, restoring them into a nice, whole, dark ball. 'I went out for a breath of fresh air.' She doesn't tell him about meeting Vincent; their conversation seems too private. 'And how was yours?' It comes out cold, but that's how she feels.

'Oh – fine thanks.' Slow and wary.

'I'm sure it was.' Her words are sharp.

'Sorry?'

'I saw you leaving with that girl last night. Nice pick-up, considering it was a community business meeting in Carter's Ford.' (She wants to scream 'men!' and stamp her feet.)

'It wasn't like that,' he says, but doesn't want to explain it all. 'I knew her from way back. I haven't seen her for years. That's all. She's nice. You'd like her.'

'Really?' She's clearly furious now.

'Really. Why? What's going on?'

'It's just that I don't pash every contact that I bump into after years.' And suddenly she realises that she is feeling jealous. And she realises that she sounds it too.

'Ah.'

'Ah, indeed.'

'A goodbye kiss, that's all it was.' He feels like telling her about Lyn, but knows not to.

'Quite a goodbye.'

'Maybe. But it was most definitely goodbye.'

'Just that?' Oh my God, she thinks, now I sound pathetic.

'Just goodbye.' Dylan Ward has a particular power of honesty when he looks directly into people's eyes. It is as if he glances straight through the cornea, the pupil, the lens. He pierces the jelly-vitreous humour fluid like a laser, until he is facing the retina lining the back of the eye. The macula itself – the area of keenest vision. And now he looks into Kate's eyes. 'Really,' he says. 'Just goodbye.'

Kate has a winsome facial expression that she slips on sometimes. She squeezes in her cheeks so they have dimples, and the corners of her mouth so that her soft lips pout like an angel fish. It gives her a look of innocence. But in this instance, she is not putting it on; it is a look of pure relief.

Dylan sees Cole turn the corner of the building and come towards them. He'd like to take her sweet face between his hands and kiss her. But he just squints the slightest, most intimate smile.

It is half an hour's drive down the bitumen, then nearly another hour on a dusty track to the river. A snake crosses in arabesques and Dylan swings the wheel to avoid it and checks the rear-view mirrors. Clip them and they can swing up underneath. A flock of budgerigars flies madly across, chattering, pulsing green and yellow. Dylan points to a bush turkey. A pair of brolgas stalks off, elegant in grey, flashes of red on their necks. A herd of Brahman cattle stands on the south side of the road, heads swinging in unison, stalks bushing from the sides of their mouths.

They aren't far down the track when Cole tells him to stop. 'Too much bloody tea,' he says as he slides out, leaving the door ajar and his notebook open on the front seat. Vincent is following some way behind, towing the boat, and when Dylan sees him in the mirror, he reaches across to grab the handle and pull the passenger door closed. Stop dust blowing in. Stretched flat, looking down, his eyes fall on words. The top of the page says 'INUNDATION'. Then a list of places and notes:

NGALGARDI COMMUNITY = Fortescue has interstate contacts.

MT GOODE STATION = Ingham. Negligible.

DAYDAWN BIOSPHERE RESERVE = Research Tedd Bakker. (Pru Bearer.) Risk.

BARKER RIVER STATION = Nick Goodson trouble? (Research Billy Parkes.)

WARRAMORRA COMMUNITY = Outflow affected? (Ask Pearson.) Munumurra. Indig connections. Don't underestimate the RCs!

NINE MILE = Chrissie Borthwick – noise, no clout. Burleigh can pull strings.

MT JANE STATION = Can McDay rally Indig?

COMMUNITY MEETING = Professor (find out who).


'OK?' asks Kate from the back seat.

Dylan sits up again. 'Sure.'

'I thought you'd had a heart attack or something, stuck down there.'

'I'm fine.' But none of it seems to gel. It's like a jigsaw without the picture on the box lid, but it doesn't seem to add up to a solar power project. Dylan sees what it's not, but not what it is.

Vincent slows to a crawl as he passes, nodding with a deeper familiarity to Kate. When Dylan signals with a thumbs-up, the old man catches something unconvincing in it.

Cole emerges from bushes, brushing ants off his shins and stamping them from his boots. When he gets back in, Dylan is looking out of his own side window, as if distracted. With a glance at him, Cole quickly scoops up the open book and tucks it back into his top pocket. Kate sees and knows Dylan has seen some clue.

'That's better,' Cole says in a voice chattier than usual. 'Thanks.'

'No problem.'

'How long to the river?'

'Half an hour. The track looks pretty good.'

———

Dylan pulls Kate aside in the confusion of packing the boat, and plunges in, in almost a whisper. 'There's something I *have* to ask.'

'What's that?'

'It's just the word "inundation". I saw it by accident in his notebook when we stopped. It seems so out of context I can't let it go...'

'You saw it in the car?' She has known this moment would come, but sees Cole pointedly watching them.

'Yeah. Back there, when we stopped on the track. The word "inundation".'

'We'll have to talk about it later,' she says.

'You know something about it?'

'Later,' she says. 'When we're alone.' But she knows the floodgate is about to open.

'I can just ask Cole,' he says, pushing it.

'No,' Kate says sharply. 'Don't do that. That'd be the worst thing you could do. Just wait. We'll talk, but not now.'

Airplane Cuttover sits in Vincent's four-wheel drive, calmly staring straight ahead as they get the boat into the water, and Cole and Kate safely stowed.

Dylan's holding the bow mooring line and Henny's at

the stern when Uncle Vincent brings the old man down, helps him on board and makes sure he's comfortable in the passenger swivel seat.

Dylan leaves the introduction to Vincent. 'This is Mr Cuttover. Senior man for Minjubal people.'

A warm 'hello' and cool 'g'day' come from the stern.

Airplane, in another loose white op shop T-shirt, but this time with BARRAMUNDI BURGLER written across the chest, sits bolt upright, and acknowledges with the slightest nod of his wild black-and-grey-haired head.

The hull is pressured by water and the air pestered by the reverberation of aluminium thrumming. Dylan perches on the transom, map folded to show the section of the Duncan River from the Crossing to Admiralty Sound. The Kimberley, at the southern edge of the global monsoon system, has thousands of creeks and streams and more than a hundred rivers, but none is as big as the Duncan River, with its 100,000 square kilometres of catchment.

'We've been travelling in this arc up the valley, north of the river.' His forefinger is graceful. Nine Mile, Daydawn, the peninsula, Carter's Ford. 'We're here, about 500 kilometres from the coast, and we'll head downstream. We'll probably camp around here...' Pointing to a bend in the river. 'We've come right round and we'll only be forty kays above Emerald Gorge, at Daydawn.'

The boat waddles across the flow.

'Be careful there,' shouts Uncle Vincent. Henny is gripping the boat's black plastic wheel and Vincent is standing behind him giving animated advice. The Evinrude sings unevenly and works harder than the progress it's causing. Dylan, alongside Vincent, holds onto the back of Airplane's seat as the boat glances off a sandbank. Kate and Cole grip for grim life.

The immense weight of the water pitches it, and whirlpools twist it one way and the other, then, suddenly, Airplane points to the right and snaps, 'Over there – go thaddaway'. Henny spins the wildly lurching boat, just missing sharks-tooth rocks that sit just under the surface.

Uncle Vincent has always reckoned a runabout's too fast. 'That's why we went walkabout.' Now he turns to reassure his guests, 'Old man knows this place like the back of his hand.'

Airplane Cuttover has lived his life with the river. He feels congenitally part of it, just as it seems to consume him. He knows its stories and feels its moods. The life in it is a familiar consommé. Giant freshwater shrimps, macrobrachium river prawns and caridina shrimps. Nearly fifty fish species, many endemic. Gudgeons, grunters, hardyheads and rainbowfish. *Eleotridae*, *Terapontidae*, *Atherinidae* and *Melanotaeniidae* perfectly, and literally, at home.

After nearly an hour on the river, they pull up at a sandy beach and collect firewood. Henny and Dylan break out the fishing handlines and Henny skylarks with the bait.

'Wanna nibble?' Shoving it towards Dylan's face.

'Get out of it.' Twisting and pushing him away.

'Come on, little fishy-fishy.'

Dylan rolls him down into the sand and Henny looks up blinking. 'Love ya like a brother and ya treats me like shit.' Peels back, laughing.

How good's this, Dylan thinks. Wild river, warm night, mates at play. Kate. He waits for the moment when he can draw her away and talk about Cole's notebook.

And Cole sits with it now, off on a flat rock.

'Join us for a bit of fishing?' Dylan asks. 'Just handlines, but there's plenty in there.' Cole shakes his head like a dog getting water off.

But Kate looks up. 'I'd like to, but I don't know much about it.' She looks across the blond shore.

'We'll show you.'

Henny has given in to the heat, ripped off his slim jeans and cartwheeled into the water in his boxer shorts. 'Look,' he shrieks, hauling himself back out and standing, triumphant, cotton clinging, arms thrown wide. 'A shag on a rock.'

'A dag on a rock, more like,' says Dylan.

Henny Breeze, still glistening, grins to no-one in particular as Dylan re-ties Kate's hook with the five careful turns of a clinch knot, then stands behind and shows her how to twirl the leaded end of the line and cast it, letting it rip off the spool's chamfered edge. Three or four goes and she's getting the hang of it.

'A natural,' whoops Henny. 'One of us.'

The lines are wet for a while, but only Henny is popping fish out as if they don't want a tomorrow.

'Let's give this away. I want to swim,' says Dylan. 'How about you?' He looks at Kate hoping for a chance to talk to her about Cole's notebook.

'Sure.'

She walks further down the sweep of the beach, to where it shelves more steeply into an eddy of stiller water. She is barefoot, her legs glossy. She's wearing a shirt and has a silk sarong around her. She unbuttons the shirt and lets it fall, and then unwinds the cloth, revealing a modest, one-piece bathing suit. After rolling the clothes into a loose ball, she bowls them underarm past the tideline, then edges forward, places her palms together and curls forward in a dive. The water devours every intimate part of her as she passes through the surface and into steely blue. Then she launches up through the surface, hair streaming backwards, face pearly with drops, beaming towards him. Come on in, she says, it's gorgeous.

'Our Dyl's a goner,' says Henny. 'Yep, gone for all money.' Dylan has stripped off his shirt and jeans and plunged in in his boxer shorts, stroking gently alongside Kate.

'Good thing, too,' says Vincent. 'And a good place for it.'

'Whaddya mean, Uncle?'

'Don't give me that,' with mock venom. 'You can feel it. This place. The power of the river.'

'Yeah,' grins Henny. 'I s'pose I can.'

'Anything that happens here happens in the sanctity of the river.'

'Yeah, Uncle,' agrees Henny, but his attention span has failed him. 'Hey, Kate,' he yells. 'Look out for snakes in there. A *big, bad* snake. HA!'

They swim on round the next bend in the river, frog-kicking abreast. The massive triangle of a red rock wall rises hundreds of metres above them.

'I'm cold,' she suddenly says. 'Let's get out. Warm up a bit.'

'Sure.' And they veer off to the left bank, which is bathed in the early sun. 'Over here,' he says.

The smooth, grey rocks are already warm and Kate lies facedown on them, turned away from him, shivering slightly, feeling their heat slowly penetrate her. Him lying next to her on his back. The comfortable feeling of cold retreating.

'Can you tell me now?' he says. 'About Cole's notebook.'

'Not now,' she says, so gently. 'Not in this moment. Please, let's just have this moment. Let's not talk about other stuff. Just savour this. To remember it. Like this. In this amazing place.' She can't handle the bubble bursting. Not yet. She has no plan other than to delay it. To avoid it for now.

She feels like they are almost there. She and Dylan are almost complete – and she can see the irony of this one moment in her life being snatched away by the old her. She is resigned to the fact that the deceit will come out, and she can predict Dylan's reaction, and yet it seems to her that the person implicated is no longer really her. It is some earlier version. Not the 'her' that is here, by the river, with these people, feeling this ease, feeling these things.

And she realises that she is no longer doubtful of the change in herself – this change which seemed so fast, so, well, unlikely. She sees herself not as shifting away from what she was, but towards what has always been inside. She just feels comfortable.

Dylan wants to press her – to somehow force her to tell him what's going on. At the same time, what is growing between them is all the more precious for being so unexpected. It has dissolved his insularity, even dulled his guilt, and he is already scared of losing it.

'Leave it for now,' she says, perhaps sensing all this, 'and I promise that we'll talk about it when we really have to.'

She moves her hand to touch his, then turns to lie with her cheek to the rock, facing him. Fingers caressing fingers.

———

By the time they have swum back, the fire has flared and died to cooking coals. 'I'd better get dinner under way,' says Dylan, and busies himself with preparations. They eat and, replete, settle back into the cooling sand.

'I'll clear up,' says Henny.

'And I'll help,' says Kate.

'No need,' says Vincent. 'It's our job.'

'I'd like to.'

'Fair-nough.'

And she squats at the crooning river's edge beside Henny, who mixes clean sand and water into the pans and scrubs them round.

'Works well,' she says.

'Uncle taught me. When I was a nipper.'

'A useful lesson.'

'Yeah, Uncle's full of 'em. Best man I know.' He looks at her and smiles. 'Your bloke's a close second.'

'My bloke?'

'Yeah,' he says. 'You the last to know?'

'Good tucker,' Vincent Yimi says quietly away from the light, as Dylan bends over boxes with his head torch, sorting out coffee, port and chocolate. Spoiling them.

'Thanks, Uncle.'

'Going alright?'

'You tell me. There's something going on. Something that we don't know about. Cole's onto something – something about "inundation".'

'Probably just looking at where it's safe to spend their money without getting it wiped out by the Wet season. Makes sense. You know how it is. Roads, sheds, whole communities get sent down the river, then you build 'em up again – costs a fortune – and next season the new lot goes down the river to join it.'

Plausible enough. 'That makes sense,' he says.

'But he's not an easy one, the boss bloke. Like one of those old, cunning barramundi. You're not sure if you've really jagged the bastards. They might take the bait, alright – might even seem to swallow it down – but you still can't be sure you've got 'em, even then. Might just throw it back up, long time later. Reject it, just like that, when you think they've taken it hook, line and sinker.'

'Yeah,' says Dylan. 'Just like one of those. Meaner, though.' He wants to say more to Vincent, but knows he must speak to Kate first.

'Still,' says Vincent, 'you've hooked yourself an angel fish.'

'What do you mean?'

'Come on,' says Vincent. 'You can see. You just ain't lookin'.'

Dylan looks up so that the torch's light flares at Vincent. 'Actually, yes I am. Looking.'

'Good,' says Vincent. 'Good.'

'But we're from different worlds.'

'When two people get together, they create a new world,' says Vincent.

The stars start to crowd over them in the slot of sky above, between the gorge's walls, and the river settles into an even, creamy, all-night song. Airplane Cuttover suddenly speaks in a low tremolo. 'This place is about respect. You visitors should know this. You should know this is a place of tribal law. Tribal law is strong.'

He breathes slowly. There's a long pause, but then it is as if the same sentence, the same thought, is just picked up… 'Respect for the country. For the animals and plants. Respect for other people. For their feelings. Respect for yourself and your own feelings. The country loves us, but the country can punish us.'

Respect echoes around the gorges of the indigenous north and Kate hears it like a gentle, distant night sigh.

'You are here and I will give you this story,' says Airplane. 'It's my story, but I'll give it to you. Then you can tell it too.' His most precious gift.

'In the Dreamtime three strangers came to the country, near Sing-out Pool. They hadn't been welcomed to the country but when they came to a spring they bent down to drink the cool water. The country's keeper was a big water snake that lived in that pool, and when they bent down he ate them. They should have waited to be welcomed. They could have dipped a rock in the water and wiped their sides with the rock, then thrown it into the water. That's tradition – lets that water snake smell the visitor. It's important to announce yourself and your intentions. To be honest. That's showing respect.'

Airplane pauses. 'Our people are good people, the people of Minjubal, and I want you to know that.' He waves his right arm in a big arc. 'They live all around here and you can help them. I ask you to do that. You have a story here now.'

Jack Cole stands, with just with a blunt goodnight, ready to retreat to the tent he's got Dylan to put up way off from the group. Dylan has hung an LED lantern by it so Cole can find his way, and it throws out a halo of sharp light.

Henny walks over and offers him a bottle of water, but he just shakes his head. No looking up. The young buck shrugs and turns away. 'Coffee,' says Cole to his back.

Henny spins and eyes him. Weighs it up, then thinks 'what the hell'. Fed up with it. 'A *please*'d be good.'

The silence is too long. Still Cole doesn't look up. 'Coffee.' He barks it, low and menacing.

Henny feels Cole lining him up head-on, squints at the top of his head and says nothing. He knows he should just stoke the fire and boil water, get out the plunger and put in however-many spoonfuls, but he just can't find it in himself.

'Co-ffee,' says Cole, looking up to eye him, intonating *imbecile*.

Henny just launches in. 'There's a nice way of asking for something and a shit-for-brains way of asking for something.'

'Don't give me any lip. Just do what you're told.' The air is iced. 'You people.' Cole spits it.

'You heard what the old man said about respect. You and your like could do with getting some.' Henny reckons in for a penny, in for a pound.

'And it's you who's going to teach me, is it?' Cole is invigorated by the action. He feels everything uncoiling inside him. Feels his guts loosening. Then he's on his feet, squaring up. 'You're going to teach *me* to respect *you*?'

The movement alerts Vincent, a long way off. 'What's up there?' he shouts.

'I don't think you want to go there, sonny.' Cole's warning is hissed and sinister. He steps forward and pokes Henny in the chest to drive the point home.

Vincent sees it. 'Hey, you blokes. Settle down.'

He flashes a glance at Dylan, who's immediately on his feet. But before he takes a stride, Henny lashes out with an arcing black fist that catches Cole on the hard edge of his jawbone, skewing his head right, cricking his neck. He falls sideways, his feet catching one on the other and making it look worse than it is, and topples backwards and lands in the reedy scrub, sprawled and blinking.

Then a slim shimmer catches his eye, and Cole looks left and sees the snake in the lantern's bluish light. He instinctively raises his left hand, palm forward, to protect his face, watching the serpent through spread fingers. Its head is poised a fist's width above the ground, aimed at him. He sees the cut of its eyes and the minute sway of its head. The snake is a big and dark red, with what appears to be pinkish flecks down its body. It has a beautiful pale pink head. It is slender and dry, its whip tail ending in a fine taper. It seems calm and elegant. It is like a lean whip of lightning. There is something more calculated than malevolent about it as it licks the air with a dark, forked tongue. And then it comes at him, like a sliver of muscly lightning, and Cole closes his fingers and his eyes.

Henny Breeze sees the snake dart in, too, and knows everything that happens from here on is going to be bad.

Cole shrieks more from fear than from the pain of the first punctures, though the taipan's hypodermic fangs are as long as a thumb nail and whack venom deep into his subcutaneous tissues. Then it strikes again, hitting him this second time on the fleshy saddle of his hand, then again and catches his forearm. The three jabs have come staccato, rat-a-tat-tat. *Oxyuranus scutellatus* milking in 120 grams of potent juice in instants.

Dylan is there in a flash, Vincent stomping in behind him, scared witless. The snake retreats a couple of metres, then just turns and studies them, in no rush to vanish completely. Like it's taking in what it's done. When they look again, it has vanished.

Henny is motionless, hands now hung by his sides. Part of him thinks it's justice, just like the old man talked about, part of him is in panic. As he looks off down the long, moon-silvered snake of the river, weighing it up, Cole springs to his feet then rails at him, grabbing his T-shirt by the neck, punching him once with his right fist clenched, then opening his hand and slapping him repeatedly. Henny just takes the punishment as Dylan and Vincent try to pull Cole off. When they part, Dylan holds on to Henny and leads him backwards, away, and Vincent steps towards Cole, who clenches his fist at the old man. 'You people are worth shit,' he roars, ready to lash out.

'*Stop that.*' Airplane's voice with the raw strength of a young man, comes across the gorge like wind. 'Don't you lay hand on him.' He stands on a rock, a silhouette against the evening sky – somehow not the frail man he was. 'You have no rights here.' The force of the old man's words stops Cole. He lowers his hand. 'Besides,' says Airplane. 'Your anger is killing you.'

The venom is a cocktail of strong toxins. Mainly proteins, their sole objective is to shut the victim down and kill him. They would've helped the taipan to digest him, if it could have swallowed him whole. Paralysis, coagulopathy, rhabdomyolysis and haemolysis. Some of the toxins damage red blood cells, some cause the cardiac muscle to seize, many wreak havoc in the kidneys, but most people who die simply stop breathing. The trick is to stop the poison getting pumped around the lymphatic system.

'You gotta lie down,' growls Uncle Vincent. 'Stay stock still.'

And, in this moment, Cole looks at Vincent, childlike. 'What do you do for it? What do you give me?'

'Just got to get you to the hospital in Carter's Ford. They know this stuff. But we gotta keep you still.'

'But that's hours away. Couldn't I die in minutes?'

'You'd have died in minutes if you'd kept beatin' that boy, that's for sure.'

'Christ,' says Cole, slumping into the sand. 'Oh Christ.'

'Henny, get the first-aid kit,' instructs Dylan into his ear. 'There are three wide bandages in there.' And Dylan kneels, with Vincent beside him and Kate now just behind them, and beckons Cole to hold his arm forward.

'Did him three times. Bam-bam-bam,' says Henny excitedly to Kate.

'Just get the bandages,' says Dylan, more forcefully.

Starting at the fingers, Dylan winds on the bandages, right up to the armpit and then over the shoulder. He makes a loop of another and feeds it behind Cole's neck, and hangs it through, then secures it to his body.

'Was it what I think it was?' Dylan asks Vincent as he works steadily, keeping the pressure tight and even.

'Taipan. I seen 'un up the peninsula once when I was a kid and the old man told me. Never seen one here before, this far south. Not in the valley. Some call 'em the *fierce snake*.'

'I thought it was a taipan. You're right – Queensland, Northern Territory and more to the north in the Kimberley usually, I think.'

'You can get 'em but it's real unusual. Grant you that. He musta had a good reason.'

'What the hell was that all about?' Dylan has eventually taken Henny to one side.

'He was getting up me and I had a go. Makes it all look like my fault, but it wasn't.'

'Reckon the country's got all sorts of justice,' says Airplane, materialising from the dark to stand behind them now.

'I'm not scared of countryside,' Cole whispers weakly.

'Well, that's what it'll be if it kills yer,' Henny retorts under his breath.

When Dylan's finished bandaging, Cole curls on his side, whimpering, oblivious. Soon he will have an excruciating headache, nausea will wash through him and he'll be vomiting. Pain will surge through his abdomen and he'll become confused as transient hypotension tightens its grip.

Dylan tells Kate, 'That's all we can do at the moment. Perhaps you just sit with him – keep watch while Henny and I pack things up. It'll only take a couple of minutes, or I'd leave it all. Besides, there's the rest of the group to think of. We are where we are and if anything else goes wrong we'll need our gear.' He tries to smile reassuringly. 'But we've got to get him to a doc as fast as we can. And we've got to try to keep fluids in him.'

'Will he make it? Is he going to die?'

'We just have to be quick,' he says again. 'Vincent, I reckon get the boat ready and started, and old Uncle in, if you will. Get all the torches ready – it's going to be tricky in the dark, and we'll have to take it slowly, which isn't going to help. Try the radio and see if we have reception yet, then we can warn them. They'll need the monovalent antivenom.' Then he says loud and forcefully, 'Let's be on that river and out of here in under five minutes folks. And let's all be careful in the dark.'

He sends Henny to pack the cooking and camp gear, and whispers to him, 'Real fast, bro. Real fast,' then he heads back towards Cole's tent. He throws the flap back and takes the lantern in with him. Cole's briefcase is open, just inside, and the light from the lantern falls on papers stacked by it, others strewn around. He kneels to gather it all up, and feels like he's being punched. Maps – Duncan River. Limit of inundation. Emerald Gorge. Dam site. Projected water pipeline. Notes – 'Solar power proposal as cover'. 'Assess potential fallout'. He stares blankly, pulling all the papers into the briefcase, comprehending in a flash. On a whim he grabs a holder of business cards from one of the small compartments in the lid of the briefcase. They all have Cole's name, but different titles. 'JACK COLE. STRATEGIC ADVISOR TO GOVERNMENT' says the top one. 'JACK COLE. ANALYST & CONSULTANT.' And 'JACK COLE. BOARD MEMBER, TRADE & INDUSTRY ADVISORY PANEL.'

And then Dylan reads, 'JACK COLE. GROUP MANAGING DIRECTOR. ACTION PROPERTY DEVELOPMENT.' And, on the flip side, 'PROUD DEVELOPERS OF...' and the list includes 'TUART CREST'.


Jack Cole has vomited through green to a dry-retching. He has already experienced double vision and the muscles surrounding one eye are starting to show signs of paralysis. His heart is racing and he's struggling for shallow breaths. The toxins are working on his vocal chords and throat and he finds it difficult to swallow. Ptosis and paresis, tachycardia and tachypnoea, dysphagia and dysphonia; a savage medley.

Dylan crouches in a halo of light in the tent, his brain running in haphazard spirals, and so fast that it is as if everything else is stationary. Thoughts crash in from all angles. Kate. What about Kate? She is part of it. He can't breathe. All their moments together seem to swirl into a weird disorder – a jumble of deception. What was it all? A joke? He feels poisoned.

And then, somewhere in the background, beyond his thought, there is a low drone. Airplane Cuttover, settled cross-legged by the fire embers, bony ankles jutting, sings a low chant. Dylan grabs the briefcase and walks towards him, and the old man meets Dylan's stare.

'Hey Dyl. I thought you said to get a hurry-up.' Henny is hauling his third load to the boat.

'Coming,' Dylan says. 'I'm on it.' And he drops into automated action.

'What's up?' Kate asks quietly, expecting the worst, seeing Dylan shocked white and thinking the worst for Cole.

'It's that bastard.' He signals to Cole. 'It's you.'

'What? What is it?'

'A dam, a water pipeline to the city. I've just found it all in his tent. That's what this is all about. Flooding this place. Inundation. Deceit.' He spits that last word.

'No – no. It's not like that. Can we talk about it? I need to tell you how it all began. How things changed for me.'

'You knew all along. All those times we were together, alone. The other night, when you could have said something, you never did. On the river, swimming. Just then.'

'I got caught between them and you. Between – I don't know – what I do and what I feel now. It's just not like you make it sound. You have to understand.'

'Understand what? That you lied to me all the way through? That I got it all wrong – what I feel for you, what I thought was between us…it's all part of some deceit.'

'No, no. It's real. What I feel is real too. She is on the verge of tears.

'Let's just get going,' he snaps, and turns away.


Cole has been laid on a swag on the floor of the boat, a light set near him. He's curled up tight. Henny has firmly squeezed the throttle and the engine gives out a mad buzz. The boat leaves a white tear down the dark water. They all point torches forwards, Kate wet-eyed, Dylan with his jaw set, purposely not looking towards her. He just has to do the right thing and work all that out later, he tells himself. He can't think about anything. Can't think about her.

Vincent stands beside him, peering forward over the low

screen, thinking it's all about Cole's state. 'Looks touch-and-go to me.'

The rupture or destruction of red blood cells; haemolysis. The destruction of striated muscle cells; rhabdomyolysis. An abnormally low concentration of oxygen in the blood; hypoxaemia. The bluish discolouration of the skin resulting from poor circulation or inadequate oxygenation of the blood; cyanosis. Paralysis of truncal and limb muscles.

Dylan would rather think about the progression of the effect of toxins in Cole than the crazed chemistry in his own body.

# Twenty-six

The boat radio-call has worked and an ambulance is waiting by the vehicles at the river's edge. They've set their spotlight towards the river. When they see the boat, and casting long shadows, two paramedics bring down a stretcher and shift Cole onto it. One at the head, one at the foot, Henny and Dylan either side, they carry him up the bank and slide him into the ambulance.

'Room for you, too,' the paramedic says to Dylan.

'You go. We'll sort everything here and follow you into town,' says Vincent.

'And me,' says Kate, braving Dylan's coldness and ducking in as he starts to close the rear doors.

They avoid one another's eyes.

'How long since the bite?' The ambo snaps on latex gloves.

'Near enough an hour and fifteen minutes,' says Dylan. 'And he was volatile straight afterwards – before I could get the pressure bandage on.'

'That'd explain it.' Paralysis grips Cole, and he's gobbling breath from the oxygen mask. 'It's unusual to lose anyone within four hours if everyone's done the right thing, but pumping the lymphatics...'

'Definitely an inland taipan,' adds Dylan. 'It hit him three times. Unusual this far south, but definitely taipan.'

'We'll go the VDK anyway.'

The venom detection kit confirms taipan poison, and identifies the genus. Of about 2,900 species of snakes, it's the deadliest in Australia.


Carter's Ford District Hospital is hidden behind palms and a wire fence, all brick and mission-brown paint and cyclone mesh across the windows. All lit up. There's a narrow concrete path to the front double doors, spongy lawns with sharp grass, golden arcs from the reticulation water's minerals, and a smokers' bench with cigarette butts in a terracotta plant pot.

To one side, the in–out driveway leads under an awning, and that's where a young doctor, two nurses and an orderly are ready with a gurney for Cole's arrival.

It happens fast. Cole is instantly subsumed by uniforms and corridors, forms are filled, details given, and a lull comes crashing in. Kate and Dylan stand in an uncomfortable silence.

'We have to talk.' Kate turns to Dylan.

'Look,' he says. 'I've been wanting to talk since I saw Cole's notebook that day – now it's all too late. There's nothing to say...' The words hurt. They are what he feels he must say – should say – but at the same time they feel all wrong.

'No,' she says. 'We have to.'

There's a little pagoda with a terracotta tile roof and slatted seats on four sides. 'Let's walk over there,' she says, and unexpectedly – boldly – reaches for the hand limp by his side, takes it in hers and starts to pull him towards it.

He says nothing, but feels strangely happy to be led.

They settle in the warm night, him with boots spread, hands in prayer, head forward and looking down at the concrete, her twisted towards him, one knee over the other, still holding his hand in both of hers.

'You must be thinking you hate me,' she says. 'And you're probably right to.'

'I don't think I hate you. I don't know what to think.'

'Well, you're right that I knew what was going on. We were here to look at the water resource. That was part of the brief.'

'So you lied to me...' He pulls away from her.

'No, I didn't. The solar project's for real. Maybe I didn't tell you everything – not about the water – I couldn't.' She feels choked. 'Please, just give me a chance to tell you about it, and if you walk away then, so be it. But please just let me do this.'

'OK,' he says and she draws a big breath.

'I could only see the water proposal from the city perspective. From the view of good governance. Looking at options.'

He snaps a glance at her. It sounds like spin.

'Let me finish,' she says. 'Please.'

'That's where I come from. That's what my whole life has been, until now. City, career, government. From there, with millions of people and a water shortage, it looks like a serious option, bringing it from here, where there's lots of water and not many people. But nothing's decided – that's exactly the point. That's why this looked like a valid exercise,

to come and see who was here, what the implications were.'
She pauses. 'To see the lie of the land.'

Her silence implores.

'But I saw the truth of the land. I never would have
believed that things could change this quickly – that I could
feel so different; have changed so much. Changed, or just let
the real me come through. I'm not even sure which it is, or
how to put it. But everything for me has been turned on its
head.'

She pauses, gathering her feelings, braving her fears.
'There's no lie in anything's that's passed between you and
me.'

She stands and walks across the concrete, then turns to
him. 'I'm sorry I let you down. You're so perfect; you don't
even know what that feels like. I am desperately sorry. I just
feel – desperate.'

But he does know what all that feels like and now, put to
the test, Dylan doesn't want to walk out on it.

# Twenty-seven

After the ambulance leaves the riverside, Vincent Yimi, Henny Breeze and Airplane Cuttover all sit for a while. A stunned silence.

Then, 'What do you think's going to happen?' whimpers Henny. 'If he dies will I go to jail? They'll say it was my fault. That I killed him.'

'It wasn't like that. We was all there,' says Vincent forcefully. Then, sympathetically, 'Stop fretting. It'll be alright.'

'But Uncle...'

'It'll be alright. And Dylan and Kate were there. They'll say, too. Knocking a man down is one thing, him getting bitten is another.'

'Bitten by a *taipan*.' Suddenly Airplane speaks with a compelling, slow clarity. 'A taipan's a particular creature. Usually sleeps in the mud in the Dry season. Flies to the sky as a rainbow in the Wet. Sends down the rain.'

'Him being there was odd – seeing him at this time of year even more unusual,' says Vincent, half asking, half stating.

'Taipan protects its people,' says the elder, simply. 'Punishes those that break the law.'

*Once Taipan was a man and a great law maker. Spiritual man. Witch doctor. If a person had swallowed the bone of a goanna, he could suck it out. Spit it away. If he pointed a bone at a person, they'd die. Taipan could make thunder and lightning. He was clever. He had three wives and one son. And that sun came across the blue-tongued lizard's wife, who was a black water snake. And they became one – man and woman together. And that blue-tongue he found out and followed them and killed Taipan's son. The lizard's terrible revenge. He took the boy's heart and blood to Taipan, and it broke his heart. He decided to leave the Earth. Fly in the sky. Watch over us. Act on injustice. That's his job now. Taipan protects his people, but punishes those that break the law.*

Airplane Cuttover tells the story slowly, authoritatively. He delivers each sentence, then waits to let it settle. Gives time for thought. Delivers the next.

Then he fixes his gaze on Henny Breeze. 'You need to know all that, boy. This is your culture. This is what you have.'

It takes them over an hour to pack up the gear and get the boat out of the water. Then Vincent tows it back to town, carefully nosing down the track under headlights. It's a slow business, with Henny behind in Dylan's four-wheel drive.

He leaves Henny and the boat and tells him to hose it down and flush the engine, like he's been shown before, and then takes Airplane home. By now it's after midnight.

'Big business that,' he says to the old man, as he helps him out of the vehicle. They walk to Airplane's front door together, and the old man doesn't reply. 'Got your key?'

But Airplane just turns the handle on the unlocked door and walks in. He nods Vincent to turn on the light, and Vincent flicks the switch. The room has a tiled floor, two mismatched armchairs and a sofa half buried under a dump of clothes and other stuff. A TV, but it has a cloth draped over it. A pile of CDs and radio equipment on the floor in the corner, which young blokes gave the elder, none of which are plugged in. And against the window, an old kitchen table with a single chair, where Airplane spends much of his time. Where he paints.

There are shabby canvasses strewn across the table, acrylics in a mishmash of jam jars, brushes sticking out of a vase. The painting directly in front of the chair is half finished. To Vincent, there is the unmistakeable, serpentine line of a snake alongside a river. The inland taipan can be any hue from dark brown to straw, but Airplane Cuttover's painting is unmistakeably the copper colour of the taipan by the river.

Vincent looks at the old man, who peaceably meets his gaze. A long exchange.

Vincent finds another chair in the kitchen and brings it to the table, and there they sit in silence until the little corellas start screeching in the early dawn, greeting the new day.

Vincent Yimi drives round a bit. His country. His place. His town. He drives the streets slowly, in second gear – walking pace really – past the houses, the parks, the lives. With the vehicle's window wound down, as it always is, he just skews sideways and slouches half through it, and watches it all pass gently.

He thinks of going to the hospital to find out how things are, but he knows Cole won't die. The inland taipan's the world's most venomous snake – toxin fifty times more potent than the Indian cobra – but there is no documented case of a human dying from a taipan bite. He knows Cole won't die, but not because of that. He knows it from the old man's face. He knows everything from looking into Airplane's eyes.

He ends up at the community centre, rings the hospital and they say Cole is stable. And then he picks up a white plastic bag from under his desk, with his fishing handlines in it, and tramps out.

'Where you goin'?' asks Betsie Pie, who's in early herself, tidying up.

'The river.'

Dr John Little is called to Kununda District Hospital in the night to handle his first potentially lethal snake bite. Three months out of the city and he's never seen such a close shave. It has every ingredient of a fatality – a highly venomous snake, patient movement after multiple strikes, a relatively long and difficult trip to the paramedics.

'Looks like he really got a good dose,' he says. 'He'll pull through but it could easily have gone the other way.' He looks at the couple before him – fraught, wrung out. 'It's been a nasty shock for you two, too. I heard you were way down the river. You did well getting him here, the shape he was in. Best thing you can do now is go and get some sleep. There's nothing else you can do here. Call us in the morning to see how he is.'

'Thanks, doctor,' says Dylan. 'We appreciate everything you've all done.'

'Yes,' says Kate. 'We do.' And Dr Little notices the most subtle gesture, as, almost imperceptibly, she moves her hand towards Dylan's, and gently takes his little finger between her thumb and index finger, gripping it softly.

They walk empty streets back towards the river. Way off, a dog barks in a yard and another answers. There's the sound of a car a couple of blocks down. The windows must be wound down and bassy music floods out into the night, in a crescendo that passes quickly. The dry trees rustle under the slightest breeze.

The hotel's reception is lit, locked and eerily empty, and Dylan doesn't turn towards it. She glances at him but he just looks straight ahead as he walks, leading her. His head is in turmoil, his heart physically hurts. But he is with her, in this moment, and he has the sense of hoarding it – of clinging to and cherishing this moment, and the ones behind it. A storehouse; a treasure in an unsure future.

They walk around the back of the hotel and across a wide lawn towards river gums lit by moonlight. And beyond them is the Duncan River. It is wide and slower at this point, and it smells more earthy. 'Come. Down the bank here,' he says. And he helps her down to a clear area near the water itself, and they sit, side by side in the cool grass and let the river draw the poison from them, sucking it into its relentless flow.

Neither can bring themselves to speak, for fear of what might be said. For fear of a then-unavoidable ending.

.

They sleep together but they do not make love. They just lie in each other's arms in the cool white cotton sheets and let the few hours that are left of the night pass. They hold each other as demons race in and roar around their heads.

And through those hours, the question hangs in the air... *what are we going to do now?* And each answers it alone, and privately.

The shutters' slats cast morning sunlight across the room in thin trapezoids. Dylan slides from the bed, unhooking her arm gently, not waking her, and showers as quietly as he can.

'Gotta go out for a bit,' he says, leaning forward to kiss her on one cheek. 'You stay there. I might be a couple of hours.'

'I'll be here,' she says.

He sees the four-wheel drive in the hotel's car park, where Henny's left it, and finds the key up under the back bumper, as they'd arranged. He turns his mobile on, flicks to the contacts and dials Vincent's number, but it's switched off. He dials the Carter's Ford Community Centre, on the off-chance, and Betsie Pie answers and says Uncle Vincent's gone fishing.

The therapy of being with the river.

Dylan works slowly up through the gears and drops back to a low cruise when he's away from the town. He feels he's broken into clear air again; crossed some line. He pulls up at Uncle Vincent's favourite spot on the Duncan River and sees the dual cab parked under trees, by the gravelly sand that the river left behind last Wet. The duck-feet marks of Vincent's thongs flip-flop away from the vehicle.

Dylan pads barefoot across the sandbars, fine grit sticking to him. It rubs between his toes and climbs up his bare legs. He's walked a long way downstream beside the river when he sees Vincent. He sits on a domed midden, where generations have shucked mussels and eaten giant freshwater shrimps and river prawns. In his silver Elvis glasses, hair oily and slicked back and skin glistening, history and the ethereal Duncan River seem to envelope him.

He doesn't look up and Dylan doesn't speak, but just edges up and sits slightly lower, a couple of body-lengths away. They look into the water's dark nothingness separately and together. Time passes and Dylan knows to let it pass silently until the moment comes.

Vincent flinches, as if he has returned from somewhere else.

'Better spit it out, son, before it chokes you and I have to give you the kiss of life. You wouldn't like that. I haven't shaved in days.'

Head still sunk, Dylan shrugs in appreciation. An ice-breaker. 'I've got something to tell you, Uncle, and I don't know how to do it.'

'This is me, and you know how to talk to me,' says Vincent quietly.

Dylan tells him about the dam, the reservoir, the water pipeline. Everything he knows, until he is past the stage of being distraught, and just empty. 'I told you that we were here to help you all, but this could destroy you,' he says. The country lost, the place drowned, the people gone. A giant, silver snake wriggling to the city, stealing the water.

'No, son, it won't destroy us,' says Vincent. 'We'd still be around.'

'But I'm responsible. God knows what will happen now.'

'They were planning it before they found you,' says Uncle Vincent. 'Anyways, it's an old chestnut. The idea's been around for donkeys'. Every now and then they dust it off and have a look at it. Makes sense to have a look-see first. You gotta do that.'

'But...'

'Sssshh, boy. Ssshh. One bad politician and his bouncer don't equal a policy. And never go round saying the whole basket's rotten just because you've got a bad egg. Ain't fair on the others. Ain't just.

'Besides, nothin's actually happened, if you think about it – except we've got a nice new solar power scheme.'

There is a long quiet, and the river passes. It passes in a steel-and-brown snake, the most natural, unperturbed thing in the world.

'Look at it. Freshwater. Imagine if you're gasping for it – you gotta look around for some – that's natural. Human instinct. We've always done it – one waterhole dries up, so you walk on and look for another. I don't blame 'em. There's a lotta people down there and they've got to drink. There's a lotta water up here in the Wet. I see how it looks. But how it looks isn't always how it is.'

His beliefs and words pass as smoothly and calmly as the river runs.

'Besides, if they carry on with it this time, they'll have us to reckon with. There might only be a handful of us, by comparison, but we know how to say our piece.'

'Not trouble, though.'

'Nah, not our style. Mob rule's disgraceful in my book. Reasoned argument, that's what I reckon. We're intelligent adults.' But then he grins '...although, we could always strap you to a bulldozer or concrete you into one of them dragons. You got the experience, after all.'

How can he be so unruffled? 'You don't seem shocked.'

'Nah,' says Vincent. 'Way of the world. Always an idea coming up, and gen'rilly they cause trouble somewhere down the line. Not to worry about it yet, though. No good lighting a fire you might not need.'

Vincent tugs on his handline, which is snagged underwater somewhere, but he makes no attempt to release it – he just sits looking at the river, spool loosely in one hand, line in the other, focused on the spot where it disappears into the water.

'I can believe it of Cole,' says Dylan. 'If I'd been smart enough, I probably could have guessed that something was going on. Something under the table. But not of Kate.' He hangs his head. 'Well, I can believe it – it's a fact – but, well, all that's difficult.'

'Don't be hard on her,' says Vincent placidly. 'Caught in the middle. Nasty place to be.'

'Yeah, but she was part of it.'

'She was to start with – but what do you expect? That was her place. She spent her life in that place. Her family, her culture. It was how she thought, and fair enough, too.'

'Was?'

'Oh yeah. I saw the fight going on in her. Twistin' her up inside. All that stuff hidden in her and change going on so fast. It can happen like that – see things differently – you just change your mind. Like a blinding light. *I got the faith.*

*Hallelujah. God be praised.* HA! An' she got more than that, m'boy.'

'More than what? What do you mean?'

'She's smitten.'

'That's a funny old word.'

'None better.' Yimi flashes a big, warm smile. '*Smitten.* Just like you, pal.' He beams. 'Anyways, you said "was" too. You said "she *was* part of it".'

'Yes. She's working on what to do. She knows this stuff from the inside. She asked me to give her some time, but if she can't pull anything off, I'll go to the media. They'll have a field day.

'She asked me not to tell anyone, but she'll know I had to speak to you. I know she's dreading facing you – but she'll do it. Face up to it.

'Anyway, can we keep this to ourselves for a few hours?'

'A few hours?' Vincent's laugh is melodious. 'You whitefellas're always in a rush. A few hours is nothing. We been here tens of thousands of years, and the river's been here a darn sight longer. Back to the rainbow serpent, remember.' His face creases into a shiny topography as he smiles. 'Yeah,' he whisper kindly, 'I think we can wait a few hours more.'

They lapse now into a comfortable silence.

'Know something?' says Uncle Vincent loudly after a while, not looking towards Dylan.

'I used to think so.'

Vincent smiles. 'You can't change the world. And that's not the point. That's *exactly* not the point, my boy. The point is that you can't let the world change you.' The words wrap them. 'Don't matter whether you're a blackfella or a whitefella, as long as you're a goodfella.' And now Vincent looks upon him kindly. 'And you're a goodfella.'

'Maybe, maybe not,' says Dylan. 'I think I'm certainly a gullible one.'

'The world's complicated these days,' says Vincent, 'but most people in it are pretty simple. They want to earn lots of money, climb up the ladder, get a nice car, get noticed. People like us aren't like that, so it's harder for us. We're the odd ones out. We give a shit.' He smiles. 'But that's alright, we can be that and they can be what they are.'

They sit, staring at the river benevolently sliding past them, the colour of dried blood.

'Thanks,' says Dylan eventually.

'My pleasure,' says Vincent. 'And now,' he adds. 'You'd better get going. Your missus'll be wondering where you are.'

Vincent smiles reassurance.

'She's a good girl,' he says. 'A good heart. I like her.'

# Twenty-eight

'He's looking considerably better than when he arrived,' says Dr Little, for whom one hospital shift has run into another, as it so often does. 'No harm in dropping in to see him now. He's compos mentis.'

'Good,' says Dylan. 'I was hoping for a word.'

'No excitement, though,' says Dr Little. 'We need to keep him calm.'

Dylan follows the directions to a shared room, which Cole is in alone.

'I thought you'd turn up.' Cole struggles to prop himself more upright against the pillows. 'It's no use grovelling. There's going to be serious trouble over this. That young Abo's in it up to his neck. And so are you.'

'There's going to be trouble, alright,' says Dylan. 'But I didn't come about Henny. Or me.'

Cole squints, weighing him up.

'The water pipeline, the dam, the reservoir. I know about it all, and all about you.'

He expects surprise and hopes for alarm, but instead Cole just nods slowly, and then smiles.

'None of your business.' Cole laughs affectedly. 'You're just the bus driver, remember? Now, go and buy me an air ticket home.'

'It's not going to be that easy,' says Dylan, looking for words.

Cole smiles, pulling his cheeks high, clowning, 'And what exactly do you think you can do?'

'I'll blow the whistle on the whole thing. We'll tell everyone.' But it feels unplanned and empty. He already feels out of his depth.

Cole snorts, notes the 'we', but purposefully aims his barbs just at Dylan. 'It's way over your head, son. Have you got any idea who you are dealing with? You reckon we haven't thought this out? You think we haven't got a plan for people like you? Think very carefully before you try to play with the big boys. You can't even imagine the repercussions. You have no comprehension of where this might end up. No idea what we are capable of.' The roared threats hit Dylan in solid gusts. Like the searing hot air driven before a bush fire. The sheer force makes him blink and step backwards.

'Now get out and close the door behind you.' Cole's final and frightening boom.

The sheer force of Cole's voice makes Dylan turn towards the door.

'Pathetic', Cole stage whispers once Dylan's outside, adding quietly, 'just like his old man.'

Cole calls the nurse and barks for her to find his mobile. 'Now, out,' he snaps at her. He thumbs through his address book and presses Michael Mooney's number.

As soon as Dylan had left their room at the hotel, Kate jumped out of bed and dialled first the hospital, to hear that Cole's condition was much improved, and then the Minister's office.

'He's out at a meeting, Kate,' says Liz. 'He'll be about an hour. Is there any message?' Kate contemplates ringing his mobile, but decides against it. 'OK,' Liz says. 'I'll tell him you rang and that you'll call back.'

As Kate showers and rifles through her bag for something nice to wear, her mind is working in the old way. She finds a couple of sheets of headed notepaper and a cheap pen with the hotel's logo stamped on it in the dresser's top drawer, and sits out on the verandah listing points, making notes, drafting out what she'll say to Michael Mooney.

She doesn't write down the ace she's prepared to play, for fear Dylan might stumble across these notes, too.

Less than an hour has passed when she dials again.

'He's not available, I'm afraid, Kate.' Liz now sounds unconvincing.

'I really need to speak to him.'

'Look, I don't know what's going on, but Michael's definitely not available and he isn't going to be.'

'Oh, I get the picture,' says Kate. 'Could you tell him I won't be in for a few days, please? No, I'm not sure how long. I'll let you know. Thanks. Oh, and could you tell him I'll be emailing him straight away. He'd be wise to read it.'

She hadn't wanted to put it in an email, but there's no choice. And there's no option but to go in all guns blazing. One big hit.

She drops back into parts of her old self and is glad Dylan isn't there. She wants to play hardball, and she doesn't want onlookers.

She taps out the email on her laptop:

'Michael,

'I write to let you know how things have ended up, in case you haven't heard. Jack Cole is in Kununda District Hospital. He was bitten by a snake last night, but this was handled well and his condition is stable. I have just spoken with the hospital and understand arrangements can soon be made for his transfer home. Despite what Jack may tell you, this was very much the result of his own actions. I'm happy to fill you in on the details of this at a later stage, but I write now about other issues.

'First the good news. There's been a strong reaction to the solar power plan. I know this was our fallback position, but having met with the well-connected organisations and individuals who will benefit, I have come to realise the very real values of the project. You have always talked to me about visionary government and this is it. I do advise that there's good political mileage in it – and not only that, but it's the right thing to do. It is cost-effective and the government will surely benefit from taking the high ground.'

She pauses, then launches into the crux of the email. 'But now understanding more of the area's social, historic, conservation, agricultural, tourism and spiritual values, I must tell you I have concluded that the Duncan River valley is not suitable for the water project.' In bullet points, she lays out practical arguments. The displacement of people, the loss of productive land, the loss of habitat for species already under stress, the loss of significant cultural sites, all set against the colossal expense and what would clearly, to her, be a concerted and prolonged political opposition.

She tries to explain that even if the government had the numbers to push it through, 'for the greater good', against local, environmental and cultural opposition, it would at best be an absolute political nightmare for years. If they tried to hang the next election on it, it could easily cost them.

She reiterates that he would be surprised by connections that people here have, despite anything Cole might tell him. 'I believe there would be significant and organised opposition to a dam proposal, as there has been twice in the past. These things go national, then international.'

And then she adds, 'What's more, I don't think any of us can be proud of the way we've gone about this – the subterfuge of this assignment. It is obvious to me, as it surely would be to others, that deception is not the way to go about government. Particularly where it is being used purely to further one person's political ambitions.

'I see it clearly now. I can't believe I didn't see it before and I'm not proud of my part in it. These good people – taxpayers and voters – deserve better from their elected representation. I believe there would be a very real political risk for you and the government if the media were to be made aware of the deceit.' A threat only thinly veiled.

But Kate knows even this is not enough. She has spent years in the shadows beside Michael Mooney, radar scanning for the ever-present threat of political disaster. She has learnt to spot it a long way off, and to understand its cataclysmic speed and uncompromising brutality. And she now wonders whether all those years of unrelenting hours and the enormous pressure was simply to educate her for this moment. For learning how to identify and avoid political disaster has given her an explicit knowledge of how to create it and threaten to deliver it.

She taps the Return key again, and lays it on the line. 'Michael, only you and I know how very close we have been in the past – something, I'm sure, you'd prefer the media, your colleagues in parliament, your family, your constituency and the public to remain unaware of, particularly at this crucial juncture in your career. But I'm looking at quite a different future, and with that comes the opportunity to clean out skeletons from the closet. How completely I do that remains to be decided, but I am prepared for any consequences this may bring me.

'I had spoken with Liz about a few days' leave, but I have since decided to tender my resignation. I should give three months' notice, but I am sure you will agree it's better if I don't return, in the circumstances. I am sure that you would prefer it if we made a clean break and I just disappeared off the scene – and I am as prepared to do this as I am to come back and face the music.

'I look forward to your decision.

'Kate.'

The deal is clear enough. Kate hooks into the hotel's wireless broadband and hits the Send button without another thought. She feels like she has reached inside herself, cut out a tumour and lifted it from her innards.

She knows she has given Mooney no choice. She knows she'll quickly be replaced and forgotten. And that is OK. All those years, all those late nights, and all that loneliness have served their purpose.

Michael Mooney is used to cut-throat politics, but he feels garrotted. One unremarkable indiscretion, and now this. The bitch. His mind spins. Could he weather such a controversy? His family, his friends, his political allies and enemies and, most importantly, his reputation – his legacy. And Simon Whittaker already looking for an excuse to move him to the backbenches.

Mooney knows how to weigh up the odds, and when risks are simply too great.

Kate checks her Inbox a couple of times and there's no reply, then she sits back out the verandah with a handful of the magazines that were fanned out across the room's coffee table. She looks for her horoscope. It's ridiculous, she thinks, but she always looks for her horoscope. Sagittarius. 'Half human, half horse, you are hunting ideas and experiences that will draw you into a greater awareness. You love adventure, travel and philosophy – anything that will stretch you beyond your immediate surroundings.'

See looks for Dylan's. Cancer. 'One of the zodiac's enigmas – a pool of contradictions. They are compassionate and caring towards friends, family and lovers, yet there are those ever-changing moods. Like their symbol, the Crab, Cancerians appear hard and insensitive on the outside but below are soft, deep-feeling and very special.'

Half an hour later, when she clicks the laptop's Send & Receive button, an email bings in from Michael Mooney, who has had another enraged call from Jack Cole – a rant to which he offered little in reply. The email's subject line says WITHOUT PREJUDICE in capital letters, and expressly forbids its republication.

'Kate, I was disappointed to receive your email, as the reason for the methodology of the water research work was not to deceive the electorate – rather, not to alarm them about a fringe proposal which, even at the early stages, was unlikely to progress.'

It is more than an interesting spin. It stops her in her tracks. Mooney has immediately weighed things up and made a decision. (Even without anyone there to apply a rubber stamp on his conclusions, she thinks.)

'The onus is upon government to pursue and consider a wide range of proposals and options. Not to do so would be to fail the mandate handed to the government by the electorate.

'This proposal is unworkable at present. I shall inform Jack Cole of the position.

'I have taken on board your comments on the solar power scheme.

'I appreciate the clear nature of your correspondence and I agree with all the terms of severance you suggest.

'Yours sincerely.'

And that, she thinks, appears to be that.


Michael Mooney looks out from his panoramic office window over the snaking river; so powerful and yet so impotent against topography, gravity and providence. Impotent, you might say, against fate.

He feels woozy and grasps his chest. At first he just feels short of breath, his chest constricted and tight, but then a fist of pain smashes the centre of it. It feels likes something is trying to crush it. With every racing heartbeat, the pain seems to increase behind his breastbone, pulsing through his left side and spreading to his arms and stomach. His shoulder feels heavy, his hand goes numb.

There's a real constricting sensation in his throat. His jaw and teeth hurt.

And then his forehead flops onto the window with a solid thud. The pain surges unbearably through him and he curls forward, his face sliding down the cold glass, pulling the cheek's skin bizarrely upwards. He can hardly breathe.

By the time he is on his knees, coiled forward, his body contorted by pain, the angina attack has agonised Michael Mooney. He collapses, incapable of calling for help or getting pills from his desk drawer. He rolls over on his side, knees tucked up, ovoid, smelling carpet.

The sun's rays bounce off the mass of water below and, viewed from this weird angle, it looks like it's coming towards him. He feels completely hopeless.

Liz has forwarded Kate a letter of severance by email and Cole will soon be on a plane south. 'Are you sure it's all over?' Dylan asks. He's suspicious. 'Just like that? It seems too easy. Cole was so fired up – threatening all-sorts. I thought we were in for a helluva fight. How can you be sure? How did you pull it off?'

'Let's not talk about it anymore,' she says.

'I thought there'd be no secrets.'

'Just this one. Then no more. It's something I'm not proud of. Let's put all the things we're not proud of behind us. Let's have an honourable future. From this moment onwards.'

She looks so sincere.

'Sure,' he says. 'Sure. I'm sorry.'

'There's just one other thing I have to do…' she says. 'Do you know where Uncle Vincent is?'

Looking for a conclusive absolution.

# Twenty-nine

Everything has ended, everything has begun. The next morning, Dylan and Kate leave Carter's Ford behind and set off for the coast, shell-shocked.

They follow the southern edge of the Duncan River valley until Dylan says, 'You should see this,' and turns up an unmarked track, following a vague fence line with old hand-cut posts and rusted wire. He steers around shrubs as it becomes more overgrown.

'It doesn't look used,' she says.

Finally the track swings into an oasis of paperbark trees; Kate has never seen any as tall. And hidden behind them is a big pool fed from a dribble out of the river. It is perfectly round, mostly in the trees' deep shade, but its sunny edge is sandy. It is cupped in a bowl of the red rock.

'It's beautiful,' she says. 'So beautiful.'

They step from the vehicle into heat and Kate walks forward to the water. And then she turns towards Dylan and slowly lifts her two layers of silk over her head and lets them fall in the sand beside her. Her gaze never shifts from his. She is nude and smooth and unrushed. She slides into the water in a long, low glide. He sees it closing over the small of her back.

And then Dylan is beside her, cradling her. Chest deep, he holds her in his arms, and she floats and he sees her exotic, erotic, through the water, their skin touching and the silky water between. She reaches up and holds his face and kisses him.

Dylan and Kate lie in each other's arms in the shade, naked and intimate.

'I wonder how many people have done this before us,' she says. 'How many people have known this place. Lived moments here.'

*Aboriginal mothers peeled off the outer sheafs of these paperbark trees to line the coolamons they carried their babies in; their crushed leaves were used as an antiseptic.*

*The trees' bark was soaked and used to wrap and cook fish and meat, and seeds from spinifex were ground into flour. Boab nuts were eaten dry or green; the dry ones like sherbet, the green ones prepared and baked like apples. Grasses were burnt to keep mosquitoes at bay and soapbush was lathered for washing.*

'You can hear the stories in these places, if you listen hard enough,' he says.

———

But now they need the antiseptic of salt water. 'Let's head to the coast,' he says. They need the time that beaches bring.

And in Shoal Bay they dive back into bands of aquamarine and ochre; different but entirely compatible, vibrating and shimmering together. 'Let's stay somewhere nice,' she says. 'My treat.'

He drives them out of the red lattice and white tin town, past frangipanis and mango trees and towards the long, blond beach, and they swing into the in–out driveway of a hotel engulfed by palms and bougainvilleas. They check in, carry a couple of bags to the room, and are then lost in the rhythm of cicadas and ticking fans and a swirl of crisp sheets.

Late in the afternoon they take towels and walk over the road to the beach. The heat has dropped to a simmer and waves break like lines of music along its clean curve. A pretty young girl surfs on a shocking-pink board. Crabs seem to arrange their sand balls in messages. This is their place. Their perfect place. Kate and Dylan dive and whoop through waves and white spume. He turns cartwheels in the slippery suds, then sticks his legs up, ten-to-two, until she grabs them and they tumble in the froth.

A mai tai and a champagne cocktail. A massive orb of orange setting behind palms. A gentle, caressing, confidential night.

When morning light eventually slats in through the louvres and the kettle clicks off, Dylan makes tea in two mugs he's fetched from the vehicle – he just can't stand the tiny white cups and saucers of hotel rooms.

'Mademoiselle,' he says, putting it on the bedside table beside Kate. 'Crocodile Tea.'

She frowns questioningly.

'*Make it snappy.* An old family joke.'

'I want to meet this family,' she says.

'Did they get what they wanted?' Elaine Ward asks on the phone, after she has told Dylan that Mitchell's well.

'Not really,' he says. 'But I did.'

'That sounds odd. You sound different.'

He wants to tell his mother that he feels he's rolling in warm velvet and cool linen at the same time. Sinking his teeth into lime and drinking in maple syrup. Diving into cold water and floating in tepid salts. Exhilarated by height and safely lying on the earth. Jangling with electricity and completely soothed.

'It'd sound daft if I described it all,' he says.

'You don't have to,' says his mother. 'I can hear it in your voice.'

Kate just sends her family an email, copied to each, saying she's pulled the pin on the department and is going travelling up north for a little while. 'I'm travelling with someone – with Dylan, who was running our trip. So I'll be safe. I'll work the practical things out later. I've got a little money put away. I don't know where this is going, but as much as anything, I just have to get off the treadmill. I'm happy.' She leaves them to read between the lines.

# Thirty

Michael Mooney had lain on the carpet, eyes wide and watery, a chronic panic attack prompting an acute angina episode. He was mesmerised by the river, and it had seemed to come alive and wriggle towards him, jaws agape, fangs glinting. Ready to administer venom, swallow him whole, suck him down and melt him with enzymes.

Liz had eventually found him gasping like a stranded goldfish.

By the time the paramedics got to him, hooked him up and stabilised him, he looked like yesterday's counter lunch, barely warmed up.

A day later, when Cole rings again, mobile-to-mobile, and now also hospital-to-hospital, the odour of Mooney's vulnerability is impossibly attractive. 'Don't worry about the water pipeline,' he bedside-whispers. 'I can handle all of that for you.'

'It is handled.' Mooney speaks softly through still-pallid lips.

'It is?'

'I've already corresponded with Kate Kennedy,' Mooney says in shallow breaths. 'It's all agreed.' He doesn't tell Cole that she has resigned.

'Ah,' says Cole, thinking on his feet. 'What has she said? Precisely what's agreed?'

'That's between me and her.'

'And Ward? You know they're on together? He's in on this.'

Mooney can barely focus on the details.

'What has she said?' Cole demands again. 'The water project's an election winner, Michael. A no-brainer.'

But confidence has evaporated from Mooney. 'It's all over, Jack,' he says. 'All over. We'll do the solar, but that's it.'

Cole is flabbergasted. He goes straight into damage control, without bothering to push for more details. 'I don't know what she's said, but ask yourself one thing – can you trust her?' He hisses it. *Can you trust her?* It is his refrain of last resort, and he trusts it.

Mooney doesn't answer. He just presses the button to end the call. Yes, he thinks, I can trust her.


When Simon Whittaker is informed about Mooney's illness, he asks to be put through to his Chief of Staff, but the call diverts to Liz. He and Liz go way back. She helped on his first campaign, was his electorate admin officer when he was elected, came with him to the House when he became a junior minister, and stayed with him in the Department of Premier, right up until her persuaded her to take the secondment to look after Mooney, who was not only an unproven new minister, but whom he appointed under duress, bending to powerbrokers. So Mooney needed both safe hands and watching.

'Hi, Liz,' he says. 'I've just heard about Michael. It must have been a shock for you to find him – how are you?'

She's always been impressed by Whittaker's empathy. 'I'm fine, but thank you for asking.' She's also always been very proper, never taking their friendship for granted.

'I was trying to get hold of his Chief of Staff, Kate Kennedy. Could you put me through to her, please?'

'I would have been pleased to, Premier, but Kate has resigned. She's just been in contact from the Kimberley, where she's doing some private research for the Minister. She is there with Mr Cole.' Liz knows she is telling far more than the few, well-chosen words she speaks.

'Jack Cole?'

'Yes, Premier.'

Jack Cole and Kate Kennedy in the Kimberley. Doing what? Whittaker's hackles rise. He looks at his watch. It is 4pm. 'I think we can drop the "Premier" bit, Liz. I think we'd better talk. I'll be there in twenty minutes.'

'Certainly, Premier.'

Whittaker nods to Liz to lead into Mooney's office. The river below is ruffled by the afternoon sea breeze.

'We'll need to put someone in temporarily to hold on to the portfolios,' he begins. 'I'm sure you can guide them through where Michael is on things.'

'Well, yes Premier. And there is a lot going on…he's given himself a lot of pressure, one way and the other…' she hints.

'And we aren't just talking portfolios, are we, Liz. How come Kate has resigned like this? It seems out of character.' He leaves a silence for Liz to fill.

'Yes, but if I might say, between us, that it's probably good for him, in the long run – depending on how things have been finalised personally between them,' she says. 'Probably better for everyone…him, the government, the party, his family…' Propriety limits her to suggestion.

'I think I see.'

'I'm sure you do.'

'And Jack Cole? What are they doing in the Kimberley?'

'I do feel a little awkward – compromised – Simon…'

'Let me make it easier for you,' he says kindly. 'Essentially your contract is with the people of the State, not with Michael Mooney. And your moral imperative is to do the right thing by them.'

'Thank you, Simon. Very well. I think I can tell you everything.'

Simon Whittaker is seething. He calls a meeting of his closest confidantes – a mix of ministers and advisors. He gives them most of the picture. 'I'm putting out a media statement,' he tells them.

'Quite right. It'll leak so you'd better get in first,' says a frontbencher. 'The only problem with lying is getting caught.'

'No, Paul. The only problem with lying is that it's wrong. That's why I'm putting out a media statement.'

Whittaker pauses and scans the room. 'Let me take the opportunity to make one thing clear. There is no place for this sort of behaviour in government. There is no place for dishonesty, either representing the government or personally. There are no compromises on that. Full stop. We are never going back to the '80s, when that sort of thing was rife.'

'But Michael was onto something with a water pipeline,' cuts in Paul Minchen again.

'Just in the same way that Mooney can't push ahead with a scheme the way he has – motivated for his own political means – he can't cancel the idea either, for, shall we say, his own personal reasons. Michael didn't come up with the idea of a pipeline – it's been around for four decades. It's been looked into before. It's timely to look into it again, but not like this. I won't have behaviour like this.

'That's why the media statement will say that Michael is indisposed and I will be taking over his portfolios myself, with a Minister assisting. That's you, Paul. It will say the government has decided to look into the Northern Water Pipeline option as a part of good governance.

'You see, this was all Michael had to do – be honest about it and do it in the public interest rather than his own. It's as simple as that. It's a matter of trust.'

Whittaker pauses for effect. 'And on that last point, I will consider that anyone communicating in any way with Jack Cole to have breached that trust.'

# Thirty-one

In every sense, the country calls them back. This land is magnetic. Dylan arranges to truck the hire vehicle back to the city, and Vincent says he'll come into Shoal Bay and pick them up and they can use the dual cab as long as they want. 'There's other ways for me to get around.'

They shop for supplies. Dylan buys CDs with softer sounds and a country twang. Young Kasey Chambers and Kris Kristofferson grown old. He can't believe his luck when he finds a dusty Ramblin' Jack Elliott and a pre-loved Woody Guthrie. Kate's never heard of them, and she buys an Aussie acoustic boxed set. 'Something different for me.'

He buys her elastic-sided boots and a feminine Akubra Coober Pedy hat with an opal in the band. She buys him new bandanas and a belt with an arrowhead buckle. They walk hand in hand, and sit in the shade with mango smoothies.

'Where shall we go?' she asks.

'Somewhere red,' he says.

'With places to swim. Will there be swimming?'

She sounds so wonderfully innocent.

They could head back out through the valley – there's ragged ranges and dramatic country out east. 'I'd like to spend some time with Billy and Amy at Erindale. I really want them to meet you. I'm sure you'll like them. And it's such a wonderful place. Well-run, diverse, carefully handled.'

'I'd love to,' she says, already feeling part of something. Sensing the fabric. Feeling its softness and strength.

Then up through Kununda to the coast. Fish for barramundi, feel the oozy tidal pulse of the gulf country and desert winds that seem to suck all the moisture from you.

'Sounds good,' she says. 'Anything sounds good.'

'No regrets?'

'None.' Kate has cauterised the practicalities of her life. She has simply, consciously put them to one side. It was something she never knew she could do.

They plunge back into that country – off the bitumen and into the interior's biotic boutique, and fall into the lyrical rhythm of cerulean morning skies and velveteen nights. They love the red, pindan earth, and they make love in it.

Scuffed arcs in the ochre dust around her show Kate's brief, playful resistance. But she is in his grip. She slithers happily around him. They kiss, her neck muscles contracting. In pleasure and ever-slower, her shiny, tanned legs circle and signal a sweet, complicit hopelessness. Her mouth is dry but she is crazy with happiness.

They are locked in a mesmerising, slow spectacle. They are absorbed only by life; and he loves her a little more, a little more.

Dylan wants to lie here and ingest the essence of her. She looks as soft and sleek as mercury poured onto the ferociously red grit ground. He crams in closer so that he can see the sparkle like diamonds in her eyes.

# Epilogue

'Water is sometimes sharp and sometimes strong,
sometimes acid and sometimes bitter,
sometimes sweet and sometimes thick or thin,
sometimes it is seen bringing hurt or pestilence,
sometime health-giving, sometimes poisonous.

'It suffers change into as many natures as are the different places
through which it passes. And as the mirror changes with the
colour of its subject, so it alters with the nature of the place,
becoming noisome, laxative, astringent, sulfurous,
salty, incarnadined, mournful, raging, angry,
red, yellow, green, black, blue, greasy, fat or slim.

'Sometimes it starts a conflagration, sometimes it extinguishes one;
is warm and is cold, carries away or sets down, hollows out or
builds up, tears or establishes, fills or empties, raises itself or burrows
down, speeds or is still; is the cause at times of life or death,
or increase or privation, nourishes at times and at others does the
contrary; at times has a tang, at times is without savour, sometimes
submerging the valleys with great floods.

'In time and with water, everything changes.'
– Leonardo da Vinci

# ACKNOWLEDGMENTS

This is a work of fiction and any resemblance to persons living or dead, or specific places, is coincidental. But I have spent more than two decades travelling and writing in the Kimberley, in the north of Australia. Many people have contributed to my general knowledge and understanding, and I thank them. I have many friends there, and have shared many conversations. There have been thousands of occurrences and observations. Perhaps a million moments and thoughts.

My heartfelt appreciation to Virginia and Max Ward, and to my mother, brother, sister and other family and friends.

It is a pleasure being a UWA Publishing author. My thanks to UWAP director Terri-ann White, editor Anne Ryden, Anna Maley-Fadgyas, Kiri Falls and Britt Ingerson.

Turn over for other great books by Stephen Scourfield from UWA Publishing.

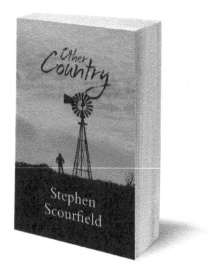

*Other Country*

'Down here,' he says, 'that's Australia.' Then he points with a single, direct finger, above the line. 'But up here. This is the other country.'

Linked by a common hatred of their violent Old Man, The Ace and his younger brother Wild Billy Parkes hit the road into northern Australia to make their own history. Two very different brothers, one held by the past, the other grasping for the future, they grow into men among tough blokes who prefer silence to emotions.

Their story, set in a landscape as harsh as the lives lived in it, is both desperate and filled with hope. There's the other country that is out there, and there is the other country within; what you make of each is up to you.

Affecting and deeply resonant, *Other Country* is Stephen Scourfield's award-winning first novel.

'...immediate, dramatic and stark. Poetic as well as vernacular, it suggests Proulx, McCarthy...an impressive novel.' THE WEEKEND AUSTRALIAN

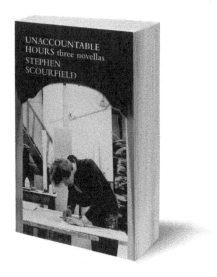

*Unaccountable Hours*

This collection of three novellas follows the fortunes of a maker of musical instruments, the ethical dilemma of a biologist and birdwatcher, and the romantic friendship between a young man and an aged woman – all firmly set in and defined by the Australian landscape.

In 'The Luthier,' musician Alton Freeman devotes his life to crafting a violin that will reproduce the perfect sound of Bach's Partitas and Sonatas, as played by his idol, musician Monica Erica Grenbaum. 'Ethical Man' follows the biologist and birdwatcher Bartholomew Milner, who lives stringently according to his 'Milner's Ethic', and is put to the ultimate ethical test whilst on a research expedition in the Australian outback. 'Like Water,' tells the story of an unlikely friendship and subsequent romance that develops between two kindred spirits, Matthew and Beatrice – two soulmates born generations apart.

**www.uwap.com.au**